Unrestrained

Hot in the Saddle

CIANA STONE

Ellora's Cave
Romantica Publishing

What the critics are saying...

ꟾ

SCOUT 'N' COLE

5 Hearts "The first two books in this trilogy were excellent, however, this one goes way beyond. I didn't want it to end. It's a truly captivating story with sizzling erotic love scenes and lots of tension. [...] I'm impressed with Ciana Stone's writing and look forward to reading more of her work in the future. [...] For an outstanding quality novel, check out *Scout 'n' Cole* and the other books in this series." ~ *The Romance Studio*

CONN 'N' CALEB

5 Hearts "After reading the first three books, all of which stand alone as does *Conn 'N' Caleb,* I was looking forward to see what Ciana Stone would do with Caleb, the youngest brother of the Russell siblings. I wasn't disappointed. She created a rather unique and intriguing premise that entertained me through out. Another element that piqued my interest was the introduction of a race of humanoid aliens that I wouldn't mind knowing more about. Excellent dialogue as always with a Ciana Stone book and memorable characters made this a very worthwhile book to read." ~ *The Romance Studio*

An Ellora's Cave Romantica Publication

www.ellorascave.com

Unrestrained

ISBN 9781419959851

Edited by Sue-Ellen Gower.
Cover art by Syneca.

This book printed in the U.S.A. by Jasmine-Jade Enterprises, LLC.

Trade paperback Publication October 2009

UNRESTRAINED

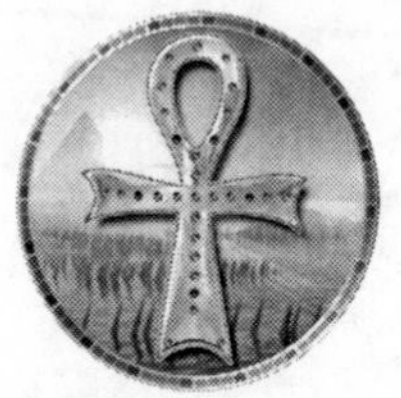

SCOUT 'N' COLE

Dedication

ꕤ

For the "real" Cole – a cowboy who can make a night spent under the stars the most exhilarating experience in life.

Acknowledgements

ꕤ

My deepest appreciation to all the people who were so instrumental in the creation of this book:
Grandpa – gone but never forgotten. For all you taught me about life,
and our connection with the earth and all that dwells on it.

Trademarks Acknowledgement

ꕤ

The author acknowledges the trademarked status and trademark owners of the following wordmarks mentioned in this work of fiction:

Camaro: General Motors Corporation

Dial soap: Dial Corporation, The

Gulfstream: Gulfstream Aerospace Corporation

Jack Daniels: Jack Daniel's Properties, Inc.

Chapter One

ꟹ

She arched against him, crying out as an orgasm claimed her. He rode her, refusing to let the swell of sensation abate, stretching out the pleasure until her cry was but a long wordless scream of pleasure. She writhed against him, wanting it to go on and on.

And the alarm rang.

Scout cursed at the offending sound that jolted her from the dream and checked the time on the clock. Five a.m. Quickly silencing the noise, she sat and swung her legs over the side of the bed, shoving thoughts of the dream aside.

Today she'd step into the ring, so to speak, to defend the family honor. For the past five years, the US Geological Survey-Fort Collins Science Center on the Mountain Lion Ecology, had sponsored a hunt. They invited the top hunters and trackers in the world to team up with rangers and specialists with the Center to tag mountain lions for the ongoing study. It was a no-kill competition, yet a fierce one.

This was the first year she would be the only member of her family in the competition and she fully intended to win. Even if it meant physically dragging whomever she was teamed with the entire way.

That was the real challenge for the hunters and trackers. The specialists from the Center were trained in animal biology, behavior and group dynamics, but were not necessarily skilled outdoorsmen. The rangers were normally more skilled in surviving the wilderness, but generally not that knowledgeable about the species itself.

Scout had never participated in the competition. Even though she'd signed up last year, she'd had to drop out. Her reputation may have been as one of the best trackers in the country, but she also specialized in tracking big cats. There were not a lot of trackers who wanted to hunt the big cats. Not everyone had the patience for it. And not everyone had been trained by Jededia Windrider, the legendary tracker and backcountry survival expert.

Scout had not only been trained by Jededia, she was his granddaughter, raised by him after her parents were killed in an auto accident when she was five days old. She only knew her parents from old photos and barely remembered their faces from those faded images, but Jed's face would be etched into her mind forever. He had been father and mother to her, as well as teacher and friend.

His death last year had left a hole in her heart that nothing would ever fill. His passing left her alone. No family and few friends. Scout felt something of an anomaly, comfortable in the wild, and a fish out of water in mainstream society.

Not that it bothered her. At least not often. There were times when loneliness crept up on her, but when it did, she accepted that as long as she lived the life she had chosen, loneliness would be a factor. Maintaining a relationship when you were gone most of the time was impossible. She knew. She'd tried. And she'd failed. And resolved not to make that mistake again.

Since the end of her short-lived marriage, she'd focused on work. Her first job was with the IUCN. Six months later, thanks to her contributions to a study on the Mountain Lion Ecology in Rocky Mountain National Park and the Northern Colorado, she was approached by CAT, the Cat Action Treasury, the IUCN Species Survival Commission's specialist group, tasked with producing action plans representing species-specific knowledge.

Now Scout was considered one of the foremost authorities on the cat family, with a specialty in the Puma concolor or Mountain Lion, most commonly referred to as the cougar. She was happy to have earned a good reputation but could have cared less about the political and bureaucratic aspects. She left that to the people who were adept at such matters, and focused her energy and attention in the area she was best suited. Namely the wild. It made her happy being out in the wild. It didn't matter if she was tracking or just taking a solitary hike. When she was outside, away from people, she could breathe.

This morning she contemplated the event before her. Last year she'd been scheduled to participate, as had Jed. It was to be their first time competing against one another. Scout was hesitant, but he had insisted. He was growing old, he'd told her, and needed to know that she'd learned all he'd tried to teach her. If she had, then her youth should give her the edge to beat him.

His death a week before the competition had knocked her for a loop. The fact that he was murdered had filled her with rage and a need for revenge. She'd spent six months trying to solve the mystery of who had killed him. Neither she nor the state law enforcement had been able to find the guilty party. This told Scout that whoever it was, he was a skilled hunter. Sneaking up on Jed would have taken a great deal of skill. The kind of skill only people such as those entered into the competition possessed. She intended to pay close attention to all the participants before and after the hunt.

And she intended to win. She'd prove to Jed that she'd not let him down. That she'd learned what he'd taught. That he could be proud of her.

Within the hour she was navigating the twisting roads, watching a shroud of fog that crept in fingers across the blacktop. It was still a few hours before dawn, and the temperature was hovering right at fifty degrees. A good day for a hunt.

Chapter Two

ꟸ

Cole wandered through the assembly, catching bits and pieces of conversation. It was a diverse group, and already a segregated one. The hunters and trackers were off to one side, talking among themselves, paying no attention to the others. The people from the Center were clustered around the breakfast table and the rangers signed up for the hunt were gathered together on one side of the room, discussing the merits of the hunters and whom they hoped to be teamed up with.

The most common topic of conversation seemed to center around Windrider.

He was curious. Jedediah Windrider was a legend, a master tracker who could track anything. Cole had even heard stories about him tracking ants across bare rock like the old Apache Scouts were supposed to have been able to do. Cole hadn't realized the old man had a family. But then, not much was known about Windrider. He showed up when called and then vanished back to wherever he came from, as mysterious and elusive as the animals he tracked.

But Jed was murdered a year or so ago. So it had to be Jed's son the men were discussing.

Cole hoped he got teamed up with Windrider. If the man was half as good as his father, they should be able to win the competition. And Cole was a man who played to win. Just like his brothers.

That thought brought a smile to Cole's face, softening the hard lines and making his hazel eyes crinkle at the corners. He'd have a story to tell his twin brother Clay the next time they spoke.

Which reminded Cole that he hadn't talked with Clay in nearly a month. The last time they spoke, Clay and his wife Rusty were gearing up for a national rodeo. Unlike Cole and Clay's father, Rusty had encouraged Clay to pursue his career as a pro bull rider. This year Clay was riding in the nationals and Rusty swore he was going to win.

Cole hoped she was right. He'd only known Rusty for a little over a year, and had seen her only four times but he liked her. She was spunky, tough, bull-headed, funny and sexy as hell. A perfect match for his brother.

Seemed to Cole that all the Russell men except him and the youngest brother Caleb had gotten pretty damn lucky when it came to finding wives. His oldest brother Chase had a wife who was a real traffic stopper. And as in love with Chase now as she was in the beginning.

And Clay had scored in a big way with Rusty. She was one of the top trainers in the country of horses for barrel racing, and since she and Clay had gotten together, had become the top-ranked barrel racer in the world. She had a way with horses that was downright spooky.

But then, she was a witch. Just like Ana. Cole thought it ironic beyond mere coincidence that two of his brothers had married witches. He'd often wondered if there was a sexy witch out there in the world waiting for him.

That brought a snort that had a couple of people giving him strange looks. If there was a woman for him out there, he'd never know it. He had no interest in bars and clubs or anything that had to do with city life. Since the day he'd finished graduate school he'd turned his back on that life.

Life as a ranger suited his solitary nature and his need to be away from people. Sure he had to interact with people in his job, but by and large his days were spent alone out in the vastness of the park, patrolling or being involved in rescues of lost hikers or accident victims.

It had been months since his last date. He still got a bad taste in his mouth when he remembered it. The woman was in her mid-twenties, blonde, built like a centerfold and about as environmentally aware as a bag of rocks. Conversation with her was restricted to either what movie star did what, or whether she should have a chin implant to make her profile look better.

That was one of the most miserable evenings Cole could remember. She had been completely disinterested in what he did, had even laughed and called him Smoky the Bear.

Cole pushed aside thoughts of the miserable date as Tim Matthews, the Director of the Rocky Mountain National Park, came up behind him. "You set for this, Cole?" Tim asked.

"Yep," Cole replied.

Tim took a look around the room. "Scout hasn't shown up yet?"

"Scout?"

"Windrider."

"Any relation to Jed?" Cole asked.

"Yep, and hand-trained, old-school fashion by the old man himself pretty much since birth," Tim replied. "I'm gonna grab a cup of coffee and get things rolling."

"That's a ten-four," Cole replied.

Something nagged at Cole's memory. Something about Windrider. But what? He searched his memory. Suddenly it came to him. A ROMO report he'd read last year on mountain lions, discussing the nature and potential for human-mountain lion interaction in ROMO, or Rocky Mountain National Park.

Capturing the lions had proven a monumental task. That's what had brought Windrider onto the scene. Within a year of Windrider coming aboard the study team conducted or assisted with twenty-six safe captures individual mountain lions in Larimer County and ROMO. The animals were fitted with GPS collars and released.

Which meant that Windrider had a definite edge in the competition. He knew the lay of the land and had a personal commitment to the preservation of the species.

Cole wondered if Scout looked anything like his father. Jed had been a big man, with sharp features, hard eyes and long graying hair. His native heritage had been quite apparent.

A murmur in the crowd behind him drew his attention. He turned and saw the top of a dark head making its way through the crowd, the person being stopped every few seconds by one of the hunters or specialists who had suddenly congregated around the mystery person.

Scout greeted the men she knew, gave polite greetings to the ones she was introduced to, and continued making her way to the front of the room. The crowd thinned and she saw the man standing off by himself.

No way! He looked just like the bull rider whose career she'd been following, and who she'd been having very delicious and erotic fantasies about for the last few years. *Yumm.* Her insides started to purr at the thought. *Rein it in* was her second. She was there to win. The last thing she needed to think about was sex.

Tim Matthews stepped into her path. "I was starting to think you weren't going to show."

"Not likely. How're you doing, Tim? Donna and Tommy okay?"

"Good, and good," he replied. "He's signing up for T-ball this spring. First time."

"And I bet you signed up to coach," she said with a smile. Tim was the most devoted husband and father she'd ever met.

"You bet."

"Let me know the schedule and I'll come cheer you on," she said and took a look around. "So, you have the roster drawn up? Who're you gonna saddle me with?"

Tim laughed. "Actually it's a blind draw. Speaking of which, I need to get the show on the road."

"Have at it," she replied and wandered over to one side of the room where she could watch everyone as Tim called the meeting to order.

The crowd fell silent while Tim greeted everyone and explained the rules. It was a three-week hunt. The team with the most tags won. The Park was closed down for those three weeks and access to the surrounding wilderness was being patrolled to keep people out. However, they were warned to report anyone they encountered via their radio headsets so that any civilians could be removed from the area.

"Now, this hat contains the names of all the specialists from the Center as well as the rangers," he finished with. "My assistant here, Rodney, will call out the name of each hunter. As your name is called, please step forward or identify yourself. I will draw a name from the hat and that will be your teammate. Please wait until all names are called before you get with your teammate. As soon as we're all paired up, I'll be coordinating the drop-off points and times for the teams and will post it on the board behind me. Be geared up and ready to go at the appointed time. Any questions?"

With no questions, Tim began the process of team assignment. Scout paid attention to the pairings. She saw several people she worked with at the Center being paired up with noted hunters, and one with a hunter she was unfamiliar with.

When her name was called, she raised her hand. "Windrider."

Tim drew a name. "Cole Russell."

The name sparked Scout's attention. The bull rider she had a thing for was named Clay Russell. She scanned the crowd. Sure enough the sexy look-alike she'd noticed raised his hand and looked in her direction.

Whoa baby! the lusty wench inside her cheered. Scout pushed the thought aside with a measure of irritation at herself. She wasn't there to get a date but to compete. She nodded her head at Russell then turned her attention back to Tim.

Once finished, Tim moved off to consult with his assistant and coordinate the drop-off points. The men moved through the room, introducing themselves to their teammates.

Scout pushed away from the wall and made for the door as Cole Russell made his way toward her. She walked outside and waited. The moment he stepped through the door, their eyes met. For the space of a breath the world went silent. A thousand whispers wafted through her mind, all saying the same thing. *Trouble.*

Scout acknowledged and agreed. Cole Russell was a man who could definitely make her think of all kinds of delicious ways to get in trouble. From the look in his eyes and the electricity arcing between them, she got the idea he wouldn't be opposed to a bit of trouble. But now was not the time.

Cole was definitely thinking of trouble. The kind of trouble he could easily slide into with the woman looking up at him. She had the eyes of a cat, wary but curious, the color unidentifiable in the dark, but the almond shape as unmistakable as the heavy fringe of dark lashes. Lean with soft but angular lines, she looked almost feline. Except for those full, lush lips.

He never got past her face. That was enough to capture him and hold him spellbound. For a long moment they remained frozen, eyes locked.

"You're not what I expected," he said, uncomfortable at the sudden swelling taking place south of his belt.

The hint of a smile lightened Scout's eyes. "No? Just what did you expect, Mr. Russell?"

Cole was distracted. The camouflage tank top she wore hugged her body like a glove. And what a body. Curves in all the right places, firm and well toned.

"Let me guess," she filled the silence. "You thought I was a man. But I'm not. Come on. My gear's in my truck."

He fell in step beside her as she turned. She paused to look up at the sky. "Gonna be a good day. But might rain tonight."

"You get all that from looking at the sky?" Cole asked.

"Nope," she replied and continued walking toward her truck. "National weather service."

He grinned and the grin widened as he watched her walk in front of him, her tight little ass twitching enticingly. The grin faded as his dick started to swell. He'd have to get a grip on it fast if they were going to work together and win this competition. Spending three weeks with a raging hard-on had no appeal at all.

Scout was digging through a backpack when he reached her truck. She pulled out a plastic squirt bottle. "Take off your shirt."

"Huh?"

"Take off your shirt. You smell like a man."

Cole was taken aback by the statement. "You trying to tell me I stink?"

"Animals rely on their sense of smell and you don't smell like the wilderness. Now take off your shirt."

"No."

"Fine, have it your way." She started misting him with the squirt bottle.

"Hey!" he protested. The stuff smelled really bad. "What the hell is that?"

She continued to mist, circling around him. "It's a tea from trees and plants common in this area."

She finished then doused herself liberally with the concoction. She returned the bottle to her pack. "It'd be best if we had a fire."

"You know it's against the law to start a fire in a national park. Besides what do we need a fire for?"

"Because you showered with..." She moved in close and sniffed at him. "Dial soap. And your clothes still smell like detergent."

"How the hell can you smell that with me saturated with this...concoction?"

"Point is, if I can smell it, so can an animal." Scout blew out her breath. "Look, I know tracking isn't your specialty, but you're a ranger. You know we're not going to track down anything if we can't blend into the environment. The smell of smoke is natural in the woods."

"But animals are afraid of smoke and fire."

"Only the sight of it. Not the smell."

"Well we can't build a fire," he argued.

"Fine, then we'll do it another way. Take off your clothes. We need to get your skin saturated with this and rub your clothes in dirt or it won't be enough to kill the smell of soap and cologne the fabric has already absorbed."

"Whoa, lady!" He held up both hands, palms out and took a step back. "No way I'm taking off my clothes."

"Then get in your truck and do it. Just do it."

"No."

"Fine, then stay at least half an hour behind me." She turned to her pack, pulled out an old stained belt and strapped it around her hips.

"Like hell," Cole argued.

Scout snatched a long-bladed hunting knife in a worn holster from her pack and fastened it to her belt. "Look, Mr. Russell, I'm not trying to be difficult. I'm just telling you that as long as you smell like sex in jeans then you're not tracking through—"

"Sex in jeans?" Cole blurted.

Scout bit her lip. "You still smell like a man and animals will catch your scent a mile away. So either you have to change your smell or you have to stay behind. Your choice but make it now."

"I suppose the damn animals won't smell you?" Cole asked angrily.

"Do you?"

He blinked, and then frowned. He stepped closer and sniffed. Then took another step and sniffed again. Nothing. He moved in close, towering over her and leaned down to smell her hair.

"You smell like…" He straightened up in surprise. "The woods."

"Exactly," she said with a smile. "And you have to smell like the woods too."

"Well, barring the fire and taking off my clothes, you have any suggestions?"

Scout looked around and took off, disappearing into the trees. Cole stood there wondering if she had just run off and left him or if she was going to come back. Just as he'd decided to take off after her, she reappeared.

"Here," she said, showing him the handful of spruce berries she held. "Unbutton your shirt."

Cole started to argue but decided against it. He unbuttoned his shirt. Scout frowned at the sight of the tight tee shirt beneath the button up. "Pull it up," she said and turned her attention to mashing the berries with her right hand, using her left to contain them.

Blowing out his breath in frustration, Cole complied. Scout scooped up some of the mashed berries and looked at Cole.

Jesus, Joseph and Mary, she fought not to react. He was built. Seriously built. She started smearing her hand over his chest and abdomen, trying not to take any delight in the feel of all that hard muscle and smooth skin.

His back was as gorgeous as his front. She quickly smeared his skin, running her hands up and down his back, then up his sides to his armpits. When she finished she wiped her hands on his shirt. "Okay, maybe that'll do it," she said, returning to the truck and busying herself with using the tea from the squirt bottle to rinse the stickiness from her hands. "Once you start to sweat the scent will get into your clothes and dilute the chemical smell."

Truth be told she needed a moment to collect herself. It had been a while since she'd touched a man, and in all her life she'd never touched one who was built like Cole Russell. It took all her willpower to turn her thoughts away from his hard body and back to the task at hand.

Cole buttoned and tucked in his shirt. "So do I still smell like sex in jeans?"

Scout jerked her head around in surprise to find him grinning at her. She snorted and turned away. "Nope. You ready?"

"Yep. Let me grab my pack."

Scout watched him walk to his truck, unable to stop herself from admiring the view. He had a nice firm butt and strong legs and a stride that was both confident and strong.

Cole pulled on his pack and reached into the cab of the truck for his radio and a rifle. He also grabbed a map. "You know this area?" he asked as he turned to her.

"Pretty much. Why?"

"I was thinking about the last cat sighting," he said as he unfolded the map. "See, right here. Maybe that's the first place we should look."

"Or not. Just because a cat was spotted there doesn't mean it is now. They have a pretty big territory. An adult male's home range can cover over one hundred square miles. As a rule, females have smaller ranges, around twenty to sixty square miles. In this area the competition for habitat isn't extreme, but we can still have as many as six to ten adult males occupying the same hundred square miles," Scout said.

"Lot of ground to cover. So what do you think our target should be?"

"Depends," she replied and looked at the map for a second. "Maybe here." She pointed to an area on the map.

"Why?" Cole asked.

"One, it's nearing time for cubs to be born. Which means the mothers will have a safe place secured. And two, if I was a cat that's where I'd go," Scout replied, still looking at the map and thinking.

"Is that a valid tracking technique or just a hunch?"

"Intuition." She looked up with a smile. "And experience. Here's what I think." She pointed to the map. "We make our way from wherever our drop-off point is to here. Until this turn, then we cut across toward the east and work our way north when we reach the ridge."

"Lots of climbing to do taking that route," Cole replied.

"You got gear?"

"In my pack."

"Climbing bother you, Mr. Russell?"

"Not a bit. But why do all that useless climbing? If we take the trail to the junction here, turn west and follow the trail to here then—"

"You think cats follow a hiking trail, Mr. Russell?"

"No, I don't. But—"

"Look, I know you're more familiar with the park than I am, but trust me, I know cats and we're not going to find them following that trail."

"And we're not going to find them if we spend the whole day climbing," he argued.

"Oh no? Just where do you think that cats are going to hole up? Out in the open? Those cliffs are riddled with niches and caves. A perfect place for expectant cats to den. I say we take the west-northwest route. It's our best bet."

"I disagree."

"Fine, disagree." Scout was starting to get a little annoyed and a whole lot impatient. This fellow might be sexy as hell, a hands-down great ranger, but she knew cats and was a tracker. "You take the trail. I'll go alone."

"We're not splitting up."

"Then you best be following me," she said and started walking toward the lodge. "Turn off that radio and make sure there's no live ammo in that gun. This is a no-kill hunt."

Cole blew out his breath, folded the map and jammed it into the pocket of his jacket. Scout Windrider might be real easy on the eyes, but he was starting to get the idea that she was going to be a true pain in the ass.

"I'm not loaded with anything but tranquilizers."

"Good."

She strode ahead of him back to the meeting hall. It took nearly half an hour before they were on their way. They were trucked to a small clearing where a dozen helicopters waited.

"You have experience making aerial descents?" Scout asked as they were motioned over by one of the pilots.

"Yeah. You?"

"A few times. I'm not an expert but I can handle it."

They climbed into the helicopter and were silent until the copilot got out of his seat to help them harness up for the descent.

Scout admired Cole's proficiency. He'd obviously done this before. In minutes they were both on the ground with the helicopter headed back to base. Scout turned to look at Cole and when their eyes met she could have sworn that sparks arced through the air between them, the current was so strong.

Three weeks, she thought, for the first time in her life feeling like three weeks in the wilderness was a terribly long time. How the hell was she going to make it three weeks alone with Cole Russell if every time he looked at her all she could think about was ripping off his clothes and putting her hands, mouth and body all over him?

"You get a bead on our position from the air?" Cole asked.

"Yeah." She forced her attention back on the matter at hand. "I hoped we'd get a drop point closer, but it is what it is. I estimate a two-day hike before we reach the base of the cliffs. Sound about right to you?"

"Pretty much."

"Then let's move," she said and took the lead.

Cole nodded without comment. Silence fell around them. Silence that he noticed. Most of all because she made no sound. Not just in lack of words or sounds of her breath. She made no sound as she moved.

He kept those thoughts and all others to himself for the next three hours. In silence, he followed and observed. There was something about Scout that intrigued him. It was as though the moment she stepped into the woods she became part of them.

Her movements were like water, very fluid and smooth. They covered far more ground in three hours than he'd anticipated. They reached a basin canopied by trees and she stopped.

For several minutes she stood perfectly still, and then she turned to him. "We can take a break if you want. Report in to base camp that we're in the field and going silent, then turn off the radio."

"Isn't that against protocol?"

"We only have to report in once a day. Nothing more. So we do it now then go silent," she replied and looked him in the eyes. His first thought was of her eyes. Now that the sun had risen, he could see their color in depth and it was remarkable. Around the pupils the color was copper that faded to a warm gold as it spread out over the iris, ending in a band of dark gold that seemed to outline the unusual coloration. He could only compare them to a wild creature. *A cat,* he thought. *She has the eyes of a cat.*

"What if base tries to reach us?"

"They won't. They won't make the mistake you're making now."

"Which is?"

"Thinking that we're still back in that world. We're not. Make no mistake. We're in my world now, and as the lead in this team I have to insist that either you do this my way or turn around and go back."

"Are you always this hard to get along with?" Cole's ire was rising, despite his fascination with her eyes.

Scout regarded him for a moment. "Let me ask you something. What's your specialty?"

"Rescue and fire."

She nodded. "So, let's say there was an injured hiker up there on that ridge. You'd know exactly what you needed to do to get to him and get him down safely, right?"

"Absolutely."

"Well, it's the same thing," she explained. "I know cats, Mr. Russell. And I know how to track. So I'm going to ask you to trust me to do what I do best. Do you think you can do that?"

Cole felt a little ashamed. He'd let her bossiness annoy him. And in all honesty, he probably would not have felt the same way if she'd been a man. The fact that she was this small, incredibly sexy and monumentally vexing woman had made him forget that she was Jed Windrider's prodigy.

"Yeah, I can do that. And I thought we were past the Mr. and Miss thing."

Scout smiled. "Sorry…Cole. Now why don't you radio Tim?"

While Cole made the call, Scout wandered off a little ways. She closed her eyes and took a long slow breath.

Where are you? she called silently. *Talk to me.*

The only answer she got was a sudden stabbing pain in her hip. Her eyes flew open. Something was wrong. Very wrong. They had no time to waste.

Chapter Three

ഗ

Raymond Moss settled himself more comfortably beside the small fire. He and three other men were sharing the small cave for the night. One of the men, Bobby Howard, had worked for Ray and his father James for years. The other two were city slickers from upstate New York who had paid a hefty fee to be taken out on a hunt.

While hunting cougar was not technically illegal in the state of Colorado, there were restrictions, and Ray knew he'd breeched all of them. Cougar hunting had been prohibited in the area since 2004.

Which Ray thought was stupid. There were plenty of the animals, far more than was necessary to his way of thinking. If it were left to him, every mountain lion in existence would be killed. They were evil predators with a taste for human blood.

And they had taken Ray's father from him. James Moss had been a near legend in his day. He'd worked with Jed Windrider for years when Ray was a boy. Ray could still hear the stories his father would tell when he'd return home from a hunt. Ray would fantasize about it for weeks, dreaming of the day he would be on a hunt with his dad and Jed.

When Ray was twelve, his father and Jed had a major falling out. Jed was against killing the animals. He only hunted when an animal was wounded or had proven to be a threat to livestock or humans. Hunting for the sport was against his belief. But sport hunting was big business and Ray's father was smart enough to see that a man could make a nice living leading hunts.

He tried to convince Jed to throw in with him, but Jed not only refused, he cursed James for it. Ray could still remember the look on his father's face when Jed turned his back on him. It had hurt James more than anything Ray could remember. And it was a hurt he never really recovered from.

Ray and his younger brother Jimmy had followed in his father's footsteps and for years successfully skirted the laws and made enough from their hunts to set them up in relative style. It was a good life, aside from James being haunted by the condemnation of his old friend Jed.

A couple of years ago, Ray, Jimmy and their father set up a large hunt. They had two packs of dogs, well over the legal limit allowed, and ten desk-soft executives eager to prove their manhood and go back to their penthouse offices with stories to tell of braving the wild. To ensure that none of the men went home empty-handed, Jimmy came up with the idea of employing the latest technology.

Developed by an entrepreneur in Texas, it was a rig that housed a web cam and a hunting rifle. He set up a website that allowed people to focus in, aim and fire on an unsuspecting animal using only a computer mouse.

Jimmy was excited by the idea and had modified it to suit his needs. It was costly but worked like a charm. Ray would scout an area before taking the clients in. If he found quarry, he would feed Jimmy the coordinates and Jimmy would take his own custom-designed rig and set it up, using military camouflage tarps and natural cover like fallen branches to hide it. Using a costly satellite uplink, he could sit at base camp with a laptop.

If a client took a shot at an animal, Jimmy acted as backup. One click of his mouse and the rifle on the rig, custom fitted with a silencer, would fire. The client then would forever be able to boast of his "one-shot kill".

At first Ray and his father had been against it, but Jimmy had hounded them until they gave in. It had proven to be effective, and had netted them quite a few returning clients.

Later, when their father died and Ray was so grief-stricken he could barely get out of bed and was drinking himself to death, Jimmy had come up with another use for the rig that had not only brought Ray out of his funk, but had succeeded in making them not just hunters of animals, but hunters of men.

They would never have had to resort to that if it hadn't been for Jedediah Windrider. They'd been on the hunt for two days when Jed and his granddaughter came upon them. Jed openly accused James of breaking the law and conducting an illegal hunt, right in front of the clients. And his granddaughter Scout had lambasted the lot of them for their actions, citing all kinds of government policy and threatening to have them arrested if they didn't call off the hunt immediately.

James had capitulated to their threats, at least while in their presence. It galled Ray to see his father cave in, to humble himself in front of their clients. But as soon as Jed and Scout left, James laughed it off and said the hunt would continue. He was just putting on an act to get Jed off their asses and for them not to worry.

From that moment on, everything turned south. Four days into the hunt, the dogs cornered a female lion in a tree. The clients went nuts, firing like mad. One shot caught the lion in the right shoulder. She came out of the tree. The clients scattered like mice when the cat pounced on James. Ray pumped one shot after another into her, but before she died, she'd torn his father to shreds.

Ray knew as he held his father's mutilated body in his arms that the reason he'd died was the curse Jed put on them. Everything would have been fine if the Windriders had not interfered. Now his father was dead and Ray was alone.

In that moment all reason fled his mind and in its place appeared a fire of hatred. Hatred for the cats and for the Windriders. And a vow to his dead father that Ray would avenge his death. No matter how long it took, he would make sure the Windriders paid for what they'd done. It was his duty to see justice done. Thanks to Jimmy, he'd accomplished half his mission.

One of the clients interrupted his reverie with a question. "So are we going to be killing some cats or not?"

Ray looked across the small fire at the pudgy man. "You'll get your kill. Don't you worry. Just finish your breakfast and get packed. We head out in an hour."

He tossed the remains of his coffee into the fire and rose. Outside the cave it was an overcast, cold morning. A perfect day for a kill.

* * * * *

"We need to move faster," Scout announced as soon as Cole ended his conversation with Tim on the radio.

"We're making good time," Cole replied. "What's the rush?"

"There's a wounded cat. She needs attention. We have to find her before anyone else does or they'll put her down."

Cole stared at her, his brows drawing together in a frown. "And you know this how?"

"I just know it."

"More of that intuition?"

"Just trust me, Cole. There's a female cat out there in pain and we have to find her. If one of the other teams stumbles on her they may try and terminate her rather than subduing her."

"Might be the only way."

Scout's eyes took on a glittering hardness that had Cole wanting to take a step back, despite his superior size and weight. "It is not! You listen up, Russell. We're going to find her and help her. You try and kill her and I'll take you down."

"I didn't say I was going to try and kill her. I only said it might be the only way."

"I don't accept that," Scout said and took a step closer to him. "Look, we don't know one another, and I don't expect you to share my views but I do expect you to consider my position and expertise in this area."

Cole considered her words, trying to push aside the crackling energy that was arcing between them. He didn't quite understand it. Scout was a looker, but he'd had his share of pretty women, and none of them had ever had the effect Scout had on him. Just being in close proximity to her had him thinking of how it would feel to be buried inside her with her strong legs wrapped around his waist.

He shook his head to clear the thoughts. "I do respect and consider your expertise, Scout. But you have to at least consider the possibility that the cat will be too far gone to save. Should that—" He held up his hand as she started to interrupt. "Should that prove to be the case, then you have to be prepared to put her down."

Scout hated to consider the possibility but knew that it was only realistic to do so. Moreover, she and Cole needed to be able to arrive at a common ground if they were going to successfully work together.

"You're right," she said after a long pause. "And should that prove to be the case, I promise you I'll do what needs to be done. But only if I'm convinced there's no other alternative. Agreed?"

Cole nodded and stuck out his hand. "Deal."

Scout looked from his face to his hand then back at his face. She understood that shaking his hand was a symbol, a ritual of sorts cementing their agreement, but she was hesitant to take his hand.

She couldn't say why exactly. Not much frightened her and she wasn't a nervous sort. But taking his hand seemed to imply something on a primitively emotional level that unsettled her. If she had the time she would explore the feeling to try to understand what caused it and what it meant. But time was something they were short of.

So, with reservation she clasped his hand. His big warm hand closed around hers and then it happened. She was catapulted into another realm. Feelings and emotions bombarded her from every side, sending her spinning into a vortex of swirling images and whispered sounds.

It hadn't happened often, but she did recognize the experience. She was feeling Cole and his life experiences. It took but a moment yet felt like a lifetime that she was enveloped in his essence.

The emotions were staggeringly strong. So strong that she actually did stagger.

Cole saw her eyes cloud over like a curtain of shade had been drawn across them, darkening them to the color of an old penny. Her face paled and she inhaled sharply. Then something hit him. Not physically. It was a mental blow. His vision went completely white, like the world had suddenly exploded around him. For a moment he was completely blind.

Before alarm could register in his mind, his vision returned. At almost the exact same moment, Scout staggered. Cole held onto her hand, grabbing her with his free hand to steady her.

"You okay?" he asked.

She nodded and pulled away from him.

"What the hell happened?" he asked.

Scout turned away. "What do you mean?"

Cole took her arm to turn her back around to face him. "Something happened. Like for a second I was blind. Everything went white. And you staggered, so you felt something too."

Scout's first inclination was to deny it. But dishonesty wasn't her way, even when it was uncomfortable to be truthful. That she'd learned from Jed. And that teaching was deeply ingrained.

"It was..." she paused. "I don't know how to explain what it was, Cole."

"But you felt it."

"Yeah," she replied. She wasn't sure what he had felt but was all too aware of what she'd experienced. It still sizzled through her mind. Had it happened at another time she would have stopped and done nothing but try to translate the information that had been so abruptly thrust into her mind. But there was no time to pause and dissect the flood of information.

"You ever had anything like that happen before?" he asked.

She nodded. "A couple of times."

"So what the hell is it?"

"It's like a momentary connection. Jed called it connecting with the soul of another."

Cole's eyes widened. "What does that mean?"

"It means I get a rush of...of feeling from someone. Their emotions."

Her answer made Cole distinctly uncomfortable. Uncomfortable enough that he did not want to think about it. He kept his emotions in tight check and to himself. The idea of someone sensing or feeling what he kept so carefully locked inside went way beyond disconcerting. It made him feel vulnerable.

"So what did you feel?"

"Just a jolt," she said and turned her back on him. "It takes a while for it to make any sense and right now we've got other things to think about."

Cole wasn't sure he was convinced she was telling the truth, but he was glad she didn't want to dwell on it. He was more than willing to try to forget it had ever happened. If that was possible.

"So, you have any ideas about our cat?" he asked.

"Yeah," she said over her shoulder. "Let me see your map."

Cole unfolded the map and handed it to her. She studied it for a moment then pointed to a location. "We need to reach this area before nightfall."

Cole looked at the location she pointed to. "The only way we'll make it is to follow Timber Creek to the lake, skirt it and scale here on the west face of Ida and stay to the high ground."

"Yeah, I know. You up for a climb, Cole?"

"Born ready," he said with a grin.

"Then let's get to it," Scout said with an answering smile.

"Lead the way." Cole gestured in front of him.

Scout shook her head. "You know the park better. Take us the quickest route to the west face of Ida. We're not going to find the cat between here and there."

"You sure about that, Scout?"

"Yeah."

"Okay, then, let's go."

With no further discussion they headed out.

* * * * *

"Shut the fuck up!" Raymond Moss snarled at his clients who were yakking it up like they were huffing down the sidewalks of New York.

They abruptly went silent, looking at him in anger tinted with anxiety. "What?" one of them asked softly.

Ray ignored the question, focusing his attention on their surroundings. He could have sworn he heard something.

"Hey!" A voice from behind them had Ray whirling around.

Two men approached, one behind the other.

The man in the lead stopped fifty yards out. "Drew Jones, Park Ranger Service. Would you mind telling me how you got into the park, sir?"

Before Ray could respond, Bobby's mouth flew into action. "We heard there was a wounded lion and figured we'd help y'all track him down."

Behind Drew, the hunter Ted whispered, "What wounded cat? If there was one we'd have been told. They're poachers."

Drew did not acknowledge Ted's comments but addressed the group of hunters. "Sir, there are regulations against firearms, and a strict 'no-hunting' restriction in place. Again, how did you get those weapons into the park and what is your intent?"

"I done told you," Bobby said with a whine, before Ray cut him off. "None'a your fucking business. Now unless you want trouble, you'll go back the way you came and leave us alone."

"I'm sorry, sir, I can't do that," Drew replied as Ted whispered behind him. "Call it in."

"Hold it!" Ray jerked his rifle up to his shoulder.

"Hold on now!" Drew said at the same moment Ray fired.

Drew felt the heat from the bullet pass his left shoulder and almost immediately heard Ted's breath whoosh out. He whirled around, too late to catch Ted as he fell, the radio slipping from his fingers.

Drew crouched, trying to bring his gun around to aim at the attackers but before he could, something slammed into him, propelling him backward into darkness.

"Jesus Christ!" one of Ray's clients barked weakly. "You stupid—"

His words were cut short when the third shot from Ray's rifle hit him in the center of the forehead.

The second client immediately broke and ran. Ray took a bead on him, but Bobby pushed the barrel aside, spoiling the shot. "Christ, Ray, what the fuck you doing?"

Ray turned on Bobby with murder in his eyes. "You dumb sumbitch! Those fuckers saw me shoot those guys. We can't let 'im live. He's a witness. Get rid of him and there's no evidence against us."

Bobby seemed unconvinced. "I don't know, Ray. We ain't never done nothing like this and I ain't—"

"You want to go to prison, Bobby?" Ray interrupted. "'Cause sure as shit, if we don't stop that city boy now, our asses are cooked."

"Hell no, I don't wanna go to prison!" Bobby replied. "But we can't just run him down and shoot him. Maybe he's scared enough he won't talk. Besides, how the hell's he going to find his way out? Maybe we can just track him and make sure he stays good and lost. Come nightfall he'll freeze anyway."

Ray considered it, but was more inclined to go find the man and make sure he didn't make it out. "Look, Ray," Bobby said. "We can wipe down your rifle, put it in the dead guy's hand and fire a round or two. Then you take his gun and we'll get rid of it. We'll say you loaned him a gun because he didn't have one. We'll track the other guy and make sure when night comes that he's got no chance to make it out. That way when they find the rangers it'll look like the city boy done it and no one will ever suspect us. They'll think his partner got scared and bolted and froze to death."

Ray had to admit that Bobby's idea had merit. He smiled. Every now and then Bobby came through for him. "All right, that's what we'll do. But if it looks like that city boy's going to make it out, we might just have to arrange a little accident."

"Whatever you say, Ray," Bobby replied immediately. "You're the boss."

"Got that right," Ray boasted. "You damn sure got that right."

Bobby turned and swiped his hand over his sweaty face as Ray took care of cleaning his weapon to place in the dead man's hands. Inside of five minutes they had the scene prepared, and headed out to track their quarry.

* * * * *

Scout went still and silent as a rock, making Cole do the same. For nearly two minutes she was frozen before she turned to look at him. "Gunfire. Four, maybe five miles."

"You heard gunfire from four miles away?"

"Didn't you?"

"No. You sure you're not mistaken?"

She shook her head. "Close your eyes for a minute."

"Why?"

"Indulge me."

Cole closed his eyes. "Okay," Scout said. "Think back a few moments. We were standing here, silent. What did you hear?"

Cole concentrated, his brows drawing together in an intense frown. He shook his head and opened his eyes. "Nothing. The wind, maybe."

"No, you heard more," she argued softly. "Try again. There was an alarm. You heard it. Wings and—"

"Yes!" he exclaimed. "Birds. All of a sudden, wings and cries in the air."

Scout nodded again. "Yes, it was part of a concentric circle that began about five miles from here. A gunshot. The wildlife in the immediate area reacted, setting up kind of a chain reaction that radiated out from the point of origin."

Cole regarded her with new respect. "I get it. But I still didn't hear the actual shot."

"Neither did I. I heard its echo and the reaction it evoked."

"Do you think that means someone else found the cat?"

She shook her head. "No, she's still out there. Still hurt."

"So we continue the way we're going?" he asked.

"Yeah."

"Well, maybe I should radio in just to be sure," he suggested.

"You still don't trust me," Scout replied.

"It's not that!"

"Then what?"

He didn't have an answer except to leave the radio in its harness and gesture ahead of them. "If we cut across the creek about a quarter mile up, we'll have smoother going and shave some time off reaching Ida."

Scout smiled at him. "Lead the way, Ranger."

Cole grinned and took the lead. Scout watched him walk ahead of her, wondering if she should have told him that the origin of the disturbance lay in the direction they were headed.

* * * * *

Tim Matthews swore when he couldn't raise Cole on the radio. One of the teams had run into trouble and now the competition had taken an unexpected and dangerous turn.

"Frank!" he yelled to the ranger on duty in the main office.

Frank appeared at the door. "Any word from Cole?"

"Not yet. Listen, I need a list of everyone registered in the park. And I need someone to check every vehicle and make a list of the tags. Run them against the register. I want this place locked down. No one in or out."

"Something happen?"

Tim blew out his breath and leaned forward, propping his elbows on his desk. "Drew Jones radioed in. They came upon a hunting party. He and the tracker hailed the party and he advised them there was a no-hunting restriction in place.

"But according to Drew, one of the men tried to make excuses for their armed presence and had claimed they were out trying to help track a wounded cat."

"We haven't had any reports on wounded cats," Frank said.

"Exactly," Tim agreed. "And Drew knew that. He advised the men to surrender their weapons and leave the park. The leader of the group refused.

"The way Drew tells it, Ted was standing behind him and he whispered to Drew that he should call in. Drew reached for his radio and when he did, the leader fired. At least that's who Drew thought fired. All he knew for sure was that he felt the heat of the bullet beside him and then Ted fell, dead before he hit the ground."

"Jesus!"

"Tell me about it," Tim said and pushed himself up from his seat. "Drew tried to draw his gun but was shot before he could. When he came to, he was alone. He managed to get the radio and call in for help."

"Is he gonna make it, Tim?"

"I don't know. I hope so. A team's enroute. I just hope they reach him in time."

"Amen," Frank agreed. "Anything I can do?"

"Just get the park closed down. Tight, Frank. Real tight."

"I'm on it."

Tim picked up his empty coffee cup and headed for the pot. His stomach was already a boiling vat of acid, but right now he needed to be sharp. There was a new hunt going on, and not one to tag cats, but for four men who had shot and murdered at least one man. Nothing like this had ever happened in the Park and Tim felt responsible.

Tim's secretary Melody entered the office. "State police are on their way. They said to recall all the teams and wait for them."

"Already done," Tim replied and turned to reach for the radio.

"And they said to call Windrider," she added. "They need a tracker."

Tim paused and turned to her. "She's already out there. With Cole."

Melody's eyes widened. "You want me to call the State boys back and tell them?"

"No," Tim replied. "We'll let them know when they arrive. Right now, just get up with all the teams and have them advise us of their position so we can arrange for pickup points. And check on the status of the team headed out for Drew."

"Will do," she said and hurried away.

Tim tried again to reach Cole. There was no reply. It was not like Cole to go completely dark. But then Cole had never been out with Scout and it was like her to cut off communication.

Sometimes Tim thought she was more like her grandfather than anyone realized—more part of the animal kingdom than that of man. He had no doubt of her skills in tracking, and knew she was proficient enough to handle herself. But she and Cole were out there unaware, which meant they could stumble into trouble.

"Come on, Cole, answer," he whispered as he tried again.

* * * * *

Raymond and Bobby sat on a ridge watching their former client stumble through the small clearing in the valley beneath them. Night was falling and the man was weak, his steps uncertain. Ray had no doubt that the only thing that drove him now was fear. Fear of possible pursuit and fear of night falling and him being alone and lost, with no shelter and no food.

"What'cha think?" Bobby asked. "Make camp here tonight and pick up his trail in the morning?"

Ray nodded. "Yeah, might as well. He'll stick to the valley more than likely. No fire though. We don't want to give away our position."

"Got it," Bobby agreed. "You think he'll last the night?"

Ray shrugged. "Who knows? Don't much care."

Bobby nodded and said no more as he started unpacking his bedroll. Ray remained motionless, his eyes scanning the landscape as his mind traveled back in time…

He was almost eighteen, nearly a man, and had been working with his father for several years. His father claimed that Ray was going to be a tracker on the level with Jed Windrider. Ray found it odd that even after Jed had rebuffed and turned his back on James, James still spoke so highly of him. It annoyed Ray, but he knew the compliment was the highest his father could give.

He was feeling pretty full of himself. He'd made enough to buy himself a shiny new Camaro, had money in his pocket and had developed enough self-confidence that he wasn't shy around the ladies.

In fact, he was earning himself a reputation with them as well. A real player. That's how he saw himself. Woo them with money and a fast ride, get what he wanted and leave them.

Not that he was heartless. He simply had no interest in the girls he dated. They were only interested in the latest fashion, their looks and who was the most popular that particular week. None of them were the least bit interested in his prowess in tracking. In fact, if he made the mistake of bringing it up, a girl would normally either turn up her nose at the idea or make fun of it.

All of them except Scout Windrider. She was only thirteen, but possessed far more maturity than any of the girls Ray's own age. And she was a tracker. From what he'd heard, she was darn near a master tracker already. Ray was a bit envious of the high praise she earned, but also intrigued.

He'd watched her leave the junior high school. She never dawdled, talking with friends. She made a beeline for the bus, her stride strong and sure and her head up, as if getting a lay of the land. Those strange cat's eyes of hers seemed to take in everything. Twice she had stopped and turned, pegging him with a penetrating stare as he sat in his car watching her.

Ray had already made up his mind that the day she turned sixteen, he was going to make his move on her. By then he'd have his own place and money in the bank. Not to mention a reputation as a tracker. She'd be impressed. And she'd want him…

"You want some'a this jerky?" Bobby's voice cut into his thoughts.

Ray shook his head and rose to spread out his bedroll. No use in dwelling on the past, his father always said. Just let it go and move on. But Ray was cut from a different cloth. There would be no peace for him until he'd made all the Windriders pay for his father's death, and had rid the world of as many cougar as possible. Once that was done, Ray would be done with it and ready to move on. But not a second sooner.

With his hatred refueled, he lay back and stared at the stars, his mind at work on how best to continue his quest once he had taken care of the irritating city boy. One step at a time, he told himself. Just one step at a time. First thing he needed to do was get back to base camp and talk to Jimmy. And if he stumbled on the city boy maybe he'd just take care of that problem and get it out of the way. He waited for Bobby to fall asleep then headed out.

Chapter Four

ஐ

Tim Matthews pushed himself up from his chair as the tall dark-skinned man entered the room. Not that it was required. There was just something about the man that commanded respect.

"Captain Jonas Roberts," the man said in a deep voice, offering his hand. "CBI."

"Tim Matthews," Tim replied, taking his hand. "Park Director. Can I get you some coffee?"

"Thank you, sir, but no. Do you have a room we can use to establish a command post?"

"Of course," Tim replied. "Please come with me."

He led Captain Roberts to the conference room. He hadn't expected the Colorado Bureau of Investigation to respond so quickly to his call. Once his rescue team had extracted Drew Jones and gotten him to a hospital, he had made the call to the CBI. His men were park rangers. They were not equipped to deal with hostiles who were murdering people.

"Will this do?" He stepped aside for the Captain to enter the room.

"Fine, thank you," Jonas replied and activated his com link. "Hill, we have a location. I want com set up here in ten minutes with a backup unit in the van. Get teams one through four ready to deploy. I'll brief them in twenty minutes."

Jonas then turned to address Tim. "I want to hear everything you have on the hostiles, and a list of every man you have in the field. And— Excuse me." He activated his com link again. "Hill, what's the word on our tracker?"

"No response. Still trying," the reply sounded in his earpiece.

"Keep at it," he ordered then returned his attention to Tim. "As I was saying—"

"Excuse me," Tim interrupted, "but I think you'll want to know first up that Scout Windrider is already out there."

"You already sent her in?" Jonas asked. "On whose authority?"

"No one's," Tim replied. "She was one of the participants in the competition, partnered with Cole Russell. They've been out all day."

"I was informed that all competitors had been recalled after the incident."

"They were," Tim said. "But we can't reach Cole."

"Transmission problems?"

"I don't think so." Tim hated to admit it. "I think he's gone silent."

Jonas considered it for a moment. In all likelihood, Matthews was right. And Jonas would bet that it was at Scout's insistence. He didn't like the idea that the two of them were out there uninformed, but he also knew there was every possibility that Scout was already aware of trouble. Not much escaped her notice.

His problem was how to let her know about his teams so there were no potential problems.

"What can you tell me about the hostiles?"

Tim ran his hand over his face. Fatigue was catching up with him. "According to Drew, there were four. Two men he described as pale, out of shape and seemingly out of place. The other two he described as men you'd likely see out hunting. One was around five-ten with sandy hair, slim and wearing camos. The other was tall, six-two or -three, with dark eyes. Wore a black knit cap and camos."

Jonas nodded. "Heavily armed?"

"All men had rifles. The two described as hunters also wore side arms."

"Thank you," Jonas said. "If you'll excuse me."

Tim watched Jonas walk away, and then leaned back against the wall. What had started as a friendly competition had blossomed into something out of a nightmare. If only he had been able to reach Cole. The idea of him and Scout running into four armed men made a shiver run down his spine.

Pushing himself away from the wall, he hurried to his office to try Cole on the radio again.

*****

"We need to make camp," Cole said as Scout breasted the cliff and scrambled to her feet.

"Cats are nocturnal," she replied. "She's been hiding all day. Now that it's dark she'll be on the move."

"Be that as it may, we're not cats. We haven't eaten or rested and unless we do a little of both we're going to run out of steam."

Scout considered it for a few moments then agreed. "Okay, but no more than four hours. We need to be on the move soon."

"Deal," Cole said and looked around. "If I remember correctly, there's a shallow cave a quarter mile north."

"Lead the way," Scout replied and fell in behind him as he headed out. For the last three hours she'd gotten wind of a disturbance. The forest was on alert, the animals skittish and wary. She was fairly certain they were no more than two miles from the origin of whatever had raised the alarm. Part of her wanted to press forward. Another part warned caution.

Which was why she had agreed with Cole that they should make camp. She could use the time to listen, and to see if she could sense anything. She was quiet the rest of the way, and they made camp without speaking.

The cave was deep enough that they would be protected from the wind. A fissure in the ceiling provided a small but natural chimney. "Fire?" Cole asked.

She nodded and he disappeared outside. She prepared a place for the fire with rocks she found lying about the cave then pulled a small break-down spade from her pack and set to work digging two holes near the fire site. Once there were enough coals, she'd fill the holes, cover the coals over with dirt and put the sleeping bags over them. It was a simple yet old and effective means of heating.

Cole returned with an armload of wood, dumped it then disappeared again. It struck her as they worked in unison that their movements were those of people who knew one another, rather than strangers who had just met. That thought had her pausing to turn and look at Cole as he entered with another armload of wood.

They went about making camp like people who'd worked together for years and understood one another's rhythm. How was that possible? He stopped and found her looking at him. Their eyes met and the world went silent.

He could hear nothing but the sound of his own heart, beating hard and strong, the rate increasing with each moment that her cat eyes held him spellbound. It was only pride that kept him rooted in place when everything inside him shouted for him to close the distance between them. To take her in his arms. To feast on her lips, feed on her breasts, feel passion make her weak and then claim her, taking her fast and hard, slaking the thirst that burned in his veins.

The effect she had on him made him uncomfortable in more ways than just the immediate erection she gave him with a look. He felt like an animal. Something primal, primitive. A male recognizing a potential mate.

That was the idea that shook him to the soles of his feet. He'd never had such an immediate and profound reaction to a woman. He'd always been the cool one, the one who could hold back, wait for the woman to approach him, knowing she would and that when she did she was already his.

But Scout made no move. Not even a blink. Like an animal, immobile and wary, yet curious, she stood silently, watching. Her stillness was erotic, compelling. Instinct urged him to go to her. Pride demanded that he not.

Pride was about to lose the battle when her eyes suddenly turned up and to one side, her head cocking almost exactly like that of a cat. Cole strained to hear but aside from the wind there was nothing.

Scout felt a presence. Not far, perhaps a hundred yards, off to the right of their camp. She opened her senses, letting herself become absorbed by the surroundings. After a moment she smiled. The deer was far more unsettled by their presence than she was with its. Using the technique her grandfather had taught her, Scout sent a mental message to the deer. Not words, but feelings of peace and safely. Visions of herself and the deer. Her hand on the deer's neck, her touch and scent letting the animal know that there was nothing to fear.

She felt an answering relaxation and a moment later the rustle of leaves as the deer foraged.

Scout returned her attention to Cole to find him watching her curiously. "A deer," she said simply and went back to her task.

"Where?" he asked as he started on the fire.

"About a hundred yard to the right."

"I didn't hear anything."

She shrugged and rose to replace the spade in her pack. She shook out her bedroll, placing it near one of the holes she'd dug then looked over at him. He had the fire started and was feeding wood into it. "You hungry?" she asked.

The look that flared in his eyes had her suddenly hungering. And not for food. A totally feminine need bloomed, making her nipples pucker and a fire burn its way from her belly to her groin.

"Starving," he replied, letting her know by look and tone that his appetite was not for food either.

There was no way they were going to be able to work together and focus with so much fire between them. Perhaps they wouldn't act upon it, but until they acknowledged it, it would continue to rear its head.

"What are we going to do about this?" she asked.

The question shocked Cole. He hadn't expected her to be so direct. "That depends," he replied, deciding that the best approach would be to find out first what she wanted.

"On?"

"On what you want."

He received another shock. Scout walked over to him, her eyes never leaving his. He stood and faced her. She didn't stop until her body was pressed up against his, her head angled back to maintain eye contact.

"What I want is the problem. I want to win this competition. I *want* to find that wounded cat and save her. And I want to feel you naked and inside me."

For a moment Cole had no clue how to respond. His body wasn't having that problem. His dick was at full alert, straining at his pants. "You said problem," he finally found his tongue. Once his mouth started working, his brain kicked in as well. "The way I see it, there's nothing stopping you from having everything you want."

"Is that right?" she breathed, her voice low and husky.

"Yep."

"Well then," she replied as her hands moved inside his coat and started a trek up his body to end circled around his neck. "In that case, let's start with you. Naked."

Cole didn't need any more prompting than that. He snaked one arm around her, pulling her tightly to him while running his other hand behind her head to pull her mouth to his.

Plundered. That's the only word her mind could come up with to describe the kiss. He was neither gentle nor hesitant. He assumed control and took. And the female that had lain dormant for so long beneath the hard exterior reveled in it. Wanted more.

Her fingers tangled in his thick hair, fisted and pulled him closer, asserting her own control, diving her tongue into the warm sweetness of his mouth. The arm circling her loosened and his hand traveled lower, to cup her ass and pull her more firmly against his erection.

Scout nearly came then and there. *By all the ancestors!* She could feel his heat, smell his hunger and it shoved all else from her mind. Her hands worked at the buttons of his shirt, eager to have her hands on him, needing to touch him.

His skin was warm, the muscles beneath tight. She could feel the tension that sang inside him and understood it all too well. Her body was on fire. Her nipples literally burned and her skin felt electrified, as if it had been slumbering until this moment and suddenly awakened to a world of sensation that was nearly overwhelming in its intensity.

Scout had never felt this kind of fire, this kind of wanting. It almost scared her. But the fear was eclipsed by desire. Her hands moved between them to stroke him though the fabric of his pants.

Cole broke free from the kiss and lifted her off the ground with one arm. Her legs circled his waist, settling her wet sex against his erection, providing another bolt of pleasure and longing that had her grinding against him.

His free hand unfastened her jacket and moved inside to cup one breast, his thumb rubbing over the hard nipple, creating waves of sensation that had her gasping. "Yes," she breathed as his mouth replaced his hand, teeth scraping the fabric of her top over the sensitive nub.

That throatily gasped word almost made him come. Time and place, circumstance and reason fled his mind. Nothing existed but the woman in his arms and his need. He carried her to the bedroll and laid her down, settling his weight on her as he claimed her lips.

Her legs still wound around his waist, she tilted her hips up, pressing against his erection as her mouth slanted across his, her tongue questing within his mouth. A whimper escaped her when he moved one hand down, skimmed across her ass and rubbed firmly over her sex, feeling the damp material that gave testament to her excitement.

Without warning she suddenly shoved him off her and bounded to her feet, heading for the entrance of the cave.

"What?" he scrambled to his feet.

"Gunfire," she said, stepping outside the cave.

Cole followed her outside but did not speak. She appeared to be concentrating, her eyes moved slowly, scanning the darkness. After a few minutes of tense silence she turned to face him.

"Radio Tim. Something's not right. There shouldn't be gunfire and this is the second time."

Cole nodded and went inside the cave. He returned a few moments later with the radio. "Russell to base. Come in."

They both waited, looking at one another and the radio expectantly. When Tim's voice sounded in the silence, it seemed unnaturally loud.

"Cole? It's about time! What the hell's going on? We've been trying to reach you all day."

Cole turned down the volume before responding.

"Tim, I think we may have some poachers or illegal hunters out here. Scout heard gunfire earlier and again just a few minutes ago."

There was a pause. Cole looked at Scout who wore a serious expression on her face. Tim's voice came back over the radio.

"Cole, I have Captain Jonas Roberts with the CBI here. He'd like to speak with Scout."

"She's right here," Cole responded and gave Scout a quizzical look.

She didn't react in any way. A deep male voice came over the radio. "Scout?"

"I'm here, Jonas. What's up?"

"We have a situation. A ranger and one of the hunters were gunned down earlier today. The hunter is dead. We have vague descriptions on four men and a location. I've dispatched four teams but we need a tracker."

"Give me the coordinates. We'll leave now."

"Before you move, tell me about the gunfire you just heard. You get a direction and distance?"

"No. I was in a cave, making camp. But from the area of disturbance a few seconds after the event, I'd guess it was less than two miles from our current location and best estimate is a general north-east direction which would place it..." She looked to Cole for help.

"Somewhere past Ida," Cole offered.

"Your teams shouldn't try it at night," Scout added. "It'll require climbing and there's weather coming in."

"Affirmative," Jonas replied. "But we can't let the trail go cold and weather will decrease our chances. You up for night tracking?"

"Yes."

"Is Mr. Russell equipped to accompany you?"

Scout eyed Cole for a moment. It would be faster if she went alone, and quieter. He wasn't a greenhorn but he didn't know how to move through the forest silently. But then again, if she ran into trouble, he would be handy. Cole was a big man, strong and quick. If she were tracking four men, she would be smart to have backup.

"Yeah," she answered.

"Then get to it. Radio silence until you've located the target. Mark the location and get to a safe distance and radio in. We'll be waiting on your call."

"Got it," Scout replied, and then turned away, speaking to Cole over her shoulder as she gathered her hair up and wound it into a knot on the top of her head. "We travel light. Leave everything here except the rifle. You have any live ammo?"

"No. This was supposed to be a no-kill hunt."

"Then take the trancs," she said. "If we run into trouble, I'm going to be depending on you to take them out."

It was not until that moment that Cole realized she did not have a weapon. "What about you?"

She patted the knife sheathed on her hip then squatted down in front of her backpack and rumbled around. She withdrew a small round tin and opened it. After smearing some of the dark substance over her face, neck and the top of her hands, she pulled on a dark knit cap and stood.

Cole was momentarily taken aback. With the dark smears across her face, her cat-like eyes seemed huge and almost feral. She smeared his face, neck and the tops of his hands and wrists with the substance.

"That smells like shit," he complained.

"Only partially," she said and turned away, but not before he saw a smile.

He was certain she was trying to jerk his chain. No way would she smear shit on her face. Then again, just to be safe, he'd make damn sure his hands got nowhere near his mouth.

Scout took off her coat and donned a tight, matte, black, high-necked shirt that was mottled with other colors and matched her pants. Cole knew that once she stepped outside, she'd blend into the night like a ghost. Following her lead, he shed his coat and pulled on a tight black shirt designed for artic wear, along with a wool cap that fit snuggly over his head to his eyebrows and covered his ears.

"You ready?" she asked.

"As I'll get," he replied.

"Okay, just a couple of things," she said. "We need to move fast, but quiet. I'll take the lead. I want you to stay exactly five paces behind me. No more and no less. Move as quietly as possible and if I raise my left arm, stop and don't make a sound. Got it?"

"Yeah."

"Then let's go."

Wondering what kind of trouble they would find, or what might find them, he followed her out into the night.

Chapter Five

ஐ

Ray approached the still form on the ground cautiously. Even in the darkness of night he could see the dark stain that spread slowly outward on the ground, forming a black halo around the prone figure.

Scooping up the rifle that lay nearby, Ray kicked at his client. There was no reaction. He gave the man one more kick before he knelt down beside him. No doubt. The man was dead.

What a stroke of luck it was happening on the city slicker. The man had been stupid enough to try and build a crude shelter on the north side of an outcropping of rocks. The wind had blown away most of the branches and leaves he'd used as cover, and he was damn near frozen when Ray came upon him.

Truth be told, Ray might never have spotted him if the man hadn't groaned in his sleep. But he did, and Ray saw his chance.

And Ray was not a man to let a chance pass him by. He'd walked up bold as brass on the man and shot him twice in the head.

Now the only witness left who could pin the shooting of the rangers on him was Bobby.

Chances were Bobby would never rat him out. He knew he'd be charged as an accomplice. And since it was only Bobby's word against his and Bobby was the one with a record, there was a good chance the authorities would believe Ray if he pointed the finger at Bobby.

No, he could trust Bobby. Without him, Bobby was nothing. A loser with no job and no friends. Bobby didn't just need him, he depended on him. Ray was all Bobby had.

And he needed Bobby. He still hadn't figured out how to accomplish phase two of his plan. Until he settled the score with Scout Windrider, his father's soul could not rest. And Ray was not about to let his father down. He'd promised to avenge his father's death and that was what he was going to do. No matter what.

Pushing to his feet, he cut a look around. Chances were good that no one would find the city boy for days. Hell, maybe even weeks. No need to bother burying the body. Scavengers would take care of the disposal for him.

Satisfied that he didn't have anything to be concerned over, he continued on toward base camp.

* * * * *

Scout and Cole had been traveling for almost an hour when she stopped. He moved up close behind her. "You hear something?" he whispered close to her ear.

"No. Smell," she replied almost too softly to be heard. "Stay here."

"Hold on!" Cole grabbed her arm to stay her. "Where're you going?"

"Just want to check it out. I'll be back in five minutes. Just stay here."

Cole did not like the idea of staying behind, but figured it was best not to argue. She couldn't get that far in five minutes that he couldn't catch up to her.

She disappeared into the darkness and he crouched down, listening. The only sounds he heard were those of the night. The wind. Nothing seemed to be moving. Not even Scout.

He wondered how she did it.

Scout was prepared for the sight of death because the smell that led her was blood. What she was not prepared for was the sight of the dead man, half his head and brains spattered on the ground.

She knelt beside him and felt his skin. No way of telling how long he'd been dead by his skin temperature. He'd been out in the elements without shelter. From the looks of things he'd tried to build shelter but done a poor job of it. His rifle lay nearby, but from the position of the body he hadn't been holding it. He looked more like he'd been asleep.

Which brought up the question of who had killed him. Was he one of the people responsible for the murder of the tracker? If so, then what had happened to find him sleeping alone without food or shelter?

Pushing aside the distaste it brought, Scout touched the pool of gore beside the man's head. He couldn't have been dead long. It looked like two shots had entered the front of his head. That had to have been what she heard in the cave.

So where was the person who'd killed this man? That was something she needed to figure out and fast. Careful to retrace her steps so as not to disturb any more than necessary, she quickly made her way back to Cole.

Cole darn near jumped when Scout materialized in front of him. "There's been another shooting," she said. "A man. Shot twice in the head. I want you to follow me, and make sure that you step in my tracks. I need to figure out where the person who killed this guy headed, and to do that we have to make sure we disturb as little as possible."

"Got it," he agreed and pushed himself upright.

He followed her to the scene of the crime. Bile rose in his throat as he got a look at the man. In the moonlight the man's pale skin looked almost ghostly, and the gore beneath his head, black and grisly.

Scout paid the dead man no attention at all. With slow, steady steps, she circled out from the body, her eyes scanning the ground. It wasn't long before she stopped, knelt down, touched the earth, then started forward.

"This way," she said softly over her shoulder.

Cole hurried to where she was. She talked softly as she followed a trail he could not see. "One man. Big. One ninety or so. Not a greenhorn. Soles of his boots are worn. He favors his right leg. Not a limp, but definitely a difference in weight distribution. Could be carrying a pack. He wasn't in a hurry but wasn't wasting time by the length of the stride."

"Hold up." Cole took her arm and stopped her. "That fellow from CBI said to radio in if we found anything."

"The longer we wait, the more distance there is between us and him," she argued. "I say we follow him and when we discover where he's holed up, then we…" She stopped short and her eyes turned up and then to one side in a gesture he related to the look of an animal sensing danger.

"What?" he asked.

"Let's back up and radio Jonas," she said after a moment.

"What changed your mind?" he asked.

She dropped her eyes then turned her head away, seemingly scanning the darkness.

"Scout?"

"I need to find the cat," she said softly. "Time's running out."

Cole thought it odd in the extreme that she'd change her mind so abruptly. "Look, a second ago you were gung ho on tracking the shooter. Now you just back off and say we need to go after the cat. What's up? I need the truth, Scout, and now."

She turned to look at him. "Fine. The truth is I…hear the cat. Satisfied?"

Before he could answer she started back the way they'd come.

"Just hold on!" He hurried and grabbed hold of her arm, forcing her to face him. "You hear the cat? Granted you hear things I don't because of your experience in reading the sounds animals make, but I've heard nothing that sounds remotely like a lion. So just exactly what did you hear?"

Scout sighed. Aside from Jed, she'd never told another living soul about her ability. The way she saw it, people would either think she was a liar or crazy. Jed understood because he possessed the ability. He'd always told her she'd inherited it from his people and it was nothing to fear, simply a gift that she could choose to use for good or ill. He'd stressed using it for good. Otherwise, he warned, the gift could turn against her, and her soul would be forever stained.

Now she faced telling Cole her secret. It gave her more than a little anxiety. Perhaps because she'd had such an immediate reaction to him. She'd told herself the first few hours that it was because she'd been lusting after his bull-riding brother from afar. But she knew now she wanted him and it had nothing to do with his brother or a fantasy crush. He drew her like a magnet and it was something she could not control.

But trust was another matter. For a few moments she searched inside herself. What she'd sensed from him during the connection was still jumbled but some things had become clear. Such as the fact that he was a man of honor. And there was something else. Something he hid. About witches.

"Tell me about the witches you know," she said suddenly, acting on impulse.

His eyes widened. "How— What makes you think I know any witches?"

"You said it was time for truth," she challenged him both verbally and with her eyes. "You want truth from me, and then you have to be willing to share your truth as well."

Cole was silent for a moment, and then blew out his breath. "All right. But before I say anything else, let's get this clear. I am not crazy."

That one sentence alone gave her comfort. "Okay," she said with a slight smile. "You're not crazy. Now about the witches?"

"My sisters-in-law," he said. "Ana and Rusty. Both of them."

Scout nodded. "And do either of them have any special…affinity with animals?"

"Actually yeah, both of them."

"Then there's your answer," she offered.

"You mean you…you're a…witch?"

"I don't choose to call it that. I simply have some skills and abilities. And one of them is that I have an affinity with animals. Particularly cats."

"So you're hearing the cat, but not with your ears, right? You have a, uh, connection with it?"

"Exactly," she said with relief, thinking how amazingly easy that had been. "And I know she needs help and fast. So, radio Jonas and we'll give him the coordinates and let him and his men deal with the killer. We're not armed except with trancs and a knife, and whoever the guy is we know he's armed. Best leave the dirty work to the pros. You and I can go help the cat."

"Okay," he agreed without hesitation and pulled out the radio. "You sure it's safe to call in?"

She nodded. "He's got enough of a lead that he's not going to hear it. Make the call."

Cole pulled out the radio and called in. Tim answered. "We were starting to be concerned," he said. "You find anything?"

Cole handed the radio to Scout. "Tim, it's Scout. I need to talk to Jonas."

"He's here," Tim replied.

A second later Jonas' voice came over the radio.

"What you got?"

"Another victim," she replied. "White man, mid-forties, approximately five-ten, one seventy-five. Shot twice in the head at close range. Probably a handgun. My guess is a .44. He appeared to have tried to build a shelter. Probably was near frozen. From his clothing he looks to be a greenhorn. Probably one of the hunting party the ranger described."

"You pick up a trail?"

"Yeah, can you triangulate on the radio?"

"Can do. We're on it now."

"Okay, from my position the victim is west-south-west approximately 35 degrees, two miles at most. The killer is headed in a south-east direction, averaging…I'd estimate about two miles an hour."

"In the dark?"

"He's experienced, Jonas. No doubt about it. Knows the lay of the land and where he's headed. You have teams nearby?"

"It'll take us a couple of hours to get close. I'll have my men head in from the south and east and try to intercept. You continuing to track?"

"Negative. We're not armed. And we have another matter that needs dealing with."

"Which is?"

"Wounded cat. I suspect the killer and his party are responsible. I need to get to her fast."

There was a moment of silence before Jonas came back. "Affirmative. But I need contact from you in three hours. If we don't intercept the shooter we'll need you to pick up his trail and lead my men."

"Got it," Scout replied. "Out."

She turned off the radio and handed it to Cole. "You think they'll find him?" he asked.

"If they don't we'll come back and pick up his trail. Right now we need to head due north."

"Which means we're going to be climbing in the dark so we have to go back and get our gear."

"No time," Scout argued. "You've climbed freestyle before, right?"

"Climbing without the proper gear is dangerous anytime, but at night? Scout, that's asking for trouble."

"We don't have a choice."

"Fine." Cole wasn't sure it was the wise choice, but grudgingly agreed. Without another word, Scout started forward, leaving Cole no choice but to follow and hope they did not end up victims of their own design.

Chapter Six

ꟹ

Ray leaned back against the rock and considered what his brother Jimmy was saying.

"Ray, we both know that Bobby will freak the fuck out when he finds out you shot that guy. And sooner or later, he'll make a mistake or shoot off his mouth and then the law will be gunning for you. The only, and I mean only option we have to get out of this clean is to kill him."

"We were friends more than twenty years, Jim."

"I know. But which is worse? Doing Bobby or ending up in prison?"

Ray blew out his breath and nodded. As much as Ray hated to do it, he had no choice. He had to kill Bobby. With Bobby dead, there'd be no fingers to point at him. "So what do you suggest we do?"

Jimmy finished loading his pack and crouched down beside Ray. "Knowing Bobby, he'll sleep like a log through the night. We go back to the camp, knock him out and haul him into high ground. We put climbing gear on him, rig a line and toss him over. We wear the line on rock 'til it breaks and it looks like an accident. Plant the gun you used on him, but make sure you clean it and we get his prints on it. When he's found and they discover the gun, they'll think he's the one who killed those guys and you're home free."

Ray thought about it. Jimmy was right, and the plan was good. With Bobby dead and nailed with the murders he could go about his business, act shocked when he was told about Bobby and pretend to mourn.

"One thing," he said. "I need an alibi."

"No problem, bro," Jimmy said with a smile. "We'll head straight out to Fred's place when we finish up with Bobby and stay there for a week. Fred said we could use it any time we want. Anyone asks, we been there since last weekend."

"That should work," Ray agreed. "Okay, let's do it."

Jimmy stood and offered Ray a hand, then pulled him to his feet. Together they headed out into the dark. Now the only problem Ray had was that tingling feeling on the back of his neck. For a while, on his way to meet up with Jimmy, he could have sworn he was being followed. He never saw or heard anything, it was just a feeling. He didn't say anything about it, but kept his eyes and ears sharp.

*****

Scout grabbed the hand Cole offered as she pulled herself up over the edge of the rock. It had been a harder and longer climb than she'd anticipated. Lack of food and sleep was starting to take its toll. Had it not been for the constant sensation of suffering she felt coming from the cat, she would have stopped. But already she feared they were too late.

"This way," she said to Cole and took off at a jog.

It was twenty minutes of dodging outcroppings, working their way up short ledges and more running before they reached the opening of the cave. Scout stopped and motioned for Cole to hold his position. "I need to go alone," she said.

"No!" He grabbed her arm. "That's a wounded cat. No telling what it'll do."

"I'll be fine," she assured him. "Please. I'll let you know when to enter."

"I don't like this. I know you have experience with these animals and a…connection with them, but a wounded animal is dangerous."

"Please," she implored. "Trust me."

Cole studied her eyes for a long moment then suddenly yanked her to him, and covered her mouth with his. The kiss seared her, body and mind, speaking of passion unlike any she'd known and a promise of something more than mere desire. She wanted to lose herself in it. But the call of the cat in her mind had her pulling away.

Cole nodded. "Go."

She approached the opening of the cave, speaking softly. "It's me. I'm here. I'm coming in. Alone."

A low growl sounded from within the darkness. Scout stepped inside and stood very still, letting her eyes adjust to the darkness. Eventually shapes began to materialize. She saw the cat. Lying on her side, her breathing labored, blood still seeped from the gaping wound in her side. A cub huddled up against her belly, mewling low and mournfully.

Scout hurried to her and put her hand on the animal's side. There was so much blood everywhere. Her pants were wet with it as she sat beside the lion. Tears sprang from her eyes. She was too late. The lion had lost too much blood and from the sound of its breathing had punctured a lung.

Grief tore at her swift and hard, crippling her. She lay her head down on the lion, her arms circling the big body. With great racking sobs she cried, unable to stop it. How long she wept, she didn't know. But in time a sound filtered in. The sound of Cole's voice calling her.

"Can I please let him in?" she whispered brokenly.

Permission was granted and she called out softly. "Cole. Come in."

She turned her attention back to the lion. "You are beyond my power to heal," she said softly in the language of her ancestors, the Sioux. "How can I ease your pain?"

"What?" Cole asked from behind her.

"I'm speaking to her," Scout replied. "Come, sit with me."

Cole settled down on the ground beside her. She lifted the cub and cradled it for a moment then handed it to him. The lion raised her head and gave a warning growl. Scout put her hand on the lion's face. "He will protect your child," she continued to speak in the tongue of her people. "Tell me how to ease your pain, my friend. How to make recompense for what my kind have done to you?"

A whisper appeared in her mind. "Human female, you bear no fault for what has befallen me. I see your spirit. You walk in the world of humans, and yet you are of my kind as well. Care for my cub so that she grows strong and I will leave this life in peace."

"I promise," Scout whispered. "No harm will come to her, and when she's old enough I'll bring her back and introduce her to her own kind."

"Then I may leave," the voice whispered. "But first, you must know. I have encountered the human who hurt me before. His scent is familiar and known. He kills not to live but to feed an evil that grows inside him. He killed the old one many moons ago."

"The old one?" Scout's chest clenched. "You mean my grandfather?"

"He was one of us," the voice replied. "Like you, he valued life and honored the earth. His life was taken by the same one who ends mine."

"Please, tell me what you know of him," Scout pleaded. "I will see that he's made to pay for what he's done."

"He smells of the burning leaf human's suck, is tall and dark of hair. His eyes are cold and dead. The color of winter bark. He travels with a man who is small and hair is the color of grass in the coming time of the cold. There is no peace inside him."

"Thank you," Scout whispered. "I promise you I will not rest until I see him pay."

"I believe you."

"I'm sorry," Scout said through tears that started flowing down her face. "I want to save you. Is there nothing I can do?"

There was a long silence. "You may allow me to walk within you."

A shiver danced down Scout's spine. Jed had told her stories of such things, but she'd attributed it to myth. "Is that possible?" she asked.

"If you consent, we will live as one."

Scout didn't stop to consider. "Yes. How?"

"Step out of the shell that holds you and let your spirit join with me."

Scout closed her eyes and let the Sight take her.

Jed had taught her how to surrender to the Sight when she was a child. It was a release of sorts. She released her hold on her mortal body and allowed her spirit to rise, escaping the bounds of flesh and blood.

While the Sight had her, she saw and heard things she could not sense in her body. People's thoughts and feelings were revealed to her. She could see their essence, and touch their spirits.

Joining with another spirit was not something she'd ever attempted. Jed had not prepared her for that. In this she was on her own.

One moment she was in the cave and the next she was spiraling in an endless swirl of light. She felt a presence with her. It was comforting and inviting. She opened herself to it, embracing it. A feeling of warmth flooded her. She felt new life within her. Vital and strong.

"We are one," a voice rang in the light and suddenly Scout was in the cave, slumped over the lion's body with Cole shaking her.

"Scout?" His voice carried so much concern that tears ran down her face.

She pushed herself up and turned to him.

"Christ!" he gasped.

She didn't understand the shock on his face or in his voice.

"Your eyes."

"What's wrong with them? I see clear as day."

"Scout…you…damn. What happened? Your eyes look like a cat."

She smiled at him. "Let's just say that I feel filled with new life."

"What does that mean?"

She shook her head, watching him stroke and soothe the cub in his arms. How gentle he was with it. How caring. He did it without thinking, giving love and compassion to the tiny life that had had its mother taken from it. Quite unprepared for the onslaught of emotion, a sound between a whimper and a purr emerged from her lips. Love exploded inside her, nearly overwhelming her. Along with love came longing, strong and deep. What was happening? The strength of it scared her.

Then she felt the answer from the cat within. Here was the mate she'd longed for, dreamed of. With that knowledge came a hunger unlike any she'd ever known. "I want you," she whispered.

"Now?" he asked in surprise.

"Yes. Here. Now." The desire was hers and quite genuine, but was fed by another strength that now dwelled inside her. The mating need of the feline was not simply a matter of desire. It was a primal need that demanded.

"I-I don't understand. First you're crying like you just lost your best friend then you go catatonic and now you want to—"

"Yes. I do." She moved closer, putting her hand on his arm and running it up to his shoulder, then to his neck. Her nostrils flared, taking in his scent. Male. She licked her lips, remembering the taste of him.

"Hold on." Cole readjusted the cub in the crook of one arm and took Scout's hand away from his neck, holding it firmly. "This is just weird. Either you tell me what the hell's going on or I'm calling for medivac. You're acting…strange."

Scout was trying to make sense of it herself. When she accepted the spirit of the lion, she had no clue what to expect. She'd given it no thought. But she did understand the species. When a female cat was in heat, it was a demand that was uncontrollable and primal. There was no reasoning. It was the demand of nature. The demand to procreate, continue the species. It was the most primitive and strongest biological demand in nature.

The scientist inside her recognized that. The woman had no idea how to deal with it. She'd never felt such need. It was almost maddening.

"Something…I…" She fought to find the right words to explain it. "I wanted to make it up to her. For what was done. She said we could…join."

"Join?"

"Spirits. That if I allowed the Sight to take me, we could become one."

"That's crazy!"

"An hour ago I would have agreed. Cole, my grandfather used to tell me stories about this. I thought that's all it was. But it's not just a myth. I'm living proof. I can feel her with me. "

He shook his head and squeezed her hand. "That's…hell, I don't even know what to say to that. It's just not…possible."

"But it is," she insisted. "And I can prove it."

"How?"

"Make love to me."

"What will that prove?"

Scout felt an irrational anger flare inside her. Without thinking, she jerked her hand away and jumped to her feet. "Forget it!" She paced to the mouth of the cave. Great Spirits, her senses were alive. Super-tuned. She could see things she'd never been able to see before in darkness and her sense of smell was magnified as well.

"Scout, listen to me." Cole came up behind her with the cub still held in one arm.

She whirled on him. "I know this sounds insane. But it's true. She's in me. And the desire I feel for you threw her into heat or something and it's stronger than me, Cole. I feel like I'm on the verge of madness. I can smell you, feel the vibrations of your voice like a physical touch and I've never wanted anything as much as I want you."

Embarrassed by her outburst, she looked away. Cole reached up to put his fingers under her chin and lift her face. "I don't know what to believe right now, but this I do know. I want you too. Just not here. Not in the midst of death, Scout."

"Then come with me," she said and took his hand.

He let her lead him past the body of the cat, deeper into the cave. They wound through what seemed a labyrinth to him and emerged in a circular room of stone. A single light shaft from high above gave a spotlight of illumination.

Scout turned to face him. He gently set the cub down then moved to her. He raised both hands and cupped her face. She sighed, feeling a flush spread out over her skin. Heat simmered in her belly, burned her nipples.

"Please," she breathed as he drew near enough that his breath mingled with hers.

His lips met hers, slow and soft. Her lips parted and a purr escaped her.

Nothing had ever hit him as hard as that sound. It was beyond description. All he knew was that the moment the sound emerged from her lips, he was consumed with a need so strong that it erased all traces of reason and civility from his mind.

What had started as a gentle kiss turned into a rape of her mouth. He took. Feeding until both of them were breathing hard and fast. His hand tore at her clothing, mindless of everything but having her naked.

When she stood nude before him, he marveled at her strength and beauty. His hands moved up her sides, lifting both arms to pin her wrists with one of his hands behind her head.

Her neck arched back as he licked the hollow of her throat. Her taste was intoxicating and sweet. "You're delicious," he murmured as he moved his lips down her neck.

Scout purred in pleasure, forgetting about death and danger. Nothing else existed but the smell and taste and touch of him. Eager to feel his flesh against hers, she worked his clothes off amid the kisses and caresses.

All time slipped away as they explored each other with their hands. Cole slid his fingers into the wet folds between her legs. Scout's body quivered when his finger slowly slid into her, drawing out juice. He spread her lips and moistened her clit. While his fingers explored between her legs his tongue slowly circled her nipple, flicking across the hardening flesh.

He fueled her passion even higher with his caresses. Scout opened herself up and rode the waves of sensation his hands and mouth created. Her body was his to manipulate, his to explore. His mouth moved from her nipple to the underside of her breast, causing her to arch towards him as she sighed, "aaaahhhhh!" He ran his tongue up her cleavage to the base of her neck. There he feasted, fueling both their passions, making her wetter and more needy by the moment. She wanted him inside her and knew he was aware of her need. But he was in control, keeping the movement of his hands slow and rhythmic.

With swift but gentle force, he pulled her down to the ground. His body settled above her, his hardness pressed against the aching wetness of her sex. Her womb clenched with another stab of longing. It was almost more than she could bear, and such an unfamiliar sensation. She's never wanted a man so much.

Needing to touch him, feel him, her hand traveled down his hard chest and stomach. She stretched her fingers in the tight hair that surrounded the base of his shaft. She stroked his length with her fingertips, circling the pulsing head. Her rhythm of caresses matched his. As their mouths met and connected, they pleasured each other with their hands, lovingly stroking one another.

Cole leaned down to capture her lips with his. Scout gave herself eagerly to the kiss but wanted more. She needed him inside her. "I need you…in me," she whispered in his ear after her tongue traced his lobe. Her hand guided him into her as he positioned his body between her legs. Her body quivered as he entered her. She moved her hand from his shaft, letting her fingers feel him enter her.

He sank in slowly savoring the feel of his dick entering her warm, wet core. He felt her muscles quiver around him making his dick pulse in answer to the call of her body.

Scout kept her fingers between them, rubbing herself to his rhythm. The first orgasm had her whole body tightening around him, nearly robbing him of control. She seemed to sense it and wrapped her legs around his waist, stopping his motion.

Her cat-like eyes met his. "Join with me," she whispered in a voice rough with desire.

He nodded, unsure exactly what she asked for but wanting to give her anything she desired and more. Cole realized that her need was more important to him than his own. He needed to give her pleasure beyond anything she'd ever known, to bind her to him body and soul.

With her eyes never breaking contact with his, she began a low chant in her native tongue. Cole had no idea what she said, but within seconds felt the effect of the energy that accompanied the release of her words. Light swam in her eyes like glowing coals in a fire, sending tiny shards of light rocketing around them. Each tiny pinpoint of light was like a minute charge of energy, enervating his skin, penetrating to the marrow of his bones, into the depths of his soul.

For a brief moment he lost touch with reality. All that existed was a feeling of completeness, of being part of something far larger than himself. It was a sense of belonging so strong that when reality started to reassert itself, he fought it, wanting to remain in that other realm.

But reality won, and with its victory it brought a hunger so intense that it took his breath. He saw an answering hunger in Scout's eyes, the call of a female ready and willing to surrender. To be taken.

It was an invitation he could not have refused had he wanted to. He began to move faster and harder in her. She pulled her legs up, giving him deeper access, rocking her hips to meet him. The primal lust took control and Cole gave in to the demand.

"Scout, I need you on your knees." His voice was husky, a low sexy rasp. It struck a part of her she didn't know existed—she wanted him not just to make love to her, she wanted him to take her, to fuck her.

She rolled over and got on her hands and knees. Cole went to his knees behind her and buried his face in her. He ran his tongue from her opening to her clit. He lapped at the nub until it hardened. Scout whimpered, arching her back and pressing into his tongue. Just as she was tightening to climax, Cole rose and pushed the length of his dick inside her. He rode her climax, letting her push against him as he drove into her. Flesh slapped flesh. No sooner had the waves subsided and her muscles grew lax, he started again, driving the pace faster and harder.

She cried out, arching up on the ground, her arms stretched above her head in surrender, taking all he had to give. Her body moved in concert with his, moving to meet each stroke.

Time and again he took her over the edge, savoring the feel, the scent of sex permeating the still air and the sight of her writhing in abandon beneath him. It was a heady mix of lust and power, the power to make her body quiver and quake beneath him, elicit small cries, deep purrs and gasping screams as he took her over and over.

In time it eroded his tenuous control. He could hold back no longer. As a pulsing began in his balls, his hands tightened on her hips. An orgasm claimed him, allowing him to drive one final time into her before stars exploded behind his closed eyes.

Feeling his orgasm, Scout used her body to stroke him, plummeting one final time into the chasm of sensation. She felt him lay his chest on her back. His arms encircled her gently, holding on until his pulsing stopped.

Scout flattened out on the ground, letting his weight settle on her, feeling the rapid pulse of his heartbeat against her skin. For a time they didn't move, then Cole eased off her and rolled over onto his back, pulling her so that she was spooned against his side, her head on his broad chest.

She closed her eyes, feeling the woman purr in concert with the cat within. Just as sleep started to claim her, she felt the cub behind her. Scooping him up, she put him on Cole's belly, leaving her hand on him. Within moments all three were asleep.

Chapter Seven

ꟈ

Scout woke to find Cole watching her, one hand idly stroking the cub that was sleeping on his belly, while the other hand stroked gently up and down her bare back. Her heart filled to near breaking at the sight of him. It was the most incredible feeling, one that was new and yet familiar. Her heart recognized it. Love.

"Hey, beautiful," Cole said with a smile.

"Hey," she replied. "Looks like you've made a friend." She stroked the cub and it woke, mewing at her and suckling her finger.

"We've got to get this little guy fed," she said, pushing up into a sitting position.

"I was thinking more of feeding another kind of hunger," Cole replied.

His suggestion sent her pulse racing, but Scout refused to give in to it. She'd promised the lion to care for the cub, and if it wasn't fed it would not fare well.

"As inviting as that is, how about we take the party back to my place? We'll take care of the cub, get clean and…indulge."

Cole sat, letting her take the cub into her arms. "You're not suggesting that you're going to keep this cub are you?"

"Well yeah," she replied.

"You can't do that."

"Why not?" she asked, feeling a bit miffed at his remark.

"Because it's a wild animal, not a pet. Come on, Scout. You above anyone knows that this cub needs to be around its own kind, not become a house pet."

"Well, first of all I had no intention of turning it into a pet," she retorted sharper than she intended. "And in case you've forgotten, I work with big cats. I have a compound set up at my place specifically for rehab, and it's the perfect place for this little girl."

"And how are you doing to feed her?"

"I'll ask one of the other females with a litter," she said, rubbing her face against the cub's soft fur.

He shook his head and grabbed his pants. "Just like that, eh?"

"Pretty much, yeah," she replied. "What's the big deal anyway?"

"Nothing," he said, standing to dress.

"It's not nothing," she argued. "The mention of taking the cub home and you turn into a prickly pear. What's wrong?"

"It's just...just...this whole cat thing. You've been purring to that cub for the last two minutes and I don't think you even realize it. It's like you're...I don't know...forget it."

Scout was surprised. It wasn't until he pointed it out that she realized he was right. She'd been purring. How, she didn't have a clue. But the sound came from her throat as easily as words rolled off her tongue.

But what concerned her was the sudden distance between her and Cole. "Cole, please," she implored. "Talk to me."

Cole wasn't sure he could put into words what he felt. He'd awoken with the realization that his life would never be the same. Scout had changed everything. He was in love with her. As impossible as it was, he knew it to his bones. There would never be another woman for him.

That shook him to his core. He'd never expected to find love, and sure as hell never imagined that it would be with a woman who was part witch and as much a member of the wild as any creature that dwelled within it.

He didn't know if it could work. He wanted the dream. Hearth and home, kids playing in the yard. Could Scout live that way? Her world was living out of a backpack, tracking animals and men, living in a world where danger was always around the next corner and one wrong move could be the end.

And beyond that, could he accept what she did, knowing that every time she went out to tag a cat she could be mauled or killed? That every time the law called her in to track a criminal it could be her life on the line.

He didn't realize that the link he'd established with Scout was broadcasting his feelings as clearly as if he'd spoken.

But she did. "I understand," she said softly, walking to him to put her hand on his arm. "I'm afraid too. Afraid that I'll disappoint you, that I won't fit into the life you want—and scared that maybe this isn't real. It's all happened so fast. Maybe all we have is just right now, and when we get back it will be over."

"I don't want that."

"Neither do I. But I guess we both have to be realistic and just hope for the best. If we've started something that's meant to last then it will. If not...well, then I guess we hope that we can part ways and have good memories."

Cole cupped her face in both his hands. "I hope it's real, Scout. But I don't want to make any promises. Not yet. Not until I'm sure."

"I can live with that," she replied. After all what choice did she have? Regardless of what she felt, there were two people in the equation and she knew from experience that unless both were committed, the relationship was doomed. She had no desire to make another mistake.

And she needed time to find out if what she felt was real. She thought it was, but maybe she was just fooling herself. To be safe, she'd err on the side of caution as well.

"So, about the cub?"

He smiled down at her. "You're right. You have a place for it and are the best equipped to help it. Unless you want to take it to the Center."

"No," she said immediately and smiled sheepishly when he cocked one eyebrow. "Okay, I admit it. I'm already attached to it. But I'll make sure she's reintroduced to her own kind. And I will find a surrogate mother for her. Deal?"

"You got it."

"Then we need to go. Get this baby settled in and check in with Jonas."

Cole grimaced at the comment. "I hope he's found the shooter."

"Me too," she replied, looking away. She saw no need to reveal what she'd learned from the dying lion, or the fact that now she had certain access to those memories and knew who they needed to be looking for.

She'd talk with Jonas, but she wanted to do it alone because the guilty party was someone she had a personal grievance with and she fully intended to be part of the operation that brought him in. She owed that to Jed and to the lion.

Cole finished dressing and took the cat while she dressed. "You ready?" he asked when she looked around the cave.

"Yeah," she replied and gave the place one final look. How odd that something she'd been afraid to wish for had appeared in a cave in the middle of the wilderness in the midst of death and rebirth. How amazing that it should be so intimately connected to her metamorphosis. "Let's go."

With no further conversation they started the long trek back.

* * * * *

Tim Matthews was more exhausted than he could remember ever being. The search for the murderer was still in progress and he hadn't slept since the entire thing began. Now Cole and Scout had gone silent again and he feared something bad had happened to them.

When Cole walked into his office, Tim sagged back in his chair in relief. "Thank god! Where's Scout?"

"Pit stop," Cole said. "Y'all find that guy?"

"I'm waiting to hear from Jon—" Tim was interrupted by the appearance of Jonas Roberts, sticking his head around the corner of the door.

"We have another body." He disappeared before Tim or Cole could comment.

Tim got up and headed for the door, nearly running into Scout coming into the office.

"What's up?" she asked.

"Jonas said they think they've found another body," Tim spoke on the run, headed for the command post Jonas had set up in the conference room.

Scout and Cole fell in behind him. Jonas was standing, with his hands braced on the table, hunched over a display screen. "What'd you find?" Scout asked as soon as she entered the room.

"Take a look." Jonas motioned her over. "Live feed from one of my teams."

Scout hurried to his side and looked at the monitor. A man lay on the rocky ground, one leg bent at an unnatural angle, with arms spread. His eyes were wide and sightless. His head was turned to one side, blood staining the ground beneath him.

He looked very familiar. "Can I see his face?" she asked.

Jonas gave the command and the agent feeding them the video link moved to show the man's face.

"Bobby Howard," Scout announced.

Jonas nodded and turned his attention to the communication link with his team. "I'm sending in a forensics team. Secure the area and wait for them. Once they've finished I want the body and all evidence sent to the lab at headquarters."

"Roger," came the reply.

Jonas turned and sat back on the edge of the table. "Bobby Howard," he said, looking at Scout.

"Local guy. Worked for the Moss family for about as long as I can remember. Not married. No family."

"What do you suppose he was doing out there armed for bear, so to speak?"

Scout shrugged. "Could have been running an illegal hunt. Was he shot?"

"No evidence of that. Appears to have died from a fall. Was he an experienced climber?"

"Don't know," she replied. "I haven't really had any contact with him. Just knew him as a local who was tight with the Mosses."

"Okay," Jonas said and straightened. "We'll know more after the autopsy. In the meantime…Tim?" He looked in Tim's direction. "The park stays closed while we continue the search."

"You need me?" Scout asked.

"My men will continue their sweeps, and we'll see what we get from the IDs on the bodies. Check with the victims' families and find out who they were with."

She nodded. "Fine, you know where I am if you need me." She turned and headed for the door. "Tim, Cole."

Without another word she left the room. Cole looked from Jonas to Tim. "Unless you need me, I think I'll go home and clean up. I can be back in a couple of hours."

"No need," Tim replied. "Get some rest."

"Okay," Cole said and extended his hand to Jonas. "Captain Roberts."

"Mr. Russell," Jonas said and gripped his hand. "Thank you."

Cole nodded and left the room. Once in the hall he hurried to catch up with Scout, reaching her just as she was climbing into her truck.

"You want to come over while I get the cub settled in?" she asked.

"Sure."

"Okay, want to ride with me or follow?"

"I've got my truck. Be right behind you."

She nodded and watched him go to his vehicle. When he pulled up behind her, she started the truck and headed home.

After a few miles the cub settled itself across her leg and fell asleep. Scout used the time to reflect on what had happened. It seemed like years since she'd left home to attend the hunt, instead of days. Emotionally and mentally she was not the same. Something fundamental inside her had changed.

She wanted to attribute it all to the spirit of the lioness that lived inside her now, but that would have been a lie. Much of what had changed inside her was due to Cole. As much as she hated admitting it, it scared her how deep her feelings for him ran. And it was more than just sex, although that in itself could be described as life-altering.

Thoughts of their time in the cave brought a flush to her skin and a quickening to her pulse. What was it about him that made her feel like she was going into heat at the mere thought of his strong muscular body, or the memory of his touch?

Before she realized it, a sound between a roar and a laugh emerged from her lips. The lioness inside reminded her that despite her reluctance to admit to it, humans were as much animals as the lions. And the scent of a prime male when a female was in season was impossible to ignore.

In season? Scout thought with a laugh. *Well, in that respect humans and lions are a bit different. We don't go into heat.*

The laughter that rang through her mind was all the answer she received.

She turned onto the narrow gravel road that led to her house and cut her eyes to her rearview mirror to see Cole making the turn behind her. In a few minutes she stopped in front of the house, gathered the cub in her arms and got out of the truck.

Cole got out of his truck and their eyes met. Scout felt a searing blast of emotion rip through her so strong that tears sprang to her eyes. Her arms tightened around the cub, but her eyes remained locked with Cole's.

He approached and stopped inches away. "You okay?" he asked as he reached over to stroke his fingers down the side of her face.

She nodded, batting her eyes at the gathering tears. "You?"

"Tired, dirty, hungry," he replied.

"Look if you'd rather go home I can take care of the—"

"Not a chance," he interrupted. "We'll take care of the cub together then we'll get clean, eat and sleep."

"A man with a plan," she said teasingly, feeling the emotion ease a bit in her chest.

"Always," he replied with a smile. "Now, show me your home, Scout."

She offered him a hand. He took it and she led him around to the back of the house.

The small wooden house was deceptive to the real grandeur of the place. Behind the house, one was afforded a view that photographers and painters sought to capture. A long wide pasture stretched out from the edge of the yard, rolling for what seemed forever. Thick stands of trees were scattered the length and width of the land, giving it a park-like appearance. As far as the eye could see the land rolled and stretched, the mountains rising up in the distance like majestic guardians.

"It's beautiful," Cole said softly. "How much land do you have?"

"Twenty thousand acres," she replied, looking out lovingly over the land she called home. "Been in the family for…five generations, I guess."

"It's beautiful," he said and gave her hand a squeeze. "But I thought you said you had a place for the cub?"

"We'll have to walk aways," she said and tugged at his hand. "Come on."

She led him across the corner of the pasture when it dipped along the northern border. The trees grew thicker, and the terrain rougher. They descended down a rise then back up another, winding their way deeper into a forest that grew increasingly thicker.

When they stopped, a wall of rock stood before them. "Up there," Scout nodded. "To the right. We follow the base of the cliff about a quarter mile and there's a way up. There's a nice cave about sixty feet up, and I have one female there already with three cubs."

"So we're literally going to walk into the lion's den?" Cole asked.

"Yep," Scout replied with a grin. "You game?"

"I figure I'm safe as long as I'm with you." His reply both surprised and pleased her.

"Well okay then," she said and led the way.

The climb was short but strenuous, particularly with the cub stuffed inside her shirt and no gear, but she'd made it many times in the past so knew the foot and handholds. Cole seemed to have no difficulty following.

"This way," she said when he reached the top.

The entrance to the cave was well hidden with brush. Scout stopped outside. "Can I come in?" she called.

A low growl came from within the cave and she grinned at Cole. "Come on."

"You ask permission?" he whispered behind her. "Like the cat didn't smell or sense us?"

"Well sure she did," Scout replied. "But good manners are always appreciated," she added with a grin at him over her shoulder.

Cole stopped short when the lioness rose and faced them. Scout did not slow in the least. "Hey, pretty mama," she said, walking over to kneel down in front of the lion. "I brought someone to meet you."

She pulled the cub from beneath her shirt and held it in her arms. The lion sniffed at it then at her. A low growl sounded, then another. Then the lion opened its mouth and screamed a blood-curdling sound that had Cole running to grab hold of Scout and pull her out of harm's way, stationing himself between her and the lion.

The lion screamed again and Cole took a slow step backwards, trying to force Scout in the direction of the cave entrance. When he heard Scout giggling behind him, he stopped.

"What's so damn funny?" he asked, keeping a wary eye on the lion.

"She was complimenting you," Scout replied.

"Huh?" He was so surprised that he turned to look at her.

"She smelled you on me," Scout explained. "And said you were prime. A real alpha."

Cole cut his eyes at the cat and would have sworn that she was grinning. Either that or she was preparing to have him for dinner. "This is too weird," he said.

Scout chuckled and scooted around him to sit down beside the lion. "Look, I know you have your hands full," she told the cat. "But this little girl's mama died and unless you take her in, she's going to die."

Cole watched as Scout's facial expression changed, as if someone were talking to her. After a moment she nodded. "I know. Ordinarily I'd agree. But in this case, survival of the fittest means that I have to break a vow. I promised to make sure this baby was cared for. If you can't or won't help me, then I can try to do it on my own, but we both know that her chances aren't good. And besides, I can't teach her all she needs to know. You can."

A few moments passed before Scout set the cub down in front of the lion. The lion sniffed at it, turned it over on its belly, sniffed some more then looked at Scout. Scout's face broke out in a big smile and she threw her arms around the lion's neck, burying her face in its fur.

Cole felt a thrill of alarm when the lion nuzzled down against Scout's neck as well. But she didn't appear to be intent on harming Scout. Instead, there came the sound of purring. Two distinct and different sounds. He realized it was the lion and Scout.

They stayed that way for a little while then Scout drew back. The lion licked her, from the point of her chin all the way to her eyebrows. Scout grinned and gave the lion an affectionate stroke on the head then rose.

"We're good to go," she announced. "She's going to take the cub. I'll come back and visit in a week or so, but she'll be fine."

Cole didn't know what to say. Truth be told, since he'd met Scout Windrider, his world had been topsy-turvy.

"Come on." She offered her hand. "Let's head back to the house."

In silence they left the cave. Neither of them spoke on the walk back. Cole was trying to come to terms with what he'd seen and heard. Was it really possible that Scout had taken the spirit of the dying lion into herself?

She sure seemed to be able to communicate with lions. But how was that possible? It sure wasn't normal by any stretch of the imagination. So what exactly did that make her?

He didn't have the answers. Only questions. And focusing on those questions kept him from having to pay attention to others. Such as why he felt that she was the woman for him and that he'd already lost his heart to her. That wasn't possible either. He'd only just met her.

She stopped as they reached the edge of the yard to her house, and looked up at him. And try as he might, he could not stop the overwhelming rush of desire and longing that raged like a flood through him. Her eyes bewitched him. Her nearness inflamed him. He rose to full erection in the space of a breath.

"Clean or eat?" she asked with a sexy smile.

"Both," he replied.

"Now you're talking," she replied with a laugh and led him to the house.

Cole followed her inside, noting the homey warmth of the kitchen with its old-fashioned stove and warm earth tones. The living area was just as warm and inviting, with an enormous stone fireplace dominating one wall, deep comfortable furniture with Indian print throws and hand-woven rugs on the old but gleaming hardwood floors.

Scout led him down a short hallway with one door to the left and two on the right. "Now don't laugh," she said as she stopped at the first door on the right. "It's my one indulgence."

She opened the door and Cole bit back a chuckle. Who would have guessed that a woman more at home in the wilderness would have a thing for bathrooms? "Okay, I admit it. I'm surprised," he said as he followed her in.

"Originally there was just a small bathroom with an old claw foot tub. I talked Jed into knocking out the wall between the bath and bedroom and making one big bathroom."

"Jed did this?" Cole asked.

"We both did," she replied proudly.

Cole was impressed. The room they stood in housed double pedestal sinks, a floor to ceiling mirror with a dressing table. A small door off to one side held the toilet area and on the wall that once separated the room was a large arch, its edge trimmed in natural tile.

Beyond lay what he supposed would be a woman's dream. Soft light from sconce lighting gave a romantic glow to the room. Scattered along the edges were enormous potted plants and abstract sculptures.

And in the middle of the room was the biggest tub he'd ever seen. Composed of smooth porcelain and rimmed with tile, it was raised by one step. Smooth tile surrounded it, radiating out in a concentric pattern, making the tub the hub of the design.

Decorative metalwork rose on opposite sides of the tub, housing dual showerheads, and a heavy carved stand sat beside the tub, bearing various bottles and soaps.

"Nice," he said with a smile. "And very informative. Now I know your weakness."

Scout rewarded him with a smile sexy enough to have his dick standing up and saluting. "Then how about sharing it with me?"

"Honey, you don't have to ask twice. You want to fill that bad boy up or you want me to do it?"

"I'll take care of it," she replied. "But first..."

She peeled off her boots, socks and slid out of her pants. Cole's dick throbbed at the sight. Dark hair curled on her mound, trimmed short to provide a tantalizing view of what lay beneath.

When she pulled her tank top over her head and those lush dusky-tipped breasts rose, his mouth watered. Dropping the top on the floor, she walked over to the tub. Cole watched her firm ass sway and smiled in appreciation. When she bent over to start the water, his dick throbbed in anticipation of sinking into the slick warm pussy that was so nicely displayed.

Scout turned and headed back toward him. "Shuck those dudes, cowboy."

"With pleasure," he said and peeled off his shirt.

Scout felt a flush of heat work over her skin at the sight of his broad chest, chiseled abdomen and muscular arms. By all the ancestors, he was so fine it nearly took her breath. Her nipples began to tingle, and without realizing it, one hand slid down to cup her own burning sex.

She saw Cole's eyes follow the path of her hand. He loosened his pants and his cock sprang free, hard and ready. Her mouth watered at the sight.

He stepped out of his pants and closed the distance between them. Without a word, he scooped her up in his arms and carried her to the tub, stepping into it. His lips sought hers as he allowed her to slide down his body.

Scout thought she was going to come then and there. His kiss was possessive and dominating and his hands moved to her ass, pulling her firmly against him so that his erection was trapped between them. It was enough to have her pussy weeping, wetting her inner thighs with longing.

She worked her hand between them, sliding it down the length of his hard cock, and then lower to fondle his balls. The answering tightening her touch evoked gave her a thrill, driving her desire higher.

"Hmmm, that feels good," he murmured.

"This will feel better," she replied and released him long enough to turn on the double showerheads. Warm water cascaded down on them. Scout reached for a bottle and poured shampoo into her hand.

"Kneel down," she suggested.

Cole complied, sinking down in front of her and running his hands around her body to fondle her ass. As she shampooed his hair, his fingers played on her skin, dipping into the cleft of her ass and running down its length to her anus, not probing, merely feeling.

She almost lost concentration, the feeling was so electric. Once she finished his hair she pulled the showerhead down to rinse him. "Stand up," she said in a voice she almost did not recognize as her own it was so roughened with desire.

He stood and she took a bar of sweet smelling soap in her hands. Cole submitted to her ministrations and she enjoyed taking her time, soaping every inch of his magnificent body, lingering on his balls and cock, stroking him slow and firm.

His cock was like silk-covered steel in her hands. She reveled in the feel of him, leaning forward to flick her tongue over his nipple then nip it lightly. The answering intake of breath she received from him had her stroking faster. She felt the build up of tension in his body and it was like a drug, fueling her own fire, making her sex spill with need.

She'd never before felt such a need to pleasure a man, to lose herself in the feel and smell and taste of him. It was akin to addiction, the need was so vast. She didn't understand it, but for the moment she didn't have to. She surrendered to it and let it take her.

Cole reached down to stay her hands. "You're gonna do me in," he said in a husky voice. "Besides, I want a turn."

His words created a wave of hunger that nearly staggered her with its power. Without a word, her hand stilled and she handed him the soap.

Cole felt the threatening climax subside when she released him. As much as he would have enjoyed the release, he didn't want to come. He wanted the feeling of need and longing to last as long as possible, to feel the hunger tearing at him until he could no longer resist its demands.

He wanted to take Scout to a place she'd never been, to give her pleasure so intense that she became his.

He pushed her to her knees before him and started to wash her long thick hair. When he felt her mouth close on the head of his dick he couldn't suppress a sudden spike that had him pressing forward into the warm recesses of her mouth, driving his dick deeper.

Her fingers toyed with his balls, worked around and behind them, probing his anus. All the while her mouth moved on his dick, each stroke taking him deeper into the wetness.

He wasn't sure he could hold out. She was driving him too close to the edge, asserting her own control.

"Honey, please." His hands tightened in her hair.

Her answer was to suck him harder and faster. A deep purr came from her throat, making his balls ache and his belly tighten. Imprisoned in the warmth of her mouth, her hands caressing his testicles and anus, he couldn't fight it. His surrender was sudden and powerful, and the moment he let go, an orgasm took him. His hands fisted in her hair, pulling against him as his dick pulsed and spurted. A lassitude came over his legs and he sank down onto his knees. She would not release him, but sank down with him, on her knees, her mouth sucking the last of his cum.

The sight of her on her knees that way with her ass in the air brought surprising new life to his dick that shocked him.

"Hmmmm," she murmured and worked her way up his body, kissing and licking until her tongue traced its way up the side of his neck and she captured his ear lobe between her teeth.

"Hmmm don't even touch it," Cole replied and grabbed her by the hair to draw her lips to his. She tasted of him and a sweetness that was all her own. She writhed against him, allowing him to take her mouth, her hard nipples raking across his chest, creating trails of fire on his skin.

His lips left hers and moved down the side of her neck, over the top of one shoulder then to the tantalizing bud of her nipple. Scout arched back when his lips closed around the sensitive tip. He supported her with his arms, bending her back like a bow, suckling hard.

He was rewarded with a blast of energy from her that nearly staggered him. Raw, uninhibited primal hunger. He felt, smelled and tasted it, knew beyond all doubt that she was his for the taking.

It was an offer not to be refused. He continued to torture her breasts, one hand moving down her body and dipping into the wetness of her pussy.

She whimpered and spread her legs, pressing against his hand, riding his fingers as he penetrated deeper, questing for that sweet spot that he knew would send her spiraling.

A short cry announced that he'd not only found her secret spot, but that it was so alive that only one stroke had her working toward orgasm.

Cole held onto her and pumped his fingers inside her, each stroke driving her closer to the edge. A rush of wetness preceded a vibration that ran through her body before her pussy started to spasm around his fingers. Her hands gripped his upper arms, fingers digging into his skin as the climax rolled through her.

It was like an aphrodisiac, swelling his dick to full erection as if he had not just come.

"Please," she gasped as the climax started to subside. "More."

Cole didn't hesitate to comply. He sank down into the tub, lying back and pulling her on top of him. "Take it, baby," he said, watching her eyes for reaction. "Let me see how much you want me."

Light seemed to flare in those golden eyes before the pupils swelled, nearly eclipsing the gold. She straddled his body, taking his dick in her hand and slowly, inch by inch, impaled herself on his length.

Once fully seated, she started a rocking glide, back and forth, higher then lower, the movement slow and seductive. Cole moved his hand to the vee of her thighs, his fingers working into the folds of her sex, imprisoning her hard clit between thumb and finger.

A gasp exploded from her at the touch. She arched back, bracing herself with her hands on his thighs. The sight of her, bowed back with breasts high and his dick filling her pussy, was enough to make a man lose his mind. Her pussy was hot and slick, gripping him as she rode him.

Harder and faster she moved. Her clit grew tighter and harder, signaling a coming release. Cole felt his own climax build as she vibrated on and around him. He rolled her clit, squeezing harder and she screamed, a sound all female but perhaps not all human it was so primitive and strong.

At the moment of that scream he felt her orgasm. It literally radiated from her pussy, down the length of his dick and throughout his body. Unable to control it, he quaked beneath its power, his seed shooting inside her in great throbbing waves.

Cole had no idea how long it lasted. A moment or an eternity. It could have been either. He had no way of knowing. He was lost in sensation, a climax that claimed both body and soul. He felt, actually felt Scout with him. Felt her passion and her love.

It shook him to his soul, searing him. He felt the claim he had on her and her acceptance of it. Moreover, he realized the claim she had on him. Like it or not, he was branded.

When she sagged, melting down on top of him, her breath still fast and her heart pounding against his chest, he wrapped his arms around her, feeling, for the first time in his life, complete.

For a long time they lay beneath the jets of water, letting it pour down over them. When the heat began to fade from the water, she pushed herself up and looked down at him, a troubled expression on her face.

It speared him with alarm. "What's wrong?"

"We...I...look, I want you to know that I'm clean. I mean you're not in any danger of STDs or anything."

Cole nearly laughed in relief. "To be honest, I hadn't thought about it. Guess we weren't exactly smart. But I'm clean too. Got papers from my last physical to prove it, if you need it."

"No." She shook her head. "I trust you."

Cole knew in his gut that those three words meant more than anything anyone had ever said to him, and that she did not give them lightly.

"And I, you," he replied. "So no worries."

Scout nodded, keeping silent about what lay in her mind. She had no doubt that they were safe from disease. But pregnancy was another matter. There was no guarantee there. And what if she ended up pregnant? What would that spell for them?

What would it spell for her?

She wasn't sure she was ready for the answer, so she forced it to the back of her mind. "I don't know about you, but I'm starved."

His stomach rumbled and they both laughed. "Well, I guess that's my answer," she said and got off him. "What say we fix something to eat?"

"Do you cook?" he asked as he got to his feet and rinsed off in the cooling water.

"I'm not exactly the best cook in the world, but I made the world's best blueberry pancakes and western omelettes."

"A woman after my own heart," he said with a grin.

She grinned and started to step out of the tub, but he took her arm and stopped her. "Scout?"

"Yeah?"

"I just want you to know that this isn't a casual thing for me. And I don't think it is for you either. I don't know where we're headed, but I do know that I want to find out."

"Me too," she said and stood up on tiptoe to graze his lips with hers. "And we will. One day at a time."

"Works for me," he replied and licked at her lips, parting them with his tongue.

"Hmmmm," she murmured, sinking against him for a moment then pulling back. "Damn, Cole, you sure know how to make it tough on a woman."

"You ready for round two already?" he asked teasingly.

"Don't tempt me. At least not until I get some fuel in me. Then we'll see how much round two you have left in you." She turned to get out of the tub and he laughed and popped her lightly on the bare behind.

"Then get ready, honey, cause once I get refueled, it's on."

She laughed and tossed him a towel. "Promises, promises."

He laughed along with her, feeling suddenly as if the pieces of his life were starting to fall into place. At long last.

Chapter Eight

ജ

Tim Matthews stood as Captain Jonas Roberts entered the room. "Captain," Tim greeted him. "I didn't expect you."

"We need to talk." Jonas and gestured to the chair in front of Tim's desk. "May I?"

"Please," Tim replied and sat down.

"Our investigation is complete," Jonas announced.

"So soon? It's only been three days." Tim was surprised. He'd expected it to take longer.

"We put a rush on it," Jonas said. "This is how it stacks up. Apparently Bobby Howard arranged a private hunting expedition for two men from upstate New York. We spoke with the family of the deceased, and both stories match up. The men paid for a week hunting excursion, complete with guide, and a guarantee that they'd bag at least one mountain lion. Howard had promised to have the heads mounted and shipped to them after the hunt."

"Now, what we think happened is that Howard or one of his clients shot and wounded a lion. My men found a lion body in a cave while they were searching. It's been shot. From all we can put together, Howard and his clients were hunting for the cat to finish it off when they ran into your folks from the contest. Words were exchanged and shots were fired. Your men were hit. One killed and the other fatally wounded. As he has since died, we have no way of verifying, but it appears that the shots were fired from a weapon we found on Howard."

"After the incident, we suspect Howard and his clients had a falling out. Maybe they got scared. He killed them to keep them silent and while making his escape, he fell and was killed in the fall."

Tim considered it. "Okay, but before Drew died he said there were four men."

"Maybe he was wrong," Jonas replied. "There's no evidence to support his claim. And ballistics confirm that the victims were all killed with the same weapon, which was found on Howard and bore his prints."

"Then I guess the case is closed," Tim said. "Does that mean we can reopen the park?"

"Yes," Jonas said and stood. "I am going to want a statement from your ranger, Cole Russell. Is he on duty today?"

Tim stood as well and walked around the desk. "He's on call. Now that we're reopening, I'll call him in and have him do a patrol of the high country, check the trails before we officially reopen. You want me to call him in now?"

"Why don't I meet him here around 11:00?" Jonas asked. "I have some things I need to take care of this morning."

"I'll make the arrangements," Tim replied and offered his hand. "Thank you."

"Just doing my job," Jonas replied. "See you at eleven."

Tim returned to his seat at the desk as Jonas left. He called Cole at home and got his voice mail. After leaving a message, he tried the cell number.

* * * * *

Cole was lying, sweaty and panting, on top of Scout when his cell phone rang. They both looked in the direction of the noise, and he rolled off the bed and started rummaging around in his clothes on the chair in front of the window.

"Russell," he answered when he finally located it.

"Hey, Tim…yeah? What'd he say?"

Scout sat up, looking at him expectantly as he listened to what Tim was saying. Finally he said, "Yeah, I'll be there."

He ended the call and tossed the phone on the chair before returning to sit on the bed. "Tim said that the CBI concluded their investigation."

"That was fast," Scout commented.

"Honey, it's been three days since we've left this house. A lot can happen in three days."

"Yeah, there is that," she agreed with a smile. "So what'd Tim say?"

"Apparently the guy, Bobby Howard, is responsible for the shootings. They had evidence that he arranged a private hunt for two New York guys, and that it was his weapon that killed them and the hunting party."

"So that's it?" she asked with a frown.

"According to Tim. Anyway, Captain Roberts wants me to give a statement. Just a formality. But I have to be in at eleven."

"How long do you think it'll take?" she asked. "I should check in at the Center. They'll be thinking I've up and quit."

He grimaced. "I have to go on patrol. Check the trails. I'll be out for at least two days. Maybe three."

She gave him an exaggerated pout. "Three days?"

"What, you think you can't survive three days without me?" he teased.

"It isn't a matter of can't," she replied, falling back on the bed. "More of a matter of now I'm spoiled."

"You saying I've ruined you for other men, honey?"

She grinned. "Don't get all full of yourself, cowboy."

He stretched out on top of her, pinning her hands to the bed above her head. "I'd rather you be full of me."

"Hmmm, now you're talking," she said sassily and tilted her pelvis up, grinding against him.

"Unfortunately, I have a job," he said and nipped at her chin before sitting back up. "What say I stop by when I finish my patrol?"

"Sounds like a plan," she replied. "If I'm out, just get the key from under the planter at the back door and let yourself in."

"You going to be at the Center?" he asked.

"Yeah. I'll go check on the cub then head on over there. Got some research data I need to go over and start scheduling tagging teams for later in the summer."

"Then we'll meet here in three days," Cole said and pulled her up for a kiss that threatened their resolve to get up and head for work.

"Okay." He rose from the bed and started to dress. "I need to get home for clean clothes so I'm going to take off. Be ready, darlin'. I'm going to have a powerful hunger when I get back."

"Oh, don't you worry, I'll be ready," she replied and followed with, "Be safe."

"And you," he replied.

"My middle name," she said with a grin.

"Like hell," he laughed, and left.

Scout fell back on the bed and stared at the ceiling. It was hard to believe that they'd been holed up in her house for three days. Three days of delicious, mind-blowing, ovary-bursting sex. Three days of talking and laughing and coming to terms with what was happening between them. Three days of falling in love.

I'm in love, she said to herself, then dared to say it aloud, "I'm in love."

A smile dawned on her face and she jumped out of bed and danced around. "I'm in love, I'm in love, I'm in love, I'm—"

The shrill beep of her cell phone interrupted her dance. Thinking it might be Cole, she snatched it up. "Windrider."

"Scout?" Jonas Robert's voice came over the line. "We need to talk."

"When and where?" she asked, knowing from the tone of his voice that whatever it was, it was serious.

"I'm ten minutes from your place."

"I'll put on the coffee," she replied and hung up.

She quickly dressed in jeans and a tee shirt, pulled her hair back into a ponytail and hurried to the kitchen to put on a pot of coffee. It was just finishing when she heard a vehicle pull up.

Scout went to the front door and opened it. "Come on in," she said as Jonas got out of his SUV.

He followed her inside, took a seat at the table and was silent until she set a mug of coffee down in front of him and took a seat at the table across from him. "What's up?"

"You hear about the investigation?"

"Yep. Heard you think it was Bobby Howard who was responsible."

"You don't buy it."

"Not for an instant," she replied. "He didn't have the brains or the balls for either, Jonas. The ranger, Drew, said the shooter was a tall, dark-haired man. That doesn't describe Howard and we both know it."

Jonas nodded and stared down at the cup in his hand for a moment. "I agree," he said at last. "This hasn't been made public, so no need to tell you to keep this to yourself."

She nodded and he continued.

"Ballistics confirm that the killing shots came from a weapon found on Howard. But when we traced the gun we discovered that the gun was purchased over twenty years ago by Jed."

Scout's eyes widened. "What?"

"As a gift to James Moss," Jonas replied.

She leaned back in her chair, her eyes narrowed in thought. "Jed probably gave it to him when they went into business together."

Jonas nodded. "So how did it end up with Bobby Howard?"

Scout considered for a few moments exactly how to reveal the information she had to Jonas. She'd known him a while and he was a stand-up, no-bullshit guy. But whether he'd accept her source was an unknown. Finally she decided that the only way to find out was to lay it on the table for him.

"Ray Moss planted it on him after he killed Howard."

"That's a pretty big leap," Jonas commented. "You got anything to back it up?"

"Check Jed's autopsy report. You'll find that the bullets that killed him came from the same weapon. And if you check the county jail records, you'll also find that Bobby Howard was locked up on a DUI the day Jed was killed, which means he didn't have the gun at the time."

"That doesn't prove Moss did it."

"No, but it proves Howard didn't."

"Proves he didn't murder Jed. Doesn't do squat for the case at hand."

Scout chewed her lip for a moment. "How well did you know Jed?"

"About as well as he'd let anyone know him, I guess. Why?"

"You ever wonder how it was so easy for him to track or how he seemed to be able to understand things based on animal behavior?"

"I chalked it up to one of those Native things people aren't supposed to understand."

She chuckled. "Well put. And a surprise coming from you."

"Just because I'm a by-the-book guy doesn't mean I discount what I can't see or understand."

"Okay, then here's something to chew on. Jed had an affinity with animals. Most every animal there is. But particularly cats. He could…communicate with them."

"As in Doctor Doolittle?"

She smiled. "Something like that. It's an ability that runs through the family."

"And this helps us how?"

"I have that same ability," she said. "When Cole and I were out there, I sensed a wounded lion. After I gave your team the coordinates to follow the shooter, Cole and I went to find the cat.

"We found her in a cave. She had one cub and was dying. She told me who the killer is."

Jonas studied her for a long time. "Okay, let me guess. Raymond Moss."

"Yep."

"Okay, two problems with that," he said. "One, it's unreliable intel. No way to validate or corroborate with the 'witness'. Two, Moss has an alibi."

"What about his brother Jimmy?" Scout asked with rancor clear in her voice.

"You have some kind of axe to grind with those two I should know about?"

"You mean aside from the fact that they murdered my grandfather? No."

'That's good. And yes, his brother and a fellow who owns a fishing lodge on one of the lakes is his alibi. It seemed solid. Bottom line is we still don't have a case, Scout. Any way you cut it, your allegations won't stand up. We've got to have something tangible to go on."

"So he just gets off Scott free?" she asked heatedly.

"Until we have something to go on, yes. But for what it's worth, I think you're right. Howard's life reads like a casebook. Weakling bad-boy wannabe who hooks up with a tough crowd that validates him, at least to himself. He's the lackey, doing their bidding. Doesn't seem to have that much in the way of brains, and depends on the Moss family for all his emotional, social and financial support. And he's a coward. Petty crimes land him in jail. He even does some time. But inside, he's the bitch, not the daddy, which means he isn't a leader and not tough enough."

She was quiet for a little while, thinking, and then looked up at him. "So, what if I bring you something tangible? Something that at least proves the Moss guys are conducting illegal hunts? Will that be enough to open an investigation on them?"

"What kind of proof?"

"I don't know. I haven't found it yet," she replied. "But I will."

"I can't sanction this, Scout. You go out looking and you're on your own."

"Story of my life," she said. "Just promise me that if I do bring you something you'll consider it."

"You have my word."

"Good," she said and stood. "Then if you don't mind, I have to get moving."

"I'll get out of your way," Jonas replied and stood. He started out of the kitchen, but paused at the door to look back at her. "Don't do anything stupid, Scout. I don't want to have to retrieve your body—or lock you up."

"No worries," she assured him. "I'm just going scouting."

"Make sure that's all you do," he warned.

"Gotcha," she agreed. "I'll be in touch."

Jonas nodded and left. Scout wasted no time. Changing into camouflage pants, a matching tank top and boots, she strapped on her knife, packed water and a blanket into her backpack and headed out.

Her first stop was to see the cub. The mother lion had taken her in completely and the cub was busy playing with the others of her litter. Scout spent some time with the mother, telling her what she was trying to do, and asking if the lioness had any ideas.

Luckily, she did. Scout listened to the information and made up her mind to follow up on it. It could be just what she needed to get Jonas to go after Ray Moss. She thanked the lioness and headed out.

As she traveled, thoughts of Ray killing Jed surfaced and brought with it fresh grief and rage. Vision of him falling, wounded and bleeding, filled her mind. She could not stop it. Other images crowded in, the lion within her remembering the pain and rage from the bullet that ended her life. She tried to push back the rage, knowing she needed a clear head. But the anger supplied by the lion that inhabited her, mixed with her own and grew until she was rendered immobile, standing in the shelter of a thick stand of trees, shaking with fury.

She'd never felt such fury. Her mind was consumed by it, making her heart race and her body vibrate. She felt as if she would burst out of her skin, like there were thousands of live wires beneath the surface, tingling and electrifying.

It was frightening. It was consuming. And it was out of control. She couldn't take it. It was going to destroy her. The fight or flight instinct kicked in. Since there was no enemy to fight, flight was the only option left to her. She looked around wildly, trying to see her course, which way to run, where to escape.

Then reality deserted her. She saw the world around her fading, blackness creeping in from the periphery until her vision was only a pinpoint of life. Death was upon her. She knew no other explanation. That thought stunned her into calmness a moment before the darkness claimed her.

Chapter Nine

ꟹ

Cole was still thinking about the conversation he'd had with Jonas Roberts three days earlier when he pulled up in front of Scout's house late in the evening. He'd told Jonas what had happened while he and Scout were out in the wilderness. Well, not all of it. He'd omitted the part where Scout joined with the lion and they had wild sex in the cave.

But Jonas had seemed to sense that he was holding back. He'd asked twice if there was anything Cole had left out, anything he wanted to add. Cole had said no. But the lie had gnawed at him ever since.

Only how could he tell the CBI captain that Scout claimed to have taken the spirit of a lion into herself and that they'd gone at it like two sex-starved teenagers with a dead lion lying in the cave with them?

He wanted to talk to Scout about it. Now that he'd had time to step back from it, it seemed impossible. Things like animals communicating with animals might be real. Hell, he had proof of that from his two sisters-in-law, both of them witches who possessed the ability to communicate with animals. But things like the spirit of an animal living inside you or joining with them, those things just weren't possible. It might be part of mythology and fantasy but it just wasn't real.

He wanted, no needed to hear Scout say that it was all just a mistake, that the trauma or fear or whatever had made her a little crazy and she'd imagined it. That she'd been pulling his leg. Anything. He just didn't want to believe it.

Her truck was home which meant he wouldn't have to wait. That was a relief. He went to the front door. It was locked. He knocked and waited. No answer. He called out and knocked again. Still no answer.

Thinking maybe she was indulging herself in that elaborate bathroom, he walked around back and tried the door. It was locked, so he used the key. It was right where she said it would be.

"Scout?" he called out as he entered and closed the door behind him. "You here?"

There was no reply. He went through the house. She wasn't there. He tried her cell phone and when he heard it ring in the kitchen realized that she didn't have it with her.

All he could do was wait. He went back to his SUV and grabbed his duffle bag. Once inside, he showered, dressed and rummaged through the refrigerator for something to eat.

Then he settled down on the couch in the den and channel surfed for a while, settling on a nature program. Fifteen minutes into the show his eyes started to get heavy. His last thought was that he'd close his eyes for just a little while, and if she wasn't back in an hour he'd go look for her.

A low growl had him sitting up, wide awake and heart pounding. The television was still on. He laughed at himself. That had to be what woke him. He got up to head for the bathroom and when he did alarms went off in his head.

"Scout!" he rushed to her, where she stood in the kitchen doorway. Naked. Her hair was tangled and dirty, as was the rest of her. Her skin was scratched and bloody footprints tracked the clean kitchen floor. She stared at him like someone in a daze.

He grabbed her by the shoulders. "Scout! Christ! What happened? Are you okay? I'll call an ambulance—the police. Honey, speak to me."

She did not move or react in any way. Cole swept her up in his arms and ran to the bathroom, sitting her on the edge of the tub while he turned on the water and grabbed a washcloth.

"Scout? Can you hear me?" he asked, climbing fully clothed into the tub so he could kneel in front of her. "Scout? Scout!"

She blinked once. Then again. And suddenly her eyes focused. "What the hell happened?" Cole asked.

She shook her head and slid into the tub, wincing. "I'm tired," she said, lying back into the water. "So tired."

"I'm calling an ambulance," he announced and started to get out of the tub.

"No!" She bolted upright, grabbing the wet leg of his jeans. "No, don't. Please."

"Then tell me what happened," he said, taking a seat on the edge of the tub.

"I…I can't. Not yet. Just…just let me get clean. Please?"

"Fine." He stood and stripped off his wet clothes, gathered them up and left.

Scout sank back into the water, her mind in a whirl. How the hell was she going to explain this to Cole when she could barely believe it herself? If only Jed were here. He'd know what to do, tell her where to go for answers if he didn't have them.

She felt more alone and vulnerable than she'd ever been. If she told Cole the truth, he'd think she was crazy. Unless…

No. She couldn't even entertain the idea. There had to be another way. *Come on, get it together,* she told herself. *Get clean, get calm.*

She kept those four words in her head, reciting them over and over as she washed, dried and went into the dressing area to find antiseptic and bandages for her feet. Once that was taken care of she went into her bedroom to slip into a loose shift.

Cole was sitting on the couch wearing a pair of loose cotton pants, with his elbows propped on his knees when she entered. She sat down beside him and he turned to face her. "Are you all right, Scout?"

"I'm fine."

"You sure?"

"Positive."

"Okay, then tell me. What the hell happened?"

She blew out her breath and leaned back into the softness of the couch. "I need you to promise me something,"

"What?"

"That you'll hear me out. Listen to what I have to say before you say anything. And keep an open mind."

"I'm already not liking the sound of this."

"Then forget it." She started to get up. "Go home. I'm fine."

"Hey, hold on!" he pulled her back down. "I didn't say I wouldn't listen."

"There's no point in my talking if you've made your mind up that you're against whatever I have to say."

"I'm not!" he insisted then added when she cocked an eyebrow at him, "Please."

"Okay." She settled back against the couch. "When I was a child, my grandfather, Jed, would tell me stories—myths. One of his favorites was of the skin-walkers. Have you ever heard that term?"

"Wasn't that a bad werewolf movie?"

She rolled her eyes. "Yeah, it was. But the tales Jed told me were about the *yee naaldlooshii*, which translates as 'with it, he goes on all fours'. The *yee naaldlooshii* were people with the ability to transform into an animal. They were also witches."

A sardonic smile appeared on her face. "Yeah, witches. Something I think you've had a bit of experience with?"

He gave her a sheepish grin. "A little."

"Enough. Remember that connection we had? It's been steadily coming to me."

"What do you mean?" His voice was tight, and she knew it was unsettling for him, but now that she'd decided to lay it all on the table, she wasn't going to sugar coat it. If he walked away then they weren't meant to be. That's how she had to look at it.

"I mean Ana and Rusty. Your sisters-in-law? They're in your head. What happened with Ana and her husband when he tracked her to Arizona, and what happened to Rusty after Clay went to live there. The Stikeleathers and what they tried to do to Rusty and Cole. What happened to Clara when she and Ana were kidnapped."

Cole slumped back and regarded her with lowered brows for a long time. "Did you run some kind of background check on me?"

"Oh yeah, while I was out running around the woods naked, I whipped out my handy dandy, little super-spy gadget and hacked into all your secret files."

A corner of his mouth moved up in a smirk. "Point taken. So, you got this from that…thing we had that happened."

"Yeah. So, I know you're familiar with witches, therefore you have to be somewhat open minded to things beyond the ordinary."

"Like yee…skin-walkers."

"Yeah, like that."

"I think I need to hear more."

"Okay. Let me think…" She leaned back and closed her eyes, thinking back to the stories of her childhood. "A *yee naaldloshii* is one of several types of witch in the Navaho beliefs, which is the majority of the stories Jed told me. See, his mother was Navaho and father Sioux. His father died when Jed was young, so he was raised with his mother's people. It wasn't until he was a teenager and the Elders discovered that he was a true scout that he left his mother's people and struck out on his own. But anyway, a *yee naaldlooshii* is a witch, specifically an *ánt'įįhnii* or practitioner of the Witchery Way. Now this isn't the same as *a adagash* who is a user of curse objects.

"The *ánt'įįhnii* are people who've been given supernatural power. It's commonly believed that there are far more male *ánt'įįhnii* than female and that only childless females can become *ánt'įįhnii*. From what I remember, *ánt'įįhnii* and *yee naaldlooshii* are used pretty interchangeably, although not all Navaho witches are skin-walkers."

"So essentially, skin-walkers are what? Werewolves?"

"Something like that," she replied. "But remember all I know of it until now has been from stories told to me as a child."

"Until now?"

She nodded. "After you left, I went out to visit the cub. I was planning on doing some scouting. But something happened. Visions of Jed being killed flooded my mind, along with memories of the dying lioness. It was…horrifying. I felt like my skin was being electrified and my vision kept shrinking. I thought I was dying. So I gave in to it. And everything went black.

"When I woke, the first thing I noticed was that all the colors seemed so sharp and clear. And that seemed wrong. It was night. I have good night vision, but not that good. I thought maybe it was a passing symptom. I shook my head and went to get up. But my arms and legs weren't working right. Then I realized."

She paused and looked away, feeling all at once terribly uncertain.

"What?" Cole prompted her. "You realized what?"

"That I wasn't…human."

"What?" he exploded both verbally and physically, jumping off the couch.

"Not human," she repeated.

"Oh no!" He waved his hand at her as if warding off something he didn't want to hear. "Do not tell me that you were an animal."

"Fine, I won't." His tone resulted in an immediate rise of anger. She got off the couch and walked out of the room.

"Hold on!" Cole followed her into the kitchen. "Don't just walk away. You have something to say, then spit it out."

"Forget it," she snapped at him, opening the refrigerator and looking inside.

"Hell no. You started this, now finish it. Or you want me to do it for you? You realized you were a cat, right? That you'd magically been transformed into a damn lion."

"Stop it!" she yelled at him. "This isn't a joke."

"Fucking A it isn't a joke," he yelled back. "It's fucking insanity."

Scout froze. The word insanity seemed to echo in her head and with each repeating reverberation her anger grew. "Insane?" she hissed. "Did you call me insane?"

"I said this…whatever the hell it is you've got in your head is insane. Okay, fine, I know some witches. But they don't turn into animals or— Holy fucking shit!"

Scout saw his eyes grow wide at the same moment pain lanced through her body. A split second later she was looking at him from a much lower angle. "Oh shit," she mumbled. But the words did not match the thoughts. Instead what emerged from her lips was a growl.

She almost hated to look but couldn't stop herself. She looked down at her feet. And saw paws. Big, strong, furry paws, with long sharp nails. She looked back up at Cole, who was slowly backing away from her, shock clear on his face.

"Don't be afraid," she tried to say. But this time the sound emerging from her mouth was a cross between a roar and a scream.

Oh shit! she thought. *This is NOT good.* The very last thing she wanted was the man she loved looking at her like she was a monster. She had to show him that he was not in danger.

She stepped over the discarded shift lying on the floor and slowly approached him. He continued to back away from her until he bumped into the stone hearth. "Don't." He held up his hand as if warding her off. "I mean it. Just stay back."

She stopped and lay down, purring. Maybe that would calm him until she figured out how to change back into human form. She was really new to this and didn't quite have the hang of it.

Cole watched her for a long time, and then slowly sat down on the hearth. "Okay, either I've completely lost touch with reality, or you just turned into a lion." He paused for a moment. "If that's really you then…nod your head."

Scout nodded.

"Shit on a stick!" Cole groused. "This can't be happening! Can you change back? Please?"

She cocked her head to one side, trying to indicate that she wasn't sure. He didn't get it. "Scout, I mean it. I really want you to change back."

She inched closer. He did not move, so she rose and padded closer until she was close enough to lay her head on his leg.

For a few moments he was as rigid as stone, just the vibration of fear running through him and rising in the air. She remained still, purring. Finally he lowered his hand to her head. She did not move, but purred louder.

Cole started to stroke her. "Scout, god as my witness, I feel like I just fell down the rabbit hole. This is just too unbelievable. But I saw it with my own eyes, and I'm sitting here rubbing a lion so if it isn't real then I'm too far gone for help. If you could just turn back into you, then maybe I could get a bead on all this."

She smelled his fear, and felt his uncertainty. Suddenly nothing mattered but comforting him, putting her arms around him and assuring him that he was fine and everything would be fine.

With that wish came a sudden stab of pain that had her doubling over, eyes clenched tight. When she opened them, she saw human skin. She looked up and found Cole watching her with an amazed expression.

"I'm sorry," she said softly, wanting to touch him but afraid he would push her away. "I so sorry, Cole. I…I don't know how or why this happened and I know it's too much to take in. I'm having a hard time of it myself. I don't want you to leave, but if you need to, I'll understand."

His eyes locked with hers and for the second time she connected with him. She saw his eyes roll back and his body arch. She caught him as he fell forward, both of them toppling to the floor, the connection between them blinding them both to everything except sensation and emotion.

Only this time it was different. This time she knew he could sense her, feel her emotions, and touch her memories. And she did nothing to prohibit him. She let him see it all. The loss of her parents, her childhood, her failed marriage and her grief at losing Jed. He witnessed her joining with the lioness and her fear at the first transformation that took her.

And he felt her love. She hid nothing but laid her soul bare for him.

When the connection faded and he opened his eyes, the look within them was one of astonishment. "What was that?" he whispered.

"Same as before," she replied. "Only this time it was you who got to look inside."

He pushed himself up into a sitting position. "It's all jumbled, bits and pieces, flashes. Doesn't all make sense."

"It will. In time," she assured him.

"I'm sorry, Scout," he said, taking her hand. "I reacted badly. This has to be hard on you—traumatic even."

"It was," she admitted. "Until now."

"What makes it easier now?"

"You."

He opened his mouth as if to speak, then changed his mind and pulled her to him, enveloping her in his arms. "I promise you, I'll never reveal your secret. You're safe with me, Scout. I give you my word. As long as I live no harm will ever come to you."

She pulled back to search his eyes. "I know you're sincere—now, at this moment. But please, don't make promises that you may not be able to keep."

"I never do," he said firmly. "Ever."

"Then thank you," she said gratefully. "And I promise never to..." A smile of mischief broke out on her face "Bite you—while I'm a lion, I mean. While I'm a woman...well, no promises there."

Her jest broke the tension and he chuckled. The chuckle turned into a laugh and before they knew it they were rolling around on the floor laughing, for the moment forgetting all but the joy of being together.

ChapterTen

ဢ

The first thing Scout was aware of when she woke was Cole's strong body curved protectively against her back. She smiled, stretched and turned over to face him, surprised to see his eyes open.

"Good morning," she said with a smile.

"That it is," he replied.

She ran her hand down between their bodies to fondle him, finding him hard. "Hmmm," she murmured appreciatively. "What do you want to do today?"

Cole chuckled. "Honey, you really need to ask?"

Scout laughed along with him. For the past two days they'd been like a couple on their honeymoon, the lovemaking broken only by the need for hunger or sleep. She couldn't remember being happier. She didn't want their time to end, afraid that when he left tomorrow to return to work, everything would change. The magic would end.

"Well, in that case…" She started to slide down, kissing her way along his body. Cole stopped her before she reached her destination.

"As I recall, it's my turn," he announced.

"Says who?" she argued, still wiggling lower, hanging on to his erection.

"Says me."

He pulled her back up and rolled her over on her back, taking her hands and raising them up above and behind her head. "Grab the headboard, sugar."

Scout complied, fisting both hands around one of the metal rods that formed the headboard. A delicious shiver of anticipation danced over her skin as his hands trailed down her arms, and up to cup her breasts, his thumbs stroking over the tightening nipples. She had not yet grown immune to the effect of his touch and the excitement it evoked. She hoped she never developed such immunity. She loved the delicious hunger that curled in her belly and snaked through her veins.

"You've got the most beautiful breasts," he said huskily. "Just the right size and with such delicious nipples. I love feeling them. And doing this."

He leaned down and circled one taut nipple with his tongue. She purred appreciatively and stretched, luxuriating in the attention of his mouth and hands on her flesh.

Cole took his time, teasing her breasts until she was arching against his mouth, pressing for more, thrilling in the small pain that accompanied the pleasure spiking out from her breasts, making her sex pulse with longing.

"You like that, don't you, baby?" he whispered against her skin, squeezing her breasts with his big rough-skinned hands and flicking his tongue over one tender nipple.

"Ummm, yes," she murmured.

"Tell me what else you want."

Her voice was a lusty rasp. "Anything. Everything. Just don't stop."

He chuckled and started licking and kissing his way down her body. With one hand he nudged her legs apart. "Wider," he instructed as he nuzzled the damp curls on her mound. "Bend your knees."

The sound of his raspy voice, rough with desire, ordering her, was a new turn-on. She'd never been much of the submissive type. Until now. She bent her legs, letting her knees fall to the side, baring her pussy to his hungry mouth.

Using his fingers, he spread her lips, running his hot wet tongue the length of her then up again, to circle her clit. His fingers kept her pussy spread, exposing her so that he could lick his way over every inch of her.

He sucked her clit into his mouth and flicked his tongue over it. One finger dipped inside her pussy, feeling slowly. When he found her secret spot, she felt like a bolt of electricity had suddenly hit her.

"Now, now, now," she begged, eager for release.

He stopped, raised his head and smiled sexily at her. "Not yet. "

"Yes, yet!" she argued, thrusting her pelvis up at him.

He sat back on his heels, regarding her with an expression so heated that it made juice seep from within her just looking at him. She was struck again with just how much she wanted him. How much he turned her on.

"Have you ever been spanked?" he asked.

"What?" She sat up like she'd been shot from a cannon. That was the last thing she'd expected to come out of his mouth.

"You heard me. Have you ever been spanked?"

"Uh, no."

"Well, there's a first time for everything."

"I don't think so," she argued, feeling suddenly a little uncomfortable. Not because she feared he would hurt her, but because the suggestion had caused her pussy to clench and a strange excitement burn in her belly.

"Well then I guess I'll just have to find some other way to entertain myself, won't I?" Cole asked as he grabbed her ankles and pressed forward, spreading her legs and her pussy wide.

His mouth descended on her, eliciting a groan from her. His tongue teased her clit, ran along the rim of her labia, dipped into her liquid heat then withdrew and circled her ass.

Her hands were clenched tight on the bed rails, her body quivering with need. Each time a wave swelled close to cresting, he stopped. Her moans became deeper, more along the lines of growls. The stronger her need became the more feral she became. Need transformed into its most primitive form. The call of mating came upon her and with it came the power of the lion within who not only answered the call but demanded that it be filled.

"Now, please," she gasped. "Inside me. Please."

Cole drew back and twisted, bringing one hand over the other and flipping her onto her belly. The sudden movement sent her spinning for a moment. When his hand slapped down on her ass, it brought her jerking back with a surge of lust that had wetness spilling from her sex.

"On your knees, baby," he crooned and spanked her again.

She was more than eager to comply, and pulled her knees up under her body, lifting her hips high while keeping her chest pressed against the bed. Cole's hand moved across her ass, then down her side and under her to cup her pussy, his thumb pressed against her clit as his fingers spread her labia wider.

"Now," she moaned, feeling the pressure from the cat inside threatening to take control.

He pressed against her, his hard cock wedged between his belly and the cleft of her ass as he lay down on her back, nipping at the side of her neck. The act was a catalyst she had not anticipated. Completely animal in nature, it drew the cat further into the foreground. Her hands clawed at the sheets, nails tearing into the fabric as she struggled to stay in control. She had to come. Had to satisfy the demands of both her natures. And she had to do it now.

"Now," she rasped, barely able to speak. "Fuck me now."

Cole straightened and she braced for penetration. When the first slap connected with her butt cheek, her groan came out as a growl. Not a pseudo, pretend, almost growl. But an actual feline growl.

"No!" She tried to fight it but even her speech was affected. "Now!" she screamed.

And the scream was that of a lion. It happened before she could stop it. She twisted to see Cole diving off the bed and scurrying in a crouch behind the chair at the window, his rock-hard erection fading fast.

It should not have, but it struck her as funny. More than funny. Hilarious. She opened her mouth and laughed. And out came another scream. Cole was peering at her from behind the chair as if trying to decide whether to bolt or stay and see what she would do.

And that made her laugh harder. This time the sound was less of a scream. Within seconds the sounds coming from her were those of a human. She struggled to put a lid on the laughter and saw the flash of annoyance that wiped the wide-eyed look of anxiety from Cole's face.

"Very funny," he said gruffly.

Scout just patted the bed with one hand and crooked the index finger of the other hand at him. "Come back to bed. Let's give this spanking thing another try?"

"I don't know about that," he argued. "Not exactly a turn-on to have your woman go…animal on you at a time like that."

"It won't happen again," she promised.

"Okay, but if I see one lion in the bed—" he said as he started toward the bed.

"Scout's honor," she interrupted. "Just a tiger."

"Tiger?" He stopped dead in his tracks.

"I meant you," she said with a smile. "Now come on, Cole. I think I might like this whole spanking thing." She rolled over and lifted her ass up temptingly at him. "Don't you want to give it just one more try?"

He laughed and climbed onto the bed with her. "Well, I guess that falls under the 'offer I can't refuse' category, now doesn't it?"

"Hmmm," she murmured as his hand ran gently over her rear.

His next touch was not gentle. When his hand came down on her, she flinched. A warm flush spread out over her ass. The next spank had the flush growing warmer and penetrating her body. The third had her womb clenching and her pussy weeping. By the fourth, she was whimpering and on the fifth, she screamed and raised her hips high. "Now please. Please get in me."

He did not hesitate to comply. Grabbing her hips, he pulled her back into his engorged cock, plunging deep inside her. She didn't want to. Didn't mean to. But she couldn't stop it. She came. Like a dam had broken, she came. And no sooner than it started to subside, another wave hit.

"Yes, yes yes!" she chanted, ramming back against him, wanting all he had to give, wanting the orgasm to go on and on.

"Baby, I can't—" He didn't finish the sentence. She felt the vibration run through him. Felt the sudden pulse in his cock, and the jet it released inside her. His fingers tightened on her hips, keeping her locked close to him. And his orgasm intensified her own.

She was catapulted into pure sensation. Not until they had both collapsed onto the bed did she realize it was over. And by then, lassitude had her firm in its grip. Cole rolled off her and she turned over to curl up against him, her head on his chest.

And woke to find him teasing her breasts with his lips. She reached down to find him hard and ready. And the dance began anew.

*****

Scout woke to find that a new day had dawned. Cole was sleeping soundly. She smiled as she got out of bed and went into the kitchen for a glass of water. No wonder. He'd been like a marathon runner the last few days, in a sexual way. Much more and she wouldn't be able to walk.

As she was filling a glass with water, her phone rang. "Windrider," she answered.

Jonas' voice came back to her. "I've considered your plan."

"And?"

"It's a go. I'm making arrangements now to establish contact with the target. As soon as I have a confirmation on date I'll be in touch."

"I'll be waiting," Scout replied and hung up the phone.

"Who was that?" Cole's voice came from behind her.

She turned and leaned back against the counter. "Jonas."

"What'd he want?"

"CBI business," she replied. "We don't have much to choose from but I can scramble some eggs and make toast."

"What kind of business?" he asked.

"I'm not really at liberty to discuss it," she said and pushed away from the counter to go to the refrigerator.

"Why?"

She turned to see the cross expression on his face. "I just can't, Cole. You know I work with the CBI from time to time and that work isn't something I can talk about."

"Oh, I see," he said and turned away, disappearing through the doorway.

She chased after him. "Hey, come on!"

"No, you come on." He turned on her, his face a hard mask of anger. "You tell me you don't trust me then you want to make it like I'm the one with the problem?"

His words struck deep. Scout didn't know what to say. It wasn't that she didn't trust him to keep the information to himself. She had no doubt that he would keep it in confidence. But if she told him, she was sure he would try to talk her out of being involved and she couldn't risk that. This was something she had to do. Alone.

"You know that's not true." She walked over to him. "My god, Cole, all that you know about me? How could I not trust you?"

Cole knew his anger was a little irrational. He didn't even completely understand it himself. Or maybe he just didn't want to. The fact was, now that he'd had time to digest the information he'd been given in the connection with Scout, he felt a bond with her that was stronger than anything he'd imagined. He wanted to shield her, protect her and take care of her.

And he wanted her to want that from him. He wanted to be the one she confided in, trusted. The one she came to when the world was too harsh or when she needed comfort. He wanted to be her hero.

That realization gave him a degree of discomfort. He'd never had such needs and he wasn't sure how to deal with them. And he felt a little guilty. He knew she had to trust him. Otherwise, he'd not have spent the last three days in her home, sharing her bed, seeing her at her most passionate, and her most vulnerable. And she would never have allowed the connection if there was no trust.

"I'm sorry," he said after a long moment. "I understand."

"No, I don't think you do," she replied. "I trust you, Cole. More than I've trusted anyone except for Jed. There are just some things I'm not at liberty to discuss and this is one of them. Please try and understand."

He nodded and pulled her to him. "Weren't we discussing breakfast?"

"Well, as a matter of fact, we were," she replied with a smile, grateful he'd let the tension fade. "So, what would you like?"

"Scout and honey," he said with a grin.

She pressed close and wiggled against him. "Well, cowboy, this just might be your lucky day. I think we have that very thing on the menu."

"Then serve it up, baby, 'cause I got a powerful hunger."

Scout laughed and jumped up, winding her legs around him. Her lips crushed against his, her passion every bit a match for his. Not breaking the lock of their lips, Cole carried her to the sofa, need burning hot inside him.

Chapter Eleven

ஐ

Ray Moss walked into the room he and his brother had appointed as their business office. Jimmy sat at the computer.

"So?" Ray asked.

"Everything seems to check out," Jimmy said and leaned back in his chair to regard his brother. "But I still have a bad feeling about this one."

"You're just paranoid," Ray replied. "And you just said it all checks out. Way I see it, it's a fast 25K."

"Doesn't that seem a little high to you?" Jimmy asked. "We've never been offered that kind of money for a hunt."

"You know how it is, Jim. This bastard's got more money than God and 25K to him is chump change. He sits behind a desk all day and gets to feeling like he's missing out. Wants to do something to prove he's a real man. Give him bragging rights at his club or on the golf course."

"Maybe," Jimmy replied. "Still, we need to be careful. Cover our asses. Like, for example, where are you planning on taking them? You can't cross into the national forest or you'll run the risk of bringing the state boys down on us. And from what I found out when I hacked into the CAT system, over the last six months only three lions have been spotted outside the national forest area. Which means the chances of bagging one is slim unless we cross over into the forest."

"So, we've done it before," Ray responded. "Quit being an old woman. Now that the CBI has concluded their investigation, everything's returned to normal. You know as well as I that we can avoid the patrols. Hell, we have their schedules and routes."

Jimmy stood and stretched. "I know. Maybe you're right. It's just…well ever since Bobby, I've had this bad feeling."

"Bobby got what was coming to him," Ray snapped, then held up one hand. "Sorry, bro. You know I miss him too. But that's water under the bridge. We got to look out for ourselves and this gig's going to pay fat."

"Yeah, you're right. We'll make it work. We always do."

"You got it," Ray said with a smile. "So you have everything set up?"

"Yeah. Just need to make a run across the state line to pick up some ammo." Jimmy grabbed his keys from the desk and walked across the room. "Long as we're not purchasing in the state, we're not gonna show up on the radar. Thought I'd head on out, maybe spend the night and come back tomorrow." He stopped in front of Ray.

"Someone special you're planning on paying a visit while you're gone?" Ray asked with a lascivious smile.

Jimmy grinned. "Could be."

Ray laughed and clapped him on the shoulder. "Ride'er hard."

"Always," Jimmy replied with a laugh. "See you tomorrow."

Ray watched him leave then went to the desk and took a seat in front of the computer. He logged in under his password and called up a private file, one he was sure Jimmy didn't know about.

He double-clicked on one of the files and a new window opened, displaying a grainy photograph.

Ray studied Scout Windrider. She was on her porch, her long hair blowing in the breeze. Her hands were propped on the porch rail, causing the tee shirt she wore to rise in the back, displaying her firm ass. One arm was raised, hand to her mouth.

He could see it in his mind, the way she waved and blew a kiss to the ranger as he pulled away down her driveway. Scout might be considered a world-class tracker, but she sure as shit wasn't in touch with the world around her when that ranger was anywhere near. She'd had no idea he was on the ridge watching her through digital binoculars equipped with a camera feature.

He'd been keeping a close eye on her and the ranger. They were spending a lot of time together. Who she spent time with didn't mean a damn. When the time came for him to get even with Scout Windrider, that ranger wouldn't hold a hope in hell of stopping him.

That thought brought a smile to his face. With a sense of satisfaction at the coming day that his vengeance would be complete, he turned his attention to the matter at hand, relieving another city-slicker-sucker of twenty-five thousand dollars.

* * * * *

Scout rose from the floor of the cave where she'd been playing with the lion cubs. Cole sat on a rock, watching. They'd been coming to the cave almost daily to see the cub and the lioness. Scout and the lioness seemed to be doing a lot of communicating, but every time he asked about it, Scout said it was "girl talk". He wasn't sure he believed it but he let it go.

"What do the lions think about you being a…skin-walker?" he asked.

She looked over her shoulder at him with a smile. "Our friend here has no problems with it and from what she tells me neither do any of the others she's encountered in her hunts. You ready to go? The cubs are tired and we need to get out of mama's fur for a while."

"I'm with you."

She gave the lioness a parting embrace, and they left the cave. Once they'd made the descent to the forest floor, Cole took her hand. "Mind if I ask something?"

"What?"

"Can you tell me a little more about the skin-walkers? You've been talking to a lot of Indi…uh, Native Americans lately. You find out anything else?"

"A little. Still haven't found anyone who knows a skin-walker, but some of the Elders I've spoken with know of them or someone who has known one."

"So what have you learned?"

"Well, to begin with, as we both know, the concept isn't confined to Native American cultures. It's something that appears in almost every culture on earth. Names are different as are the stories of the skin-walkers' origins and the abilities they're said to possess, but there are common threads."

"You mean what we were discussing the other night about werewolves?"

"Yeah. But we don't call them that. And skin-walkers don't just assume the shape of wolves, although that is one of the shapes they can assume. Most all of the stories describe a skin-walker as being naked except maybe for a wolf or coyote skin. I think that goes back a long way to old myths and legends. Probably back to the time when clothing was made from natural skins."

"Also, according to the Navaho, a *yee naaldlooshii* has the power to heal or kill with his thoughts and can transform into the form of any animal they choose, depending on what kind of abilities they need at the time."

"That doesn't exactly describe you," he said then halted. "Does it?"

She shook her head. "So far I seem to be confined to shape-shifting into a lion." She tugged on his hand to start walking again. "And I'm kind of hoping that I'm not typical to be honest. Most of the stories about shape-shifters are pretty negative. They're described as evil or malevolent beings. I sure as heck don't want to be something that would attack innocent people or kidnap children."

"I don't think you have to worry about that," he assured her.

"How can you be so sure?" she asked.

Cole stopped again and pulled her to face him. "Because I know you. I've had time to…to translate what I got from you during that joining and I know you're a good, honest, decent woman, Scout. You're the type that would let themselves be destroyed before you'd hurt an innocent."

Tears pooled in her eyes at his words and he felt a wave of love and gratitude pour from her and bathe him. It was a feeling he'd come to crave. It was quickly becoming as integral to his survival as nourishment or oxygen. She was with him constantly. When they weren't together, he couldn't get her out of his mind. It felt like everything else in his life was just a way of killing time until he was with her again.

He hadn't expected it, and he'd spent the last month running like hell from it, but the fact was, he was in love with her. And that no longer made him uncomfortable. In fact, it gave him a sense of happiness he'd never known.

He'd planned on telling her. Had wanted to tell her. But he wanted to do it in a special way. Plan an evening out, or something. Only Scout wasn't a go-out-on-the-town kind of woman. She'd rather get in the kitchen and cook, wearing only one of his tee shirts, than get all dressed up and go somewhere fancy and expensive.

She was watching him, her cat eyes searching his. He knew she hadn't tried to touch his thoughts. She'd promised never to do that again without his permission.

"It's okay," he said softly, suddenly wanting her to take a look.

"Are you sure?" she asked, her eyes widening slightly in surprise.

"Absolutely."

"I don't know if I can do it on purpose," she said. "But here goes."

She placed one hand on his chest, over his heart and closed her eyes. For a few moments they stood there, neither of them speaking. Cole was about to think that nothing was going to happen when suddenly he was catapulted into a swirling vortex of light.

He felt Scout with him. Felt her essence touch his. Merge with his.

And he saw what he'd never known he'd wished for his entire life. He saw his mate and her love for him.

Then suddenly he was back in the forest, with her hand over his heart, her eyes searching his, with tears streaming down her face.

"I love you, Scout," he whispered, choking back emotion that threatened to overwhelm him.

"I love you, Cole," she replied in a tearful whisper. "Forever."

With tenderness swelling inside him, he took her into his arms. Their lips met in a kiss that was as gentle as the wings of a dragonfly, slow and sweet. Her arms circled his waist, her hands moving up his back to pull him closer.

Cole knew then that his bachelor days were over. He'd found his woman.

*****

Scout watched Cole's SUV disappear down the driveway, and then returned inside the house, smiling to herself. It was still a little hard to believe that she'd found someone like Cole. Someone to love. Someone who loved her. Despite the unease the skin-walker status still gave her, she was happy, excited about the present and the future.

She'd planned on heading over to the Center to go over data from the latest study, but figured she had time for one more cup of coffee. Just as she was pouring it, the phone rang.

"Windrider," she answered.

It was Jonas. "We need to meet."

"When?"

"Now?"

"Where are you?"

"Turning onto your driveway. Be decent. I have my team with me."

"I'll put on more coffee," she said and hung up the phone.

Fifteen minutes later, she was sitting at the kitchen table with Jonas and three of his team, all with fresh mugs of coffee in front of them.

"Okay, this is how it's going to play out," Jonas said. "I met with Ray Moss last week. He knows me as David White, a wealthy executive with a petroleum company, who wants a trophy for his wall."

"Mr. White and his party, Mr. Black," he gestured to the man seated next to him, a man Scout knew as Rick Blackwell. "Mr. Green," Jonas indicated the next man, Scott Grier. "And Mr. Brown," he indicated the final man, Mike Billings. "Will arrive via private Gulfstream and be met at the airport by a limo. They will be transported directly to the location designated by Ray Moss."

"No Mr. Yellow?" Scout could not resist the tease. "Ray isn't stupid, you know."

"Trust me, he won't be paying attention to our surnames. He'll be counting his money."

"You're the expert," she said with a shrug. "So what happens next? You traveling by vehicle, horse or foot?"

"Don't know," Jonas replied. "Regardless, you'll be able to track us. A tracking beacon will be in my wristwatch. You'll have a locator, in case we're transported by vehicle. Just in case, I want you at the designated location ahead of us."

She nodded. "Okay, what's the plan after that?"

Jonas took a sip of coffee and Rick spoke up. "The plan is to nail Ray for poaching, and if possible for murder."

"How do you plan on accomplishing that?"

"Incentive," Jonas answered. "Scott will work on Moss. Convince him that Mr. White is worth a lot of money. Now, as the husband of Mr. White's only child, Mr. Green stands to inherit millions if something unfortunate should befall Mr. White."

"He won't go for it," Scout said. "He kills Mr. White, then he takes the rap and Mr. Green walks with millions. No real incentive unless it's cash up front and there's no way you'll make it believable to show up with cash."

"Agreed," Jonas said. "But we're not going at it in a direct line. First, we have Mr. Black and Mr. Green have a falling out. Mr. Green shoots Mr. Black and asks Moss for help to make it look like an accident. He spills his guts about the inheritance and that Black found out what he'd planned and threatened to rat him out. Now Moss has the goods on Green, so the footing is more equal."

"A little drinking and bragging and he might let something slip about the murders," Mike added. "If not, then that's the breaks. We get him for conducting an illegal hunt and poaching.

Scout looked down at her cup and said nothing. "Okay, let's have it," Jonas prompted after a few moments.

She looked up at him. "Maybe it'll work, but I wouldn't count on it. Ray's not dumb. Don't let the looks fool you. He hasn't dodged the law this long by being stupid. And even if he does fall for it, it's entrapment. How do you think it will ever hold up in court?"

Jonas pinned her with a hard look. She didn't flinch or look away. "It'll hold up," he stated. "You have my word on that."

"Okay," she agreed. She knew Jonas well enough to know that he never made promises he couldn't keep. "But where do I play into all this?"

"Backup," Jonas replied. "Just in case something goes wrong, I need to know we have someone out there we can count on. Someone who won't make a blunder and get discovered."

"Fine, then we play it the way you have it written. When does this go down?"

"Tomorrow. I need you to meet me tonight at the lodge we used last year so we can familiarize you with the tracking device. The lodge is only an hour's hike from the meeting point. You can make the hike in and be in place in the morning."

"Okay," she agreed.

All the men stood, said goodbye and left. Jonas was the last one to the door. He paused and turned to her. "Look, I know you want to nail Moss for Jed's murder. If we can make this work, then we can nail him."

"I have to be honest with you," she said. "I've got a bad feeling about this."

"Which is why I'm depending on you," he replied.

"I won't let you down, Jonas. You know that."

"Indeed I do," he replied and clapped his hand on top of her shoulder. "See you tonight."

Scout closed the door behind him and leaned back against it. Cole was due back around the time she needed to leave. Should she call him and tell him just to wait until she returned? And what would she tell him she was returning from?

She battled with herself the rest of the day, picking up the phone a dozen times, then hanging up before she made the call. She'd never been caught up in indecision and it wore on her as the day ticked by.

Unable to sit still, she went to visit the lions. She didn't think to take her cell phone. When she returned to the house she discovered a message from Cole. He was patrolling a high country trail and would be late. And the reception was bad so his cell probably wouldn't pick up a signal.

With the decision taken out of her hands, she gathered her things and put them into her truck, then went back into the house, sat down at the kitchen table and penned a note to Cole, telling him she had a tracking gig and would return in three to four days. She left it propped against an empty cup on the table.

After one final check to make sure she hadn't forgotten anything, she left.

* * * * *

Disappointment rose when Cole pulled up in front of Scout's house and saw that her truck wasn't there. He'd rehearsed his speech all day to get the words right and was eager to sit her down and say all the things he'd been practicing in his head.

He'd talked to his family earlier in the day and had told them about Scout. He wanted them to meet her. They were all surprised but excited. Particularly the women. When he'd told his sister-in-law Ana that he was going to ask Scout to marry him, she'd whooped and hollered like crazy and he had no doubt that she and his step-mother Clara were already busy planning a wedding.

Cole had never taken a woman to meet his family. It made him a little nervous. Not that they wouldn't love Scout, but that maybe she wouldn't like them. He didn't quite know how to handle the feeling. He'd been anxious to tell Scout about it all day but hadn't wanted to do it over the phone. So he'd rehearsed how to ask her to meet his family, and also how to ask her to marry him.

Since she wasn't there, it looked like he would have a little more time to rehearse. He let himself in and headed straight for the shower. Once he was clean, dressed in a pair of loose jeans, he padded into the kitchen to see what there was to fix for dinner.

That's when he saw the note propped on the table. He picked it up and unfolded it. Anxiety took hold in his gut as he read.

"Cole, there's something I have to do. Something that might help catch Jed's killer. I'll be gone a few days. Don't worry. Check in on the cats and I'll be home as soon as I can. I love you. Scout."

Cole put the note down on the table and wandered into the den, rubbing absently at a knot that had formed along his trapezius. What was she doing? And where could he go to find her?

It wasn't that he didn't believe in her ability to take care of herself. His fear was what might happen if she got into a situation that prompted a transformation. Should anyone discover that she was a skin-walker, it would be a real problem.

A sudden inspiration had him sprinting for the phone. He called directory assistance for the number and placed a call to the CBI. He asked for Jonas Roberts and was told that Jonas was not reachable for the next week, but if it was an emergency he could be put through to another officer.

Cole gave his thanks and hung up. Now what? He didn't have a clue. After a half hour of pacing and coming up with nothing to go on, he went back into the kitchen and fixed himself a sandwich.

He ate in front of the television, had a couple of beers and tried Scout's cell phone every half hour. Each time he tried he got her voice mail. Finally at midnight, he gave up and went to bed, telling himself he just had to believe that everything was fine. Scout was capable. She could handle herself. She didn't need him standing guard over her every minute of every day. Now if that gnaw in his gut would just go away.

Chapter Twelve

ꙮ

Scout reached the rendezvous an hour before the appointed time. The old shack sat back from the county road behind a thick stand of trees. From her vantage point several hundred yards to the east behind an outcropping of rock and thick underbrush she could see both the road and the front of the shack.

Jonas arrived at the designated time and gave her the tracking device. He didn't stay long and she was glad. She had not slept well. Several times she'd been tempted to call Cole and explain. But she knew that if she told him was she was doing, he would try to stop her. Regardless of what he thought of her skills and ability to survive in the wilderness, he was still a man, and would feel compelled to try and protect her.

She understood that need. It was part of the reason she hadn't told him. If he was involved and something went wrong then he would be in danger. Despite his strength and intelligence, he was at a disadvantage in the wilderness, pitted against men who made their living, however illegal, tracking and hunting.

Scout did not regret her decision to come alone. She only regretted that he would be concerned. And he definitely would have been concerned if he'd been with her during the night.

Wanting to warn the animal population, she'd decided to try and bring on a transformation. It was far easier than she'd imagined. A little painful, but it happened quickly. One moment she was human and the next she was feline.

It didn't take her long to find another lion. It also didn't take her long to realize that while she inhabited the body of a lion, she was not completely feline. The first lion she encountered recognized her as a skin-walker. He was not afraid or offended by her presence, but accepted her as being a relative to his kind.

She passed on the warning and he left after assuring her that others would be forewarned. After she was left alone, she felt the urge to run, to roam the land. And so she did. She passed the night scouting the area surrounding the rendezvous point, moving in ever widening circles until she'd covered more ground than the hunting party would be able to travel in two day's time.

It was nearly dawn when she returned to the small hunting lodge where she'd left her gear. She ate and lay down for an hour, then got up to prepare.

She took little with her. The locator beacon fit easily into the pocket on the leg of her pants and her knife rested in its sheath on the belt around her hips. She slid the tiny listening device Jonas had given her into her left ear and activated it. According to Jonas he'd obtained it from a military contact, and it was supposed to have a half-mile range. There was nothing else she needed so she left her supplies and bedding behind.

From her hiding place she was safe from a surprise approach, so she closed her eyes to rest until the arrival of the hunting party. Jonas' voice in her ear woke her. "Five minutes from rendezvous."

Sure enough, within minutes a long black sedan turned off the road and rolled down the bumpy path to the shack.

Scout watched as the driver got out and opened the back door. Rick was the first one out of the car, followed by Scott and Mike. Jonas was the last to emerge. He pulled out a cell phone and made a call. Scout could hear his end of the conversation.

"We're here. Where are you?" After a few seconds pause he spoke again. "I'm not paying you twenty-five thousand dollars to keep me waiting."

He ended the call and leaned back against the car.

Scout heard the vibration of the all-terrain vehicle before she saw it. A late-model Jeep, painted in matte camouflage fashion, turned off the road and pulled up beside the limo.

Ray was the only one in the vehicle. He climbed out and approached Jonas, who pushed away from the car.

"Ray Moss," Ray introduced himself.

"David White," Jonas said then gestured to the other men. "My son-in-law, Steve Green, and my associates Rick Black and Bill Brown."

"Nice to meet you all," Ray nodded at the men. "You got your gear?"

"In the trunk," Jonas replied and gestured to the driver who immediately set about unloading backpacks, weapons and supplies.

"I was under the impression we would have two guides," Jonas commented. "Where's our second man?"

"He'll meet up with us later at base camp," Ray replied. "Right now, let's get you loaded up and we'll head over there now. You boys are in for a treat. The females are just now starting to take their young out, so there should be a lot of activity."

"Good," Jonas said. "I don't intend to go home without a trophy."

"No worries about that, Mr. White," Ray assured him and watched the driver put the last of the gear in the back of his Jeep. "That it?"

"Yes, sir," the driver replied.

"Then let's get going," Ray said and climbed in behind the wheel.

Jonas nodded to the driver and took the front passenger seat, leaving his three agents to crowd into the back.

Scout watched them drive away, listening as Jonas commented on the scenery as they drove. He was giving her landmarks. Not that she needed them. She could see the little blip on the locator moving on the screen. On foot, she followed, making sure to stay off the road and out of sight.

* * * * *

Cole walked into the Ranger station and poured himself a cup of coffee. Tim Matthews passed by the door to the break room, saw him and stopped. "Hey, you're not scheduled until tomorrow."

"Had nothing else going so I figured I'd get a jump on the high country patrol. Deters reported yesterday that one of the trails was blocked by a downed tree. Thought I'd take a chainsaw and go up and clear the way."

"That can wait. We don't have many hikers in the park right now and most of them seem to be sticking to the southernmost trails."

Cole shrugged. "Never know though."

Tim turned to leave then stopped and turned back to face Cole. "Everything okay, Cole?"

"Yeah, fine."

Tim nodded. "Look, it's none of my business, but I know you and Scout have been spending a lot of time together. If there's trouble between the two of you—"

"No, everything's fine, Tim. Thanks."

"You sure?"

"Yeah," Cole replied, then changed his mind. "No. I mean we're not fighting or anything but she took off two days ago and left me a note that has me a little troubled."

"What did she say, if you don't mind me asking?"

"Said she had something she had to do that might help bring Jed's murderer to justice."

Tim blew out his breath and walked over to the coffee pot to pour himself a cup. He sat down at the table. "She talk with Jonas Roberts lately?"

"Few days ago," Cole replied and took a seat at the table. "Why?"

"Just a hunch," Tim said. "I don't think he was convinced that Bobby Howard was really responsible for the murders."

"What makes you say that?"

"He asked me a lot of questions—about some of the locals."

"Any local in particular?"

"Ray Moss. You know him?"

"Only heard of him. That he was partners with Howard. But didn't his alibi check out?"

"Yeah, his brother and another fellow vouched for him that he was up at the fellow's lodge doing some fishing when it all happened."

"But?" Cole asked.

"But it made me think," Tim said. "Now this is between you and me, Cole. Scout would have my head if she knew I was talking behind her back, but I knew her grandfather pretty well, and have known Scout most of her life.

"Ray's father and Jed were in business at one time, as trackers. But Jed dumped him because Moss didn't have the same appreciation for the wilderness and the life in it that Jed did. Jed didn't believe in hunting for sport. He only hunted when an animal was wounded or had proven to be a threat to livestock or humans. Hunting for the sport was against his belief. But sport hunting was big business and Ray's father knew there was money to be made in it. He tried to convince Jed.

"But Jed wouldn't have any part of it. He refused and when Moss went ahead, Jed cursed him."

"You mean cussed him out?"

"No, cursed him. Said that what he was doing would lead only to suffering and death."

"That's hardly a curse."

"Well, it's the way Moss' boys ended up taking it. Moss never said a hard word against Jed, but rumor has it that his sons were pretty pissed. They even went so far as to blame Jed when their father was killed in a hunting accident."

"How did he die?"

"Mauled by a lion."

Cole grimaced. "What did that have to do with Jed?"

"Nothing, but they needed someone to blame. A few years ago, they set up this big hunt on private land. All I really know for sure is that they had two packs of dogs and ten city boys eager to go out and shoot something.

"Apparently they crossed the boundary into the national forest and ran into Jed and Scout. Jed accused Moss of breaking the law and conducting an illegal hunt. In front of Moss' clients. And Scout lit into them and threatened to have them arrested if they didn't call off the hunt that moment."

Cole chuckled. "I can see her doing that."

"Yeah, she's a firecracker," Tim agreed. "Anyway, Moss gave in and said he'd stop the hunt. But apparently he just said that to get them off his ass because four days later, a cornered female lion attacked him. His sons and the clients killed the lion, but not before she'd killed Moss."

"Bad way to go," Cole commented. "But what does that have to do with Scout?"

"Word has it that Ray blamed Jed and Scout. Said they cursed the hunt. That if his father hadn't been upset over the altercation with them, he would have been on his game and the lion wouldn't have gotten him."

"That's bullshit."

"Yeah, it is," Tim agreed. "To a rational person. Problem is, I'm not real sure Ray's been rational since his father died. He and Scout damn near came to blows just before Jed died. Ray made a smart-ass comment about Jed in her presence and she went after him. Don't know what. But I do know she went after him. Physically. He had her arrested. She spent three days in jail rather than let anyone bail her out, and let it be known that if Ray came within a hundred feet of her she'd gut him."

Cole was taken aback by that. "Are you sure Scout said that?"

"That's what I heard."

"Did you ask her?"

"No, I didn't think it was wise to bring it up. Particularly considering that Jed was killed a couple of weeks later."

Cole shook his head. "I don't buy it. Scout's tough and hardheaded but she'd never make that kind of threat against someone.

"You sure about that?" Tim asked and held up his hand for Cole to wait. "Look, I love her like a sister, Cole. But she's not like the rest of us. There's part of her that's…I don't know. Wild. Jed was the same way. Like he was more part of the animals than he was with men, if that makes sense."

Cole couldn't tell Tim that it made more sense than Tim would ever realize. But he could argue in Scout's defense. "And from what I've always heard Jed Windrider was one of the most humane, wise men who ever walked. That he was against violence and never even carried a gun. That his was a path of peace."

"That's true."

"And he raised Scout. Taught her. She's the same way. She might fight to the death if threatened, but she wouldn't ever set out to harm a life. Any life. It's not her way."

What he couldn't say, was that the animal part of Scout would not see any need for senseless killing. Lions killed to eat. End of story. They did not kill for pleasure or profit or out of spite. For them, killing was necessary for survival. The part of Scout that was a lion shared that view. The part of her that was human cared too deeply for life to end it unless it was a matter of kill or be killed. He believed that.

"You're probably right," Tim replied. "But that doesn't change the fact that there's bad blood between her and Moss, and Moss was one of the prime suspects in the murders. Or that Scout's gone missing after talking with Roberts."

"She said she did a lot of work for the CBI."

"She does. Any time there's a missing person or a manhunt for a fugitive or someone on the run from committing a crime they call her in."

"Then maybe that's what it is this time," Cole suggested.

"No reports of missing persons in the last few days," Tim replied. "But hey, what do I know. The CBI might have info that hasn't been released to the public. Anyway, I didn't really mean to get into all that. I just wanted to give you a heads up."

"Yeah, thanks," Cole said and remained seated as Tim got up and left. If that was a heads up, then on what? Was Tim trying to tell him Scout had gone off with Jonas on something that was dangerous? Was he suggesting that she was getting into something that involved this Moss fellow that might get her killed? Or was he suggesting she might be off trying to take the law into her own hands?

None of it was appetizing in the least, and all of it worrisome. Cole needed to find out where she'd gone. And he needed to do it fast. The problem was, who could help him?

He got up and went to the supply building for a saw, intending to go take care of clearing the trail. As he entered, he heard the man who ran the supply department talking with another of the rangers.

"No shit. Jack said the lion saw him, stopped, and just watched until he got back on his four-wheeler and it watched him drive off. Never growled. Didn't run. Nothing. Said it was strange as hell. Damn thing acted like a person."

A chill skittered down Cole's spine. "Hey, Russ. Some strange tale. Where did Jack say he was when he saw the lion?"

"Up along the north pass, close to the border," Russ replied.

Cole nodded and turned to leave. "Thanks, man."

"Hey, you need something?" Russ called after him.

"Nope, I'm good." Cole threw up his hand and kept walking straight to his truck. Now he knew where to go for answers. The problem facing him was how to get close enough to ask.

* * * * *

Scout worked her way around the perimeter of the hunting party's base camp. It was the third day of the hunt and so far, things had not gone well. Ray's brother Jimmy had brought in the dogs yesterday and not even they could pick up the scent of a lion.

Jonas had complained long and loud last night when they returned to camp, tired and hungry. Jimmy had left with the dogs, and Ray had turned his attention to a fifth of Jack Daniels.

Several times the agent posing as Jonas' son-in-law had approached Ray. They talked and drank and talked more. But so far Ray had not taken the bait on any plot to do away with Jonas. His only comment was that if the man wanted Jonas dead he should just pull out his gun and shoot him when no one was looking and call it a hunting accident.

Scout knew that wasn't enough for Jonas to use to put Ray behind bars. Unless they either cornered a lion or something happened to loosen Ray's lips, this mission was going south fast.

She heard Ray telling the men to gear up and they'd head out as soon as his brother arrived with the dogs.

Less than an hour passed before Jimmy Moss arrived. But he did not have the dogs with him. He called Ray over to his truck, and they spoke for a few minutes, then Ray yelled to the hunting party that he and his brother were going to check something out and they'd be back inside an hour.

Scout fell in behind them. They walked about a hundred yards outside the camp and stopped.

"I told you something about that guy was familiar," Jimmy was saying when she got close enough to hear. "When I got back last night I got online to check it out. Took me almost all night but I found it. The guy saying he's Bob Brown is really Mike Billings with the CBI."

"No way," Ray argued.

"I'm telling you it's the guy! If you don't believe me then look at this." He pulled something from his back pocket and handed it to Ray.

Ray accepted and unfolded the printed sheet of paper. He was quiet for a few minutes as he stared at the paper then he wadded it up tight in his hand.

"Motherfucker!"

Jimmy nodded. "I told you something was wrong about those guys."

"Well why the fuck are they out here?" Ray barked. "You think it has something to do with Bobby and those New York boys?"

"That'd be my guess," Jimmy replied. "I tried to get up with Fred to make sure no one had been back to talk to him about us claiming to be at his lodge with him when it all went down, but I couldn't get him."

"You think he'd turn on us?" Ray asked.

"Hell, Ray, you know as well as I do that anybody'll turn if they're trying to save their own ass."

"But this report says the guy was involved in the investigation into Windrider's death, not Bobby's."

"Point is, he's CBI," Jimmy said. "Which means the others probably are too."

"But Windrider's been dead more than a year. No way in hell they're still on that. Besides, they'll never pin that shit on us. We covered all the bases. Right?"

"Yeah. We did," Jimmy replied. "But the same may not be true with Bobby and those New York guys. You made a pretty big mess of that."

"Well fuck you!" Ray snarled.

"Chill." Jimmy reached out to put his hand on Ray's shoulder. "Look man, we're in this together. They nail you for any of this or the old man's murder and I go down too."

"So what do we do?" Ray asked.

"Let me think," Jimmy said and paced back and forth, kicking at small stones and pieces of wood on the forest floor.

Ray watched in silence. And in silence Scout watched him. Rage had bloomed fast and bitter when she heard them talking about Jed's death. There was no doubt about it. They'd killed Jed. Pain and grief swelled to mix with the rage, threatening her control. The skin-walker screamed to be released. All she had to do was let go and the animal inside her would take care of both of them.

She fought against it. The last thing Jed would want was for her to stain her soul with the taking of life. Even life as low and vile as the Moss brothers. But the call of the lion inside was strong. She broke out in a sweat in a fight to stay in control of the beast that demanded blood for blood.

Scout was so caught up in her own battle that she missed hearing what Jimmy said when he turned back to Ray. But his voice filtered in, helping her push back the madness. She needed to know what they planned.

"So if we take them into the high country and force them to climb, we can rig a fatal fall," Jimmy was saying.

"Another fall so soon after Bobby might look suspicious," Ray pointed out.

"But this time it's different," Jimmy argued. "We came in from Hastings place in Ourey and hiked out to Black Canyon. That's what we say the clients were here for. As soon as we stage the accident, we take all the guns, bury them, then one of us goes for help to report the accident."

"Right, like we're going to convince a bunch of CBI guys to try and make an ascent in Black Canyon. First, it's illegal without a permit and second they can't be that stupid. No, it won't work. We have to come up with a legitimate reason to get them into Black Canyon."

"No we don't. We just head there. Two hours away from camp and they'll be lost. They either stick with us or try and find their own way out. They'll follow us. We just have to convince them that we know where the prey is."

Scout had heard enough. She had to warn Jonas and his men. And she had to get help. The problem was she couldn't go for help and stay close enough to warn Jonas. Unless.

She made her decision quickly. Working her way back from her vantage point, she found a safe place. After undressing, she put the listening device from her ear, the tracking device and her knife into her pants pocket, then wound the pants around the length of her belt. She left the sheathed knife attached to the belt, buckled it in its loosest notch, then sat down and willed herself to change.

It was not as painful as the previous transformation, something she was profoundly grateful for. She sure didn't want to give away her position and end up being the prey for a hunt.

Once in lion form, she worked her head through the looped belt. It hung like an unwieldy necklace around her neck, but it would suffice. With a goal clear in her mind she set off as fast as her four legs would carry her.

*****

Cole arrived at the opening of the cave just before noon. A warning scream from inside had him stopping short of the entrance.

"It's me. Cole," he called out. "Scout's friend."

A deep growl came from inside. "I need help," he said. "I have to find Scout."

A more intense growl came in response to his words. Having no idea what else to do, he backed up a little ways from the cave, sat down and waited. And waited. And waited.

Twilight was starting to fall when he heard a sound at the mouth of the cave. The lioness stood there, watching him.

"She's out there, and in danger," Cole said. "I need to find her and I need help."

The lioness watched him for a few moments, the turned to look back into the depths of the cave. Cole sensed that she understood, and maybe she wanted to help but she was loathe to leave the cubs.

"I'll stand guard over them," he offered. "If you can just find out where she is."

The lioness opened her mouth and released a scream that made every hair on his body stand on end. He didn't know if she was going to attack him or not, but he didn't want to make any sudden moves, so he just sat there and hoped for the best.

Which is exactly what he got. She cocked her head to one side as if listening, and then took off, disappearing from sight within seconds. Leaving him to wait.

Chapter Thirteen

ഇ

Night was falling by the time Ray called a halt to the long trek they'd led Jonas and his men on.

"We'll make camp here and resume in the morning," he announced.

"What the hell's this?" Jonas demanded. "We haven't seen shit and done nothing but walk all day. What kind of bogus operation are you running, Moss?"

"Not a damn thing bogus about this operation!" Ray shot back.

"Well we sure as hell haven't killed anything. Or seen anything for that matter," Jonas complained. "I'm beginning to think these woods are completely uninhabited. We haven't even seen a rabbit."

"Keep your pants on," Ray replied. "Tracking cats takes time. And they travel at night. Way you boys sleep, a herd of buffalo could stampede through camp and you wouldn't know it."

"Look here—"

"Look, Mr. White," Jimmy cut in. "I know it's frustrating and you probably thought it would be like shows you see on television on African safaris where there's fifty lions lying around in the sun, but it's not like that on a real hunt. We've seen tracks and I think we're moving into a populated area. We just have to be patient."

"Well, at the tune of twenty-five thousand dollars, my patience is running a bit thin."

Jimmy nodded. "I understand. Tell you what. Why don't we build a fire and have a drink? I have a bottle stashed in my pack I was going to crack out when we bagged something, but what the hell. We could all use a pick-me-up."

"Fine," Jonas agreed and stomped off.

Jimmy turned to Ray. "You keep 'em busy. I have a plan."

"What?"

"I'm gonna doctor the liquor with animal tranquilizer. It'll put them out. Then we tie them up, and haul them out of here one at a time and stage an accident."

"Carry four grown men?" Ray asked. "Not the best plan I ever heard."

"You got a better one?"

"Not at the moment."

"Then we go with this one."

"Fine."

Ray started setting up camp, sending the men out to gather wood, while Jimmy laced the liquor with enough tranquilizers to put a dozen men out for a good long while.

"This is all that damn Windrider's fault," Ray said under his breath and he passed by his brother.

"What's that?"

"Fucking Windrider," Ray snarled and spat on the ground. "Wasn't for her and her goddamn mouth—"

"This isn't the time or place to discuss that," Jimmy pointed out as he saw one of their clients returning with an armload of wood. "Besides, our time will come and we'll deal with the last Windrider."

"Wipe those sons-a-bitches off the earth," Ray agreed.

"Amen, brother," Jimmy said and stood with a smile as Jonas appeared. "Well, now that we have wood, let's have us a toast. Ray, where are the coffee tins?"

Ray rumbled through a pack and located four tin coffee cups. Jimmy filled each one to the rim, passing them to each of their clients. Then he lifted the bottle up in front of him. "To a successful hunt."

He put the bottle to his lips, tilted it up and worked his throat muscles like he'd taken a good couple of swallows. "Whew!" he exclaimed as he lowered the bottle and passed it to Ray. "That hit the spot."

He watched as his clients raised their cups and drank the tainted brew. No one seemed to notice anything peculiar. They all sat down as he and Ray built a fire. By the time the fire was burning well, two of the men were already weaving.

Jimmy grinned and waited. It wouldn't be long.

* * * * *

Cole woke with a start at the low growl that came from the mouth of the cave. The cubs, which had all been sleeping on him, all raised a ruckus and headed for the opening. Cole stood and followed, just barely able to make out the entrance. There wasn't much of a moon, only a tiny sliver, but he could make out the dark shape of the lion.

When he emerged from the cave, he discovered that she was not alone. A large male stood off to one side, watching warily. Cole looked from the big male to the female. "Okay, I have no idea what to do."

She looked over her shoulder at the male, then approached Cole and nudged him with her head, toward the male.

He didn't have to speak the language to figure out that she wanted him to go with the male.

"Can he find Scout?" he asked the female.

She nudged him again, then growled to her cubs, and disappeared into the cave. Cole looked over at the male lion. The lion stared at him for a moment then turned and walked away a few steps, paused and looked back at Cole.

Cole figured he had to be half insane. Who in their right mind would follow a wild lion out into the wilderness at night?

A male trying to protect his mate.

Cole jumped at the sound of the voice in his head. "Was that you?" he asked the lion.

Something like a chuckle rang in his mind, before the words came, *Follow me, human.*

Having no other option, Cole did just that.

* * * * *

Scout reached the place she'd left her clothing and made the transformation back to human form. It was getting easier and easier, and hardly hurt anymore. And that gave her a little pang of concern. Being a cat was exhilarating. With the transformation being so easy, would it tempt her to spend more time as a cat and less as a human? And what effect would her urge to be feline have on her relationship with Cole?

She considered those questions as she dressed and made her way soundlessly to the edge of the camp. Jonas and his men all appeared to be asleep by the fire. Ray and Jimmy were off to one side talking. She made her way up behind them so that she could better hear what they were saying, fighting the urge to go back to cat form and enjoy the benefits of enhanced hearing. She was a tracker, she could certainly get close enough to hear without being detected.

"...we don't have enough rope," Ray was saying. He took a slug from a bottle before continuing. "No way anyone will believe the four of them tried to make that kind of ascent with what we have on hand."

"Then I'll go back to base camp and get more," Jimmy argued.

"It'll take you all night! We don't have that kind of time. The tranquilizer will wear off before you get back. "

"Then we use what we have."

"Shit on a stick, Jimmy. This is fucked up. Better we let them sleep it off then talk them into climbing in the morning. I'll take the lead and you fall into the rear. As soon as the four of them are high enough to ensure fatality, I'll cut the rope. You won't be high enough to get hurt if you lag behind."

A sick feeling took hold in Scout's stomach. They were planning on killing Jonas and his men. She had to do something. But what? The only thing she knew was to face it head on.

She stood and walked into their camp, coming up behind them. "You sorry sacks of shit," she hissed.

Both men jumped to their feet. Ray's gun was in his hand by the time he was facing her. He swayed slightly, letting her know that he'd been drinking for a while. "What the fuck are you doing here?"

"I'm here to let you know that you're not going to get away with killing these men. The CBI is on its way. If you're smart, you'll turn tail and run. And I mean run fast. Disappear."

"Fuck you!" Ray snarled. "I say we kill the fuckers and you and swear you did it."

"Like anyone would believe that," she scoffed. "Wise up, Ray. They're onto you. They know you killed Jed, and those hunters and it's just a matter of time before they take you down."

"Shut the fuck up!" He waved the gun at Scout. "You fucking cunt!"

She turned her attention to Jimmy. "You know I'm right. If you kill those men, you won't be able to run far or fast enough. They'll hunt you down."

Jimmy looked from her to Ray. "She's right, Ray. We'll never get away with it."

"We will if we have a hostage," he argued. "We do them and take her."

"And go where?" Jimmy asked.

"Wherever the fuck we want," Ray replied. "It'll be days before anyone finds them—if they ever do. By then we'll be long gone."

"I wouldn't count on it," Scout said, drawing their attention back to her. "I won't go willingly, and you know I'll slow you down."

"She's right, Ray," Jimmy said. "It won't work."

"It will if I say it will! Tie the bitch up and I'll take care of those—"

"No!" Scout jumped forward then stopped abruptly when Ray raised the gun and pressed it to her forehead. "Listen to me, Ray. Just tie them up and leave them. Alive. If you do that, I'll go with you—without a fight."

"No way," Jimmy said immediately.

"Shut up!" Ray barked at him. "Let me think."

"Come on, Ray," Scout coaxed him. "You know it's me you want. You killed Jed and you've been itching to kill me too. Well, here's your chance. Only you have to let those men live. Otherwise, I promise you, it won't go well for you."

"Yeah, well seems to me we're the ones with the guns," Jimmy shot back at her.

"Honey, I don't need a gun to take you down," she said with a smirk then turned her attention back to Ray. "Isn't that right, Ray?"

Ray's face formed into a grimace and his skin flushed. Scout saw she'd hit the mark and pressed him more. "You remember the last time you pulled a gun on me, don't you?"

"That was different. The old man was alive."

"But it wasn't the old man that made it necessary for you to have twelve stitches in your head was it?"

"Fucking bitch!" he hissed.

"And not a seventeen-year-old girl either. But still. You wouldn't mind having a piece of me before you slit my throat, now would you?"

She knew she'd hit the mark dead on the head at the flare in his eyes. It made her sick to think about him ever touching her, and she'd die before she let him, but if making him think he might be able to would save Jonas and the others, it was a gamble she had to take.

"She's playing you, Ray," Jimmy warned. "Don't listen to her. You know you can't trust her."

"Shut up," Ray growled. "Just shut up. We're going to do this my way. You tie those men up good and tight."

"No."

Ray cut his eyes toward his brother. "Say what?"

"I said no. I'm not going to do it that way. We let them live and they come after us."

"You kill them and the state boys come after you with a vengeance," Scout pointed out. "Come on, Ray. You're too smart for this. You know you'll never get away with killing them. But me? Everyone knows I'm out here most of the time. Accidents happen. All the time. Who's to say I didn't just get careless?"

"Shut up!" Jimmy yelled at her. "Ray, don't listen to her. She's—"

He never got to finish his sentence. Ray backhanded him with the same hand that held the gun. Jimmy's cheek split and blood flew as his head whipped to one side. But he did not go down. Instead he went after his brother.

Scout jumped back as Jimmy took Ray to the ground. While the two of them were rolling around trying to kill each other with their fists, she ran over to where Jonas lay on the ground. She shook him hard.

"Wake up! Jonas! Jonas, can you hear me?"

He didn't move. His eyelids didn't even flutter. It scared her. Was he dead? She pressed her ear against his chest. His heart was beating. Whatever they'd given him had him out cold, though. No way she was going to wake him up. Which meant that the only option left to her was to try and take out the Moss brothers.

At almost the same moment she had the thought, someone had her by the hair, hauling her to her feet. She struck out, feeling the satisfying thud of her fist impacting his sternum. He staggered but did not release her. And he raised his gun to stick it under her chin.

"Unless you want to see me shoot these men right now, you'll stop. You got that?"

"Yeah, I got it," she agreed.

He released her but kept the gun on her. "Tie them up."

"I don't have any rope."

He gestured to the packs. "Make it quick."

Scout did as he ordered, but made sure that Jonas's bindings were tied so that he could get free. Ray didn't notice her taking Jonas' watch from his wrist and sliding it into her pocket. Or the tracking locator she slipped into his jacket. After she'd tied up all the men, including Ray's brother Jimmy, who was unconscious on the ground, Ray gestured toward his pack.

"Put that on."

She didn't argue. There was no point. And she had to get him as far away from the camp as possible. She considered transforming, but decided against it. Cats were thin-skinned. One shot from that gun of his could do serious damage. No, her best bet was to lead him as far from the camp as possible and wait for a chance to make a move against him.

But Ray had his own plan. "Here's what we're going to do. You and I are going to head northwest."

"To where?"

"You'll know when we get there. Now get walking."

Scout complied and in silence they headed out into the night.

Chapter Fourteen

ഗ

It was almost dawn when the lion leading Cole stopped. They'd traveled all night without rest. The wind had been picking up for the last couple of hours, and the distant rumble of thunder and occasional sudden burst of light from the sky let Cole know that a storm was moving in. Which made him even more anxious.

"What?" Cole asked, looking around and seeing nothing.

Our journey ends here.

With that parting thought the lion turned and left Cole standing alone, wondering what he was supposed to do. Then he heard something. A voice. He followed the sound and within minutes walked into the camp where Jonas and his men were left tied up on the ground.

Jonas was struggling against his ropes, calling out to the others. Cole raced over to him. "What happened?" he asked as he worked at the ropes binding Jonas.

"Don't know. We stopped here for the night. Jimmy Moss poured everyone drinks. I was sitting by the fire and that's the last thing I remember. He'd obviously drugged the liquor."

Jonas extricated himself from the remainder of the rope once Cole had his hands free. He stood and stretched then started checking his men. "Untie him, would you?" he asked, pointing to one o his men.

"Where's Ray?" Cole asked, moving to the man who lay unconscious nearby.

"Beats me," Jonas replied, and gestured. "But it looks like he and his brother had a falling out."

Cole looked in the direction Jonas pointed and saw a man off to one side, his hands bound behind his back, lying on his side. "Ray's brother?" he asked.

"Jimmy Moss," Jonas replied, shaking the agent he'd just untied. "Scott, come on! Wake up!"

"Wh-what?" Scott came to, blinking and looking around.

"We were drugged," Jonas replied and moved to untie the last of his agents.

Cole approached Jimmy Moss. The man's eyes were open.

"Where's your brother?" Cole asked.

"Untie me."

Cole shook his head. "Don't think so. Where's your brother?"

Jonas joined him. "Looks like you and your brother had a falling out, Jimmy. Why'd he leave you behind like this?"

"Untie me and I'll tell you."

"That's not how this is going to work," Jonas replied, squatting down beside Jimmy. "First, let me introduce myself. Jonas Robert, CBI. And now that we have that out of the way, I'll ask again. What happened?"

"Windrider showed up and Ray jumped me."

"Scout?" Cole blurted. "Scout was here?"

"Well duh," Jimmy smirked at him then sobered. "Don't feel bad. They had me fooled too. Like I said, she showed up and Ray told me their plan. They were going to leave everyone tied up, take the money and run."

"That doesn't track," Jonas said. "Bad blood between the Moss and Windriders for a long time. Doesn't figure that Scout would take off with Ray. What really happened?"

"I already told you!" Jimmy insisted. "Christ, look at me. My own brother beat the shit outta me and left me to die so he could run off with that Indian bitch."

"Whoa." Jonas acted quickly to stop Cole when Cole made a move for Jimmy.

"He's lying," Cole insisted.

Jonas regarded Jimmy for a few moments and then planted a hand on Cole's shoulder. "Come on."

He led Cole over to where his agents were moving around, trying to work out the last of the drugs. "Looks like we have a situation," Jonas announced. "Apparently Scout showed up. Something happened and she left with Ray."

"Why would she do that?" Scott asked.

"Probably had no choice," Jonas answered. "And chances are we're not going to get a straight answer out of Jimmy. "

"There are six of us," Cole pointed out. "We split up and search for them."

"You a tracker?" Jonas asked.

"No."

"Well, there you go. We could wander around out here for days and not find them. No, we call in for support." He raised his wrist and looked at it. His head immediately jerked back up. Cole saw the look of surprise.

"What?"

"I had a tracking beacon in my wristwatch."

"You think Ray took it?"

"No, I'd guess it was Scout."

"Why would she do that?"

"So we could track her," Jonas replied then looked at his men. "Any of you remember the way back to base camp?"

One of the agents, Rick, spoke up. "I have a sat phone in my pack."

"Smart man," Jonas grinned. "Let's have it."

Rick hurried to get the phone for Jonas, who immediately called in and filled his superiors in on the situation. When he hung up the phone his face was not wearing a happy expression.

"Here's the deal. Storm's too strong for choppers. High winds. Lot of electricity. We'll have to wait for it to pass. I gave them the frequency of the beacon. They'll track her from headquarters and as soon as the sky clears will send teams to her location and a chopper to pick us up."

"We can't just sit and do nothing," Cole argued. "You said yourself there's bad blood between Scout and Ray Moss. And he's got her."

"Nothing we can do," Jonas pointed out and rubbed at his right temple with one hand. "Whatever they gave us packed a punch."

"And left a nasty aftertaste," Rick added. "Anyone have a mint or gum or something?"

Jonas reached into the pocket of his jacket and when he withdrew his hand, his face was wearing a smile. "Well, well," he said and showed the others the device in his hand.

"What's that?" Cole asked.

"A tracking device," Jonas said and turned it on. Cole walked over to look over his shoulder at the display. "What's that blip?"

"If my guess is right, it's Scout."

"Can you tell where she is?"

Jonas studied the display for a few moments. "About twelve miles north of our position."

"Twelve miles? That's a long way on this terrain."

Jonas nodded. "They must've left shortly after we passed out."

"But we can track them with this, right?" Cole asked.

"Yeah."

"Then what are we waiting for?"

Jonas turned to his men. "Wait here for pick-up. If you get anything out of Moss call HQ and fill them in."

"You're going after them alone?" Rick asked. "I mean just the two of you?"

"That's the plan," Jonas replied. "You have a problem with that?"

"No sir."

"Good." Jonas handed him the sat phone.

"Keep it. In case you run into trouble," Rick said.

"Take it," Jonas ordered. "Report to HQ every hour. We're headed north. With luck by nightfall we'll reach their location. If the choppers are able to lift off, they'll reach the location before us and can pick us up once they've secured Moss."

Rick nodded. Jonas grabbed his pack and his rifle and turned to Cole. "You ready?"

"Yeah."

"Then let's get moving."

Cole fell in step with Jonas, leaving the others behind. Twelve miles was a lot of distance to cover and the direction they were headed would call for some climbing. He just hoped Jonas could keep up, because nothing was going to stop him from reaching Scout.

* * * * *

Scout climbed the rest of the way up the ridge. When she reached the top she stopped, taking a look around. Ray shoved her to get her moving again. A cabin of dark weathered wood sat in the shelter of tall trees beyond the narrow clearing. Behind the clearing, a face of rock stretched up a good one hundred feet to a narrow plateau and then rose again.

Her heart sank. The lay of the land was not favorable. With the cabin backing up to the cliff, escape was limited. The cabin looked out over the small valley they'd just left, giving an excellent vantage point. To either side were rocky outcroppings and thick brush. There was probably a way out in either direction, but it was hard to tell. This could be a sheltered plateau with no way out but the way they'd come.

She gave Ray grudging respect for the selecting the location. From a defensive point of view, it was well situated.

He shoved her again and she mounted the wooden steps leading onto the narrow porch. Keeping his gun trained on her, he unlocked the door and gestured her inside. She walked to the center of the room, turned and faced him as he closed and locked the door behind him.

"Now what?" she asked.

"Now we play," he said, dropping his pack and placing his gun on a table beside the door.

"Play what?"

"The game is called 'do what Ray says or die'."

"Then pick up that gun again," she replied, "because if you touch me, I'll kill you."

He laughed and approached her. When he reached for her, she struck out. Her fist caught him a glancing blow on the chin. She didn't wait to see what would happen. As soon as she struck she tried to run around him, intent on getting to his gun.

He grabbed her by the hair and jerked hard enough to unbalance her. She stumbled and he laughed and hauled her to her feet, slinging her around and releasing her. She flew into a wooden table, her hip impacting painfully before she rolled. Her head banged against the table as her body bowed back painfully, the sharp edge cutting into her back. Pain blossomed sharp and cutting.

And with the pain came a surge from the beast within her. All night she'd looked for an opportunity to transform. But Ray stayed too close and kept his gun on her. She hadn't had a chance. Now the beast inside was demanding release.

For a split second she resisted, then changed her mind. It might be her only chance.

But before the thought was finished, he had hold of her leg. He yanked her hard, pulling her off the table. Scout was scrambling to find something to grab hold of, trying to break her fall. But Ray was big and strong, and had a good grip on her.

She hit the floor hard enough to knock the wind out of her, but still kicked with her free foot, hoping to dislodge him. Ray laughed and reached down to grab her shirt and haul her up. She wasn't even fully on her feet when his fist caught her in the side of the head.

And the world went black.

An ache in her shoulders woke her. When she tried to move her arms and couldn't, she was pulled to consciousness fast and hard. Fear flooded her as she realized her predicament.

Her wrists were tied together and looped over a climbing stake that was driven into the wood of the wall facing the door. Her feet were inches off the floor, leaving her dangling like a fish on a hook.

And Ray was sitting in a chair across the room watching with a smile on his face. Scout felt real fear. She had no choice, she had to chance the transformation. She willed it to come. And nothing happened.

That changed her fear into genuine terror. If she couldn't change, she had no chance. He would kill her. Desperation inspired a last ditch effort. Focusing all of her energy, she closed her eyes and send out a mental scream for help.

"That's right, pray," Ray said.

Scout opened her eyes. "Not much challenge in killing something that's tied up and can't fight back. Or is that how you like it, Ray?"

"You're the one hanging on the wall," he said. "Not as much fight in you as I'd hoped."

"Cut me down and I'll see if I can't do better."

He laughed. "That's what I always liked about you, Scout. You always were spunky."

"And you were always bigger, stronger and faster," she said, playing to his ego. "Remember when we were kids and they'd have those festivals in town every spring? Remember the year you got stuck with me in the three-legged race because Jimmy had broken his toes kicking that cinder block like a dumbass?"

Ray chuckled. "Had to carry your scrawny ass the whole way."

"But we won," Scout reminded him. "Because you were faster than everyone else."

"And smart enough to know that the only way to win was to carry you."

"Yeah, that too," she agreed, then grimaced and let out a little groan. "Let me down, Ray. Please. You can leave me tied, just let me get some circulation back in my arms."

He pursed his lips, contemplating her for a few moments, then stood and crossed the room to her, picking up a long-bladed hunting knife from the table. "You try anything and I'll slit your throat."

"I won't try anything," she promised.

He grabbed her by the front of her pants and lifted her up. She struggled to get her arms to work, and finally managed to work them over the spike. Ray released her. Her feet hit the floor and her legs crumpled. She collapsed, her limbs feeling numb and useless.

Ray backed away from her, and reclaimed his seat. Scout rubbed at her legs and stretched them out in front of her, jiggling them against the floor to work out the numbness.

"Remember when a bunch of us kids dared Jimmy to jump off that big rock at Raferty's lake and he didn't know that the water was down and he sunk up to his butt in the mud?" Scout asked and chuckled. "He was mad as a hornet. Me and the other kids were really giving him the business. And he chased us down and caught me and threw me in the water and held me down. I thought he was going to drown me for sure. Probably would have if you hadn't stopped him."

"He always did have a temper on him," Ray said with a ghost of a smile appearing on his face. "And you were always such a smart-ass, daring him to do dumb shit."

"I did have a talent for that," she agreed. "And every time it got my ass in a sling."

"Wonder you made it this long. Half the town wanted to wring your neck by the time you were fifteen."

She shrugged and climbed to her feet, leaning against the wall. "But not you. Always wondered about that. Why did you pull my ass out of trouble so many times, Ray?"

"Figured you needed it. You didn't have anyone else."

She nodded and looked down. She'd just been seized with a strong awareness. There was a lion in the area. Her call had not only been heard, but was being passed on. Help would come, but she needed to get out of the cabin. She pushed away from the wall. "So why'd you turn against me?" she asked.

"I think you've got that backwards," he replied.

"What do you mean?" She walked over in front of him.

Ray rocked back in the hardwood chair, standing it on its back legs.

"Well you said it yourself last night. You nearly killed me with that piece of firewood."

"You threatened to shoot me," she argued. "What'd you expect me to do? You're the one who told me to fight back. Remember? I was eleven and those white kids were bullying me and you ran them off and told me that you weren't going to save my sorry ass again if I didn't learn to fight back. That if I didn't look out for myself no one else would."

"I didn't say split my head open," he replied, but with a grudging smile on his face.

Scout leaned down, putting her hands on the edge of the seat between his legs.

"So why'd you pull that gun on me, Ray?" she asked softly. "I thought we were friends."

"So did I."

"What does that mean?"

"It means I was wrong. Can't be friends with someone whose old man ruined your life."

"Jed didn't ruin your life," she insisted, forgetting about trying to get him to remember good times when they were friends.

"Like hell. He turned his back on my father and got him killed."

"That's not true!"

"It's the fucking gospel. If you and your fucking grandfather hadn't shown up and gotten Pop all upset he wouldn't have been unfocused and that cat would've never gotten him."

"That's a load of shit and you know it. What happened to your dad was horrible but it wasn't Jed's fault."

"He might as well have put a fucking gun to his head as turn his back on him that way! He didn't give a rat's ass what happened to my father or the rest of us. All he cared about was his high and mighty ideals—"

Scout acted before she even thought about it. She curled her fingers around the edge of the seat and lifted, sending Ray toppling over backwards. She saw her chance and took it. She raced for the door, scrambling with the lock. Flinging the door open, she ran across the porch, down the steps and across the clearing. She was halfway to the drop-off when bullets pelted the ground around her.

She froze and turned. Ray was nowhere to be seen. She took a step back, closer to the drop-off. Bullets kicked up dirt in front of her. She scanned the area, looking for the source of the gunfire.

And a lump the size of a mountain formed in her gut. Cleverly hidden, a metal rig sat camouflaged by brush and tree limbs to one side of the house. On it was mounted an automatic weapon.

Scout had heard about that kind of apparatus. They'd been banned in almost every state in the country. Some enterprising hunter came up with the brilliant idea of making hunting a sport that could be enjoyed from the comforts of home. He developed a rig and mounted a video camera and gun on it. It was operated by a wireless control, connected to a computer.

Sitting in front of the computer, thousands of miles away, a person could move the camera, scanning the area. If an animal was spotted, all they had to do was use their computer mouse to target. A click of the mouse triggered the weapon. Thus enabling someone to kill an animal while sitting in the comfort of their own home in front of a computer.

But such an apparatus needed power, she considered, and looked harder. She couldn't spot a power source. It had to be somewhere. If she could find a way to take that out then the rig wouldn't work.

But right now, she seemed to be pinned down. Another message had a shiver race down her spine. Jonas had discovered the tracking device and was coming after her. And Cole was with him. She sent her own mental message, hoping the lions could communicate it to Cole somehow. If he and Jonas approached the cabin they would be sitting ducks.

Unless she figured out a way to sabotage Ray's rig. "Okay, I got the picture. I can't run. I'm coming back in. Don't shoot."

With far less confidence that she wanted to admit, she made her way back inside the cabin.

"Lock the door behind you," Ray ordered, appearing in the doorway across the room.

Scout did as she was told. "Take a seat," Ray said.

Scout straightened the chair she'd tipped over and took a seat. Ray leaned against the doorway. "You can't get away from me, Scout. You understand that, don't you?"

"Yes, Ray, I do."

"Then you've got two choices. Live or die."

"What do I have to do to live?"

Ray grinned. "I'm going to tell you."

*****

Cole and Jonas knew they were close. But they were in a small, steep valley, with cliffs rising around them on three sides. The storm had moved in on them and the sky was filled with lightning. Jonas scanned the landscape. "Chances are he doesn't know we're coming. Which means he won't be watching for us. If we spit up and approach from the east and west, then we'll stand a better chance of one getting him in a crossfire.

"He has Scout," Cole pointed out.

Jonas' eyes narrowed fractionally then he shrugged off his pack, opened it and dug out a handgun. "You know how to use this?" He handed it to Cole.

"Yeah."

"Then here's the plan. You get his attention. I'll take him out."

"What if he uses Scout as a shield?" Cole asked.

"You don't worry. I'll make the shot. You just get his attention."

Cole shoved the gun into the waistband of his pants. "Fine. Can you make the ascent by yourself?"

"I'll manage. Let's move."

He turned away and stopped dead in his tracks. "This could be a problem," he said in a low voice.

Cole looked ahead of Jonas and saw them. Six lions. All standing motionless watching. He could only hope one of them was the male that had led him to Jonas' camp.

"Let me handle this," he said and slowly walked in front of Jonas. "We're trying to find Scout. A man has her. He plans on hurting her. Can you help?"

We have given her our word to assist you. The human she is with has a fortified structure, with weapons on metal trees that can kill anything that approaches.

Cole nodded, feeling an odd sense of relief. He didn't know how the lions would help, but it felt good to know that someone was behind them. And if Scout had communicated with the lions, it meant she was okay.

"They're here to help," he told Jonas.

"Help?" Jonas gave him a dubious look. "They're lions."

"Look, I don't have time to explain. I'm just going to have to ask you to trust me," Cole replied. "They're here to help. Apparently he has her in some kind of structure up there that has a good defense. We've got to get close enough to figure out what it is, so we stay together."

Jonas looked from Cole to the lions and back at Cole. "If you're wrong about them, we could be dead men."

"I'm not wrong."

"Then let's go."

Cole looked at the lead lion. "We're going to scout the area and find out what the defenses are. Can you take us there?"

As one the lions turned. With no other course but the one they were set upon, Cole and Jonas followed. The rain hit in a deluge, and the wind picked up. Thunder shook the ground and the sky was ripped by blinding flashes of lighting. Thanks to the storm, it took them two hours to reach the site, approaching from the east, along the wall of the cliff.

Both men hunkered down behind an outcropping of rock. "I'm going to try and work my way to the other side," Jonas said. "Wait for me here. I'll go back down and to the west."

Cole remained hidden, but scanned every inch of the landscape. His eyes passed over it the first time, but came back. What the hell was that? He worked his way closer, taking care to move slow and make as little noise as possible.

What he found made his blood run cold. There was no way to get to the cabin without being spotted. He returned to the rendezvous point and sat down to think. The lions were all lying on the ground, silently watching.

Seeing them gave Cole an idea. While he waited for Jonas to return he outlined his idea to the lions. By the time Jonas returned, the plan was set and the lions had disappeared.

"He's got cameras set up along the edge of the roof, covering every angle of approach. And some kind of rig mounted on a metal stand to the side of the house fitted with a camera and an automatic."

"There's a matching setup along this side," Cole informed him.

"Which makes a surprise attack impossible," Jonas replied.

"Not necessarily," Cole said with a smile, and quickly explained his plan to Jonas.

Jonas listened and just shook his head. "You're willing to gamble her life on a bunch of lions?"

"Yes." Cole was surprised to hear himself say it, but knew it to be true as the word emerged.

"Then we might as well get some rest," Jonas replied. "Still a couple of hours 'til nightfall. Let's find some cover."

Cole nodded, and they worked their way back from the house, settling beneath a large overhang to wait, hoping that his gamble paid off.

* * * * *

Scout got out of the shower and wrapped a towel around her body. She'd stalled as long as she could. Ray was getting impatient. She knew the lions were gathering, and understood their plan. What she had to do to ensure success was keep Ray diverted from his bank of monitors in the back room.

He'd shown her his setup when she returned to the cabin. She had to give him credit. It was impressive. He had cameras mounted on the roof, constantly monitoring the area. Motion sensors were mounted atop each camera, and two hunting rigs stood on either side of the house.

His power came from a massive generator in a basement, beneath the cabin. The gas was vented up through a pipe in the walls that ran outside in what appeared to be a double chimney.

She never imagined Ray was such a paranoid man. To have devised such an elaborate and secure stronghold was the mark of someone either very paranoid, or someone who figured that at some point in their life, they'd find themselves in a standoff and wanted every advantage they could have.

Right now Scout wished for an advantage. Ray expected her to walk out of the bathroom door, naked, and give herself to him. To do things to and with him that made her stomach churn with nausea.

She stared at herself in the mirror. Where was her inner beast? In answer to the question a low growl came from her throat. She was a skin-walker. She felt the ability strong and sure inside herself. She smiled at her reflection. With the power of transformation available to her she could face what she had to do. She turned away from the mirror. It was time.

Just as her hand closed on the doorknob, the sound of thunder and roar of the wind made to seem tame at what sounded like hundreds of blood-curdling screams and roars. "Get the fuck out here!" Ray shouted.

Scout tucked the towel more securely around her body and went into Ray's monitoring room. "Stay right there where I can see you!" he shouted, and then cut his eyes toward the bank of monitors. "What the fuck's going on?" he asked.

Dark darting shapes moved quickly and randomly across the field of vision of the cameras. As they watched, a lions face appeared, mouth open wide. Within a split second the screen was black.

"Fucker took out the camera," Ray breathed and turned his attention to the camera on the eastern rig. He panned back and forth, but could not lock onto anything. The sound outside was deafening. Scout saw sweat appear on his face, running down his forehead.

He swiped at his face with his hand and switched to the view from the western rig. Big dark shapes flitted across the field of vision. Ray's hand moved to the mouse. He clicked and a rattle of gunfire added to the cacophony outside.

Scout saw her chance and started to make her move, but at that moment the door to the cabin burst open.

Ray was on his feet, gun in hand and knocking her out of the way by the time Jonas was in the room. Cole was right behind him. Ray squeezed off five shots in rapid succession.

It was as if time had moved into slow motion for Scout. First she saw one of the male lions go down. Then she saw Jonas' body whirl sideways as the slug entered his shoulder, propelling him around. A split second later blood exploded from Cole's chest. She saw his eyes go wide. Before his body hit the floor, a scream was ripping loose from her throat. And it was not the scream of a human. She had transformed in the space of a breath.

Mindless with rage and grief at the sight of Cole being shot, she lost touch with all reason. With the strength of her lion's form, she pounced on Ray, her claws digging into his shoulders as her mouth clamped onto the side of his neck. Her back legs moved, claws digging at the backs of his legs, as he screamed and thrashed, trying to dislodge her.

Suddenly the room filled with lions. They poured through the open door, crashed in through the windows. Scout released Ray as a large male attacked him from the front. The sound of lions feasting and Ray screaming was lost to her mind. Her eyes were on Cole.

Jonas had made it across the room to Cole. His hands were plastered to Cole's chest. He looked up wide-eyed as she approached, making her aware of her form. She transformed before his eyes, falling to her knees beside Cole.

To his credit, Jonas overcame his shock and shook his head. Scout fell down across Cole's body. "No! No no no!" she screamed. "You can't die."

"He's gone, Scout."

Jonas tried to lift her off Cole but she fought away his hands.

"No, I won't let him die."

She turned and screamed to the lions. "Help me! Please!"

As if of one mind, they stopped and came to crowd around her, Jonas and Cole. A big male, the one Ray had shot, lay down beside her. "We have to save him," she told him. "I can't do it alone. Please, help me."

There is but one way, the lion's thoughts rang in her mind. *I will join with him.*

"Will that save him? You're wounded. Weak."

But I have the strength of my brothers and sisters. Unlike humans, we are able to forge one single mind from many in a united goal.

"I'll do whatever you say. But if this works, will he...?"

Yes, he will be as you are. Neither human nor lion, but one who walks both worlds.

Scout considered it. Would Cole hate her? But surely he would rather be a skinwalker than die? She had to try it. She couldn't lose him.

"What do we do?" she asked the lion.

Close your eyes and free your spirit.

She nodded and looked at Jonas. "Please, don't interrupt. Okay?"

He nodded and she closed her eyes, took a deep breath and opened herself to the Sight. Energy captured her, sending her spiraling into an endless void of white. She felt the energy of the lions with her. She felt the male lion with her. Saying a prayer to be granted the power, she put her free hand on Cole's chest.

Light like that of a sun going nova flared, blinding her. "Cole," she whispered before consciousness evaporated.

Sunlight was streaming through the opened door and broken windows when Scout woke. Jonas was lying on the floor beside her, as she lay draped across Cole. She sat up with a jerk. The male lion lay dead beside her. Had it worked? She placed her hand on the side of Cole's face. He opened his eyes.

"Cole!" She grabbed him as he sat up. "Oh god, Cole!" She wrapped herself around him, sobbing and crying his name.

Cole held her, looking around at the destruction. Jonas was sitting up, staring at him in amazement, and surrounding them were lions. What seemed like hundreds of lions crowded into the small cabin.

"It's okay, honey, it's okay," he soothed Scout and pushed her back to look at her.

She tore his shirt open, seeing the unblemished skin. "It worked," she breathed and looked at Jonas with a smile as bright as the sun. '"It worked."

"Indeed it did," he replied with a smile.

Cole stripped off his shirt and gave it to her. Until that moment she hadn't even realized she was naked. She slipped it on and turned to the lions. "I will never be able to repay you for what you've done for me. Whenever you need me, I will be there for you. Without question."

A large female walked over and licked her face. *We take care of our own, Skin-Walker. You are one of us.*

Scout's eyes filled with tears. One by one, the lions filed out of the cabin. Jonas looked over at Ray's remains and rubbed his chin. "Either of you have any suggestions as to how I'm going to write this up?"

Cole and Scout looked at one another then at Jonas. "Jonas," she said. "You've…seen things. Things that are best kept secret. I know I'm asking a lot, but—"

"Some things are best kept secret," he agreed. "But at some point you and I need to have a serious discussion."

"I know, and we will," Scout agreed and extended her hand. "Thank you."

Jonas nodded. Scout cocked her head to one side. "Choppers. Two, maybe three miles out."

"I guess we better get our story together fast," Cole suggested.

Jonas nodded, looked around then blew out his breath. "Okay, this is the way it played out…"

Chapter Fifteen

ꙮ

Cole put the last of the luggage into the back of his SUV and closed the door. It had been three weeks since the incident in the hunting cabin. True to his word, Jonas stuck with the story they concocted. Ray had snatched Scout, leaving him, his agents and Jimmy Moss drugged and tied up.

Upon arriving at his cabin, Moss shot and wounded a lion that ran off. He was holding Scout hostage. Before Jonas and Cole arrived, Scout tried to escape. Moss chased her outside and both of them encountered several lions. They ran back inside and the lions pursued them. Ray was attacked and killed. Scout made it into the bedroom, where she was hiding when Jonas and Cole arrived. By then Moss was dead and the lions had vanished, except for the one Ray had shot and it was dead.

Scout and Cole both had to give statements and stuck to the story. Jimmy Moss was awaiting trial for conducting an illegal hunt and poaching. He confessed that Ray had killed Jed, and was being charged as an accomplice.

Cole was relieved it was finally over. It'd taken Scout several weeks to recover emotionally from the ordeal. Even now she seemed unusually emotional, and would burst into tears at the drop of a hat. When he told her he wanted to take her to meet his family she had wept. When he asked her to marry him, she wept, and when it was time to say goodbye to the mother lion and her half-grown cubs, she cried again.

He didn't know what to make of it, but chalked it up to stress. She had been through quite an ordeal. He headed back to the house, and stopped to watch her.

Scout was sitting on the front porch, playing with the cubs, who were no longer babies. Their spots had disappeared and their chubby limbs had stretched out to give them the look of gangly teenagers. The mother lion lay on the porch watching.

"That's the last of it," Cole announced as he approached them.

"Then I guess it's time to go," she said and turned to the lion. "I'm going to miss you. But I'll be back. We're only going to be gone a couple of weeks."

Then we shall meet upon your return, the lion replied. *And compare notes on the experience of having life growing inside you.*

"What?" Scout exclaimed.

The lion roared her equivalent of a laugh. *A life grows within you.*

"Oh my…" Scout looked at Cole, tears spilling from her eyes.

"Baby, what's wrong?" He hurried to pull her into his arms.

"She…we…" She hugged him tightly for a moment then broke away and spun around the yard, laughing and crying at the same time as she danced.

"Scout?" Cole went after her. "What the hell's—"

"We're having a baby!" she exclaimed and threw herself on him, wrapped her arms tightly around his neck.

"A baby?"

"A baby," she sighed and melted into him.

Cole froze dead in his tracks. After a moment she pulled away and looked at him. "You're…oh god, you don't want—"

He suddenly grinned, threw back his head and yelled at the top of his lungs. "Woo hoo! We're having a baby!" He snatched his cell phone from the clip on his belt and dialed.

"Dad? It's Cole. There's been a change of plans. Tell the gals to get busy, and round up a preacher. There's going to be a wedding at the Circle R…yeah, I'm dead sure…yep, we'll be hitting the road – in the morning. See you soon."

"In the morning?" Scout asked with a twinkle in her eye. "I thought the car was packed and ready to roll."

"It'll still be there in the morning," he said with a sexy smile that started a fire burning in her belly. "Right now we got some celebrating to do."

She laughed. "Yeah, and just what kind of celebrating you have in mind, cowboy?"

"The best kind there is," he said and extended his hand. "Scout 'n' Cole and a big hot tub."

"Woo hoo!" she crowed and grabbed his hand. "My kind of party."

Cole smiled down at her. "I love you, Scout. With all my heart. And I'll be a good father to our child."

"Children," she corrected him. "This is just the beginning, cowboy."

"You got that right, baby. It's just the beginning."

CONN 'N' CALEB

Dedication

ꕥ

For the "real" Caleb – a man whose photo should be displayed in the dictionary beside the word "fine".

Acknowledgements

ꕥ

My deepest appreciation to all the people who were so instrumental in the creation of this book:
Grandpa – gone but never forgotten.
For all you taught me about life, our connection with the earth and all that dwells on it.
And to Chase, thanks again, my friend.
You're always there to inspire and cheer me on. What a guy!

Trademarks Acknowledgement

ꕥ

The author acknowledges the trademarked status and trademark owners of the following wordmarks mentioned in this work of fiction:

Associated Press: Associated Press; The

Trojan: Church & Dwight Virginia Co., Inc.

Viagra: Pfizer, Inc.

Chapter One

ഇ

She kept her eyes closed, listening to the voices of the men in the cockpit of the military helicopter. She didn't want them to know that she was awake. Or that she was no longer bound by the restraints they'd placed on her and therefore free to move around.

For the last two days every time she'd roused she'd been given another injection. This was the first time she'd managed to regain full consciousness. Her mind was still not clear. There was a heavy shroud of drug-induced fog clouding her thoughts. She needed to be able to think clearly. Her survival depended on it.

From the conversation going on in the cockpit, they were apparently flying over a place called Arizona. Keeping below radar level. That didn't surprise her either. No one wanted to take credit or blame for what was happening. The men in the cockpit were like all the others before them. They just wanted to pass her off to those higher in the chain of command and be done with her.

Knowing that time was running short, she focused her mind on a plan. The minutes ticked by. The pilot's voice alerted her to a change in their status. They were suddenly losing fuel. He wasn't sure they had enough to make it to their destination. He had to radio for instructions.

"This is Bravo Tango Charlie 227."

There was an answering blast of static. He tried again. Still nothing. Focused on the problem at hand, he and his copilot turned all their attention to checking the instrumentation, their comments made in hopeful tones. Maybe the instruments were wrong. Maybe it was a glitch.

This was her chance. She slowly sat, peeling off the blanket they'd placed over her. Keeping her eyes peeled on the cockpit, she inched toward the door. Neither of the men sensed movement until she placed one hand on each of their shoulders.

"This aircraft is going to crash," she said softly. "You must escape before it goes down. You are lucky men. The only survivors."

"The only—" The pilot never finished the sentence. The chopper suddenly lost altitude and all his attention was on battling the controls.

Standing between the two men, for a moment she was weightless. Had she not reached up to absorb the impact with hands and arms, her head would have banged into the ceiling of the cabin.

The copilot issued a mayday call, giving their location. Hope swelled inside her. They were passing over a lake. As the chopper dropped lower, she reached for the door. The copilot grabbed her, trying to stop her. The fear must have overridden the suggestion she put in his mind. She tried focusing on the thoughts again but didn't rely just on that since her window of opportunity was so small. She backed it up with physical strength and fought him with everything she had. This time he wasn't going to overpower her. She'd played nice. She'd played fair. And it'd gotten her nowhere. Except kidnapped, drugged, bound and gagged, and flying who knew where with this surly barbarian and an equally dour pilot.

It was time to get the heck out of Dodge as she'd heard on the black and white western show she'd watched at the last holding facility she'd been kept in. And this was her best chance.

The pilot was trying to find a place to land. She'd spotted the lake and knew this was the time to act. All she had to do was get free of the co-pilot who had a death grip on her wrist.

He yanked on her and she put everything she had into a punch, right into his groin. His mouth opened wide but only a strangled gurgle came out. She vaulted over to the door as he collapsed in his seat.

The aircraft did a sudden nose down, throwing her forward onto her knees. As the pilot fought to level out the plane, she scrambled to her feet and headed for the hatch.

With all the wobbling and the steep angle of the dive, it was next to impossible to push the door open. If only she had more time and didn't have to rely on brute strength. A look toward the front told her she was out of time. With a grunt, she shoved at the door. It slid open and wind buffeted her, whipping her hair around her head.

She closed her eyes, stretched out her arms and leaned forward. This was insane. She'd probably die. But she was going to die anyway. Better to go this way than the way the people waiting for her had planned. Just then the helicopter lurched. Then the world turned upside down and topsy turvy as she fell forward into nothingness.

* * * * *

Caleb rowed along, watching the indigo sky flare with those few final moments of reds and oranges as the sun disappeared into the horizon. What a great weekend it'd been so far. Just what he'd needed. No drinking, no women, no noise. Just him, a kayak and a sleeping bag.

It'd been a while since he'd come to the lake. Back when he was young, he'd come up here with his brothers often. They'd race their jet skis, drink like fish and swap tales of their exploits with women.

Those had been good times. Now they were all grown, all of them but him with families of their own. He was the last of the single Russell men. Not that he minded it. Blessed with good genes, he made out just fine with the ladies and he didn't have any complaints about his social or sex life. They were both quite active.

But now and then he needed to get away and have some time to himself. This weekend he'd found himself thinking about his brothers and how happy they were being settled down with wives and kids. He wondered if he'd ever meet a woman who'd inspire him to want to try it. So far it hadn't happened.

One moment he was stroking along the glassy surface of the water and the next thing he knew something was falling out of the sky in front of him, a dark silhouette that looked remarkably like a person.

It couldn't be. Could it? He dug in on one side with the oar, turning the kayak and watching the strange sight. A moment later the shape hit the water. He had time to think that it couldn't have been a person because the surface of the water moved as if a giant beach ball the size of a truck had suddenly plunged into it.

A second later the resulting wave from the impact capsized him. He was slammed upside down hard enough to have him passing from a startled state of confusion into a consuming darkness.

Her landing was far rougher than she'd hoped. All the way down she'd focused her mind on the image of a bubble encasing her, visualizing it hitting the surface of the water and bouncing until it came to a soft landing.

Such was not the case. How could water be so hard? Spots danced in front of her eyes, threatening unconsciousness. She fought against it, kicking to the surface. Slinging her hair back from her face, she looked around.

And that's when she saw it. A kayak bobbing in the churning water, upside-down, and a large man floating face down in the water. Fear that she'd killed someone infused her with a rapid spike of adrenaline, providing the strength she needed to roll the man over, wrap one arm around his neck and swim for shore.

It was harder than she'd anticipated dragging him on shore. She must have suffered more from the fall than she imagined. And he was one big man. Tall and muscular in all the right places. She scolded herself for even noticing how well built and handsome he was. This was not the time for her hormones to take over.

Concentrating on his physical well-being, she maneuvered him over to a truck that was parked beneath a thin stand of trees. He was breathing. Just unconscious. She had no idea who the vehicle belonged to but hoped they wouldn't mind when she spotted a rolled up bundle of fabric and grabbed it.

Turned out, it was some kind of bedding. She draped it over the man and knelt down beside him, putting her hand on his forehead. By the stars, he was divine. She could not resist admiring the strong lines of his face, and wondering what color his eyes would be when he opened them. And he had to open them. He had to. She could not be responsible for injuring an innocent person.

When Caleb suddenly came to, he bolted upright, finding himself on the ground beside his truck at his campsite.

"Are you damaged?" a feminine voice with a musical accent asked.

He jerked his head to the right and saw a woman kneeling beside him. And what a woman. She was stunning. Exotic. Her skin carried a slight tint that spoke of the East—Iran or perhaps India. But the eyes were the color of amethyst, a violet that was pale but possessed of almost a glow. Clearly she had mixed heritage. Her features were classic—elegant arched brows, a thin delicate nose and lips that could be used as a model for women who want to achieve that full kissable pout.

"What the hell happened?"

"Your vessel capsized and I brought you to shore."

"You..." He looked around in confusion. His kayak was nowhere to be seen. Caleb leaned forward, running his hands back through his wet hair before looking at her again. "Was that you? That fell from the sky, I mean?"

She regarded him for a moment. "You think I fell from the sky?"

"Lady, I know what I saw. You fell and hit the water and...and capsized me."

"Then I suppose you have your answer," she said and sat back on her heels, watching him.

Caleb couldn't help but notice the way the white T-shirt clung to her, revealing full, high breasts with hard, perfect nipples. He also noticed the slight smile on her face when she caught him staring.

"Look, I'm not crazy. I saw you falling. But from what?"

She looked away, hugging herself. Night air was falling and the temperature was dropping. Caleb stripped off the bed roll that was draped over him and wrapped it around her shoulders. "Let's get a fire going so you can get warm. I have an extra shirt in the truck if you want to put it on and we'll dry your clothes by the fire."

He got up and reached into his pocket for his keys. "Shit!"

"There is something wrong?" she asked.

"My keys. They must have come out of my pocket when I capsized."

"Then we shall search for them," she said, throwing aside the bed roll and springing to her feet.

"Hold on." He grabbed her arm.

She jerked away so fast and with such fury on her face that he involuntarily took a step back. "Do. Not. Ever. Do. That." Her words were sharp and punctuated.

He raised both hands up in surrender. "Sorry. I just meant that there's no point. Night's falling and we'd never find them anyway."

"Then you cannot open the door to your vehicle?"

"Well, I do keep a spare set of keys."

"That is very wise."

He grinned sheepishly. "Yeah, well the problem is, they're inside the glove compartment of the truck. We'll have to break a window to get them."

"Oh."

Before he had a chance to move, she stepped over to the window, balled up her fist and slammed it through the passenger window. Caleb gaped at her in shock as she turned and smiled at him. "Now you may retrieve your keys."

He was unable to respond for a moment. *First she free-falls out of the sky and ends up without even a bruise, and then she slams her fist through a window like it's papier-mâché?* What the hell kind of woman was she anyway?

"Your keys?" she prompted.

"Oh yeah, right." He didn't bother to state the obvious. He didn't need the keys now. He reached in, unlocked the door and rumbled through the duffle bag that was on the floorboard.

"Here…" He handed her a blue plaid flannel shirt, "get out of those wet clothes and put this on while I get a fire started."

"Thank you," she said with a smile, hung the shirt over the window and started stripping off her wet clothes.

Caleb's mouth fell open in surprise. He'd been around uninhibited women before, but never one who'd strip off her clothes in the same manner one would kick off a pair of muddy boots. Despite his desire to see what delights lay beneath the wet clothing, he turned away and busied himself building a fire.

Fortunately he'd stocked up on wood earlier in the day, prepared for a cool evening. Of course, he hadn't dreamed he'd be sharing his campfire with a totally gorgeous and completely out of the ordinary woman.

He grinned to himself as he watched the kindling ignite and spread. Life sure was full of surprises.

Chapter Two

ꟹ

"What do I do with these?" she asked from behind him.

Caleb had just finished spreading a plastic tarp on the ground, topped with a wool blanket. When he turned and saw her standing there, his shirt covering her from neck to mid-thigh, exposing long, strong, sexy legs and her wet clothes held in one hand, he momentarily lost the ability to speak.

Damn, she was sexy. Wet hair cascading down over her shoulders to nearly her waist, eyes watching him with the curiosity of a cat, and those lips. Those full, please-kiss-me lips. It was enough to drive a saint to sin.

"My clothing?" she asked with a seductive little smile.

"Oh right. Here, let me take care of that." He grabbed a couple of stout sticks and jammed them into the ground near the fire, draping her shirt and pants over them. "There. They'll dry in a few hours."

"Thank you," she said. "Mr.?"

"Russell. Caleb Russell."

"Thank you, Mr. Russell."

"You're more than welcome, Miss?"

"Raenea Thotthoft," she replied after a moment's hesitation.

"That's an unusual name."

"So is Caleb," she said with a smile and gestured to the pallet on the ground. "Do you mind if I sit?"

"Oh sorry. Sure. There's an extra blanket there if you want to wrap up. It gets pretty cold at night."

"Thank you, but I'm fine," she said and sank down in an Indian-style, cross-legged position.

"You rest and warm up. I'm going to change and get things going for dinner."

"Might I assist you?"

He knew her offer was for food preparation but he couldn't help but think about her assisting him in getting out of his still damp shorts. "No thanks, I got it."

She smiled and nodded then turned her attention to the fire, staring into it as if there were secrets in the flames that only she could discern. He watched her for a moment then hurried to the truck, changed into jeans and a shirt and grabbed the cooler.

Raenea stared into the flames of the fire. She had no doubt that Caleb would revisit the topic of her unusual arrival. Naturally he was curious. She didn't blame him. It wasn't every day a person fell out of the sky. Her dilemma was what to tell him.

It was against her nature to lie. But could she trust him? She'd made the mistake of putting her trust in a stranger and it had landed her here, on the run and unsure what to do.

She did sense that he was an honest and honorable man. And was obviously compassionate, giving her dry clothing and building a fire so that she could warm herself. And now preparing food.

But her experience of late had taught her that compassion could sometimes be a self-serving act. People would feed you, keep you safe from the elements and provide you with the necessities to survive, but in return they wanted to take your life from you, make you their prisoner.

She could not afford to be taken prisoner again. Now that she was free she had to stay that way. Which meant she was going to have to find one trustworthy person. She had no money, no identity papers and no way to secure food and lodgings.

And then there was the matter of the people who would be looking for her. Fear swelled inside her at the thought of being found. They claimed to be good people, interested only in the benefit of mankind through scientific exploration and research. But their methods spoke otherwise.

"You hungry?" Caleb's voice interrupted her thoughts.

She looked up at him, thinking that her mind must have been more affected by the impact than she realized because suddenly it was very clear that she needed to learn how to speak as he did, master the accent and the cadence so that she did not sound quite so much the foreigner. She'd pay close attention and hope he didn't notice the change in her speech patterns.

"Yes."

He sat down, putting the cooler between them. "Not a lot to choose from, but I have stuff to make sandwiches, some fruit, beer, water."

"Sand witches?" Wouldn't you know he'd offer something she had no clue what it was?

"Yeah, roast beef and cheese."

"Roasted beef?" She felt her stomach recoil. "You mean the roasted flesh of a bovine?"

His face crinkled in a puzzled expression. "Uh, yeah."

She shook her head. No way was she going to eat flesh. That was disgusting. "Fruit?"

He pulled a fat red apple from the cooler and she accepted it with a smile, taking a big bite. "Mmmmm," she moaned, nodding and chewing. "This is heavenly. Thank you."

He shook his head with a smile and popped open a beer. "Want one?"

"What is it?"

The question stopped him cold turkey. "What is it? You mean you don't know what beer is?"

"Oh yes, of course. A general name for an alcoholic beverage created by the fermentation of a cereal or mixture of cereals and flavored with hops."

He laughed despite thinking that was the oddest way of explaining beer he'd ever heard. It sounded like something quoted from a dictionary. "Yeah, right. So, you've never tasted beer?"

"No."

"Would you like to?"

She cocked her head to one side for a moment then nodded. "Very well, I would love to taste beer."

Caleb handed her his bottle and watched as she lifted it to her lips, tipped it up and guzzled half of it. When she lowered the bottle, her lips pursed for a moment, her eyebrows drew together slightly and then she smiled and handed him back the bottle. "Interesting and—" She suddenly belched then laughed. "My apology."

"No worries," he said and tilted the bottle up for a drink. "So, you want one?"

"Hmmm, no. Thank you."

"Water?"

"Oh yes, please."

Caleb handed her a bottle of water and watched her tip her head back and guzzle it down. How was it possible that just watching her throat as she drank was one of the most erotic things he'd ever seen?

He needed to get a grip. Turn his attention to something besides how much she got to him sexually. Like how out of place she seemed and how she'd fallen from the sky.

"So, Ran, where're you from?"

"Rain," she corrected his pronunciation then answered, "I am not really from anywhere."

"Everyone's from somewhere."

"Really?"

"Well sure. Usually people consider the place they were born or grew up as being the place they're from. So where did you grow up?"

She saw that the moment had come. Either she took a chance and was honest with him, or she had to concoct an elaborate lie. And lies tended to trap the person who spoke them, even if it took a while.

"I have no idea," she said at last.

"What?"

"I don't know where I'm originally from."

"I heard what you said, I just don't understand."

She sighed and picked at the peel of the apple. "I have no memory of my origins. My memories begin when I was…I don't know how old I was. I only know that my first memory is of being in the Song Sang in the Henan province with an elderly man, Jin, whom I came to love as a father."

"China?"

She nodded.

He frowned at her for a moment. "Well your name sure isn't Chinese."

"No, I was not given a Chinese name since it was clear by my appearance that I am not."

"So how'd you end up here?"

"It has been a long journey.

"You want to elaborate on that?"

Raenea looked down at the apple then tossed it away. The questions robbed her of her appetite. "I lived in the Henan province for many years then we moved to India. From there we traveled to Iran and on from there to Egypt. After a time we left Egypt and spent some time in Russia and the Ukraine, then on to Spain, Portugal and finally to Brazil and the Yucatan. We were in Mexico when my father—when Shen was killed."

"Which doesn't explain how you came to be here, falling out of the sky."

She sighed and studied his face for a long time. He reached over and put his hand on her shoulder. "Rain, I don't know what kind of trouble you've got, but it's a sure bet that people don't fall from the sky without a reason. And it's clear that you're hesitant to tell me what happened to land you here, but I promise you that whatever you say I'll keep in confidence and will do whatever I can to help."

She'd never heard more honesty in a man's voice, or felt more assurance of sincerity. It was as refreshing as happening upon an oasis in the desert. But still, it was frightening. Secrets, once revealed, could not be retracted.

"You're right. There are…difficulties in my life. I did not simply fall from the sky. I escaped from a military aircraft en route to a base somewhere in the southwest of the United States."

Caleb didn't know what he'd been expecting but it sure as hell wasn't that. "You…you escaped a military aircraft?"

She nodded confirmation.

"Why did the military have you? Are you a terrorist or something? How did you come to be a military prisoner? What'd you do?"

"I am not a terrorist," she replied. "I came to be the prisoner of the United States military when my father was killed in an attempted robbery in a street market. I…I killed Shen's assailant. When the authorities arrived upon the scene a man who claimed to be a representative of your government claimed that he saw what happened. He said that my act was self-defense and he claimed to be traveling with me and Shen.

They believed him and he offered to help me arrange to have Shen's body transported back to his homeland for burial.

"But instead he drugged and held me hostage for weeks, then I was transported via automobile to an airfield where I was put on a jet and flown somewhere. I am not sure where. I was kept drugged. I do not know how much time passed, only that many medical examinations occurred. I was wakened in the night to be told I was being moved. I do not remember much about it except for being transferred to an aircraft. I regained consciousness as the military helicopter I was being transported in flew over this area."

"And you escaped?"

"Yes."

"How?"

"I jumped."

Caleb wanted to believe but it was too much to ask of any sane man. "That's impossible. I didn't hear any helicopter before you landed in the lake."

"I believe I heard the pilot talking about stealth mode and keeping under the radar to avoid having the flight logged or recorded."

"Still, you'd have had to have fallen from…thousands of feet. There's no way you could've survived."

"But as you can see, I did."

He opened his mouth then closed it and picked up a stick to poke at the fire. "Okay, let's say I believe that it did happen. Why were you a prisoner to begin with?"

She was silent for a long time. Finally he looked at her. She stared at him silently. Either she was trying to cook up another elaborate tale or she had run out of lies. As beautiful as she was, she had to be lying. Her story was just too fantastic to be real.

"Well?" he asked.

She sighed before speaking. "Caleb, the wisest course of action for you would be to pack your belongings, get in your vehicle and pretend that you never met me."

"Why?"

"Because they will be looking for me and I do not wish to bring you trouble."

"What makes you think they'll be looking? Just what is it about you that makes them want you so bad?"

Again she hesitated then raised her hand, gracefully rotating it at the wrist so that her palm faced upward. "This."

To his shame, he actually yelped as his body suddenly floated up off the ground. His legs unfolded from a seated position and dangled a good two feet from the earth.

"What the hell?"

She smiled and slowly turned her hand palm down. His feet touched the ground and for a moment he felt a little weak in the knees. Was this possible? Had the accident in the kayak left him unconscious and cooking up fantasies in his mind?

"How'd you do that?"

"I do not know."

"What do you mean you don't know?"

Raenea was trying to be patient, to understand how unbelievable and fantastic it must sound and seem to him. But her patience was being sorely tested with the effect the continuous bombardment his maleness was having on her, and the fear that the longer she stayed there the stronger the possibility that she would be found and taken again.

She stood and faced him. "I do not know why it is I possess these abilities. I only know that they exist and because of that your government wants to dissect me, and I have no desire to be their laboratory rodent. Believe me or not. That is your choice. All I know is that I have to find a place that is safe where I cannot be found."

He stared at her for a few moments then reached out to grasp her hand. "This is— well, it's pretty unbelievable. I mean people don't survive falls from helicopters without a scratch, and what you just did...well, it's like something out of a sci-fi movie. I'm sorry if I seem harsh, but I'm a down-to-earth kind of guy and I sure as hell haven't ever dealt with anything like this before—well not exactly like this anyway."

"I apologize," she said, wanting to extricate her hand from his. His touch was sending tendrils of fire up her arm to spread throughout her body, igniting the primal female within her and making her long to couple with him. "I have been less than understanding. I realize this must seem quite strange to you. And I do not want to endanger you. Again, the wisest course of action for you would be to—"

"I'm not abandoning you," he said in a determined tone. "That's not an option. If you need a safe place then you can come home with me. To the Circle R."

"What is a Circle R?"

He chuckled and gave her hand a squeeze. "It's a ranch."

"Are there others who live on this ranch?"

"Well, yeah. We have a lot of employees and provide housing for some of them. And my father and step-mother live there from time to time. When they're not at the capital."

"The capital?"

"Yeah. My father's the governor of Arizona."

Fear spiked inside her. "He is part of the government?" She jerked her hand from his and took a step back.

"Of the state, Rain. He's not part of whoever's responsible for what happened to you. I promise you that."

She felt the fear recede at his assurance and wondered if she was being completely foolish placing her trust in him. But something inside her said that he was worthy of trust. She prayed her instincts were not wrong.

"Then the people on your ranch would also be at risk, Caleb. Would you endanger their lives to aid me?"

"They won't be in danger," he insisted and sat down, tugging on her hand to get her to sit beside him. "Here's what we'll do. We'll give you another name and tell everyone that you're—shit, we have to come up with a good cover story."

He fell silent and she waited for him to continue. After a time his eyebrows rose and he turned to her with a smile. "We'll tell them that you're someone I hired to work for me and you're staying at the ranch until you can get settled into a place of your own."

"You want me to work for you? Doing what?"

"Do you know anything about horses or cattle?"

"In the breeding or raising of such animals? No."

"Okay, then what about as a vet assistant?"

"A vet assistant?"

"Yeah. See, along with ranching, I'm also a large animal vet. I have a clinic at the ranch and mainly focus on horses and cattle but sometimes people bring their pets to me for vaccinations or to set a bone or something like that."

"And you would like for me to assist you in caring for these creatures?" The idea appealed to her. She loved animals and had an affinity with almost every species.

"Yeah."

"I think I would enjoy that."

"Great! Now we just need to come up with a new name for you. Got any favorites?"

"Constantia," she said without hesitation.

"Constantia?"

"Not good? Then perhaps Constance, or Conner."

"Conner? Doesn't that sound a little masculine?"

"I do not think so, but if it offends you then perhaps Connery."

"Okay, fine. Connery. And your last name will be..."

"I am not familiar with contemporary American surnames."

"Okay, how about Hoffman?"

"Connery Hoffman," she murmured. "Yes, I will be Connery Hoffman."

Caleb stuck out his hand and she looked at it then at him. "Shake on it," he said. "It's a way of sealing a bargain."

"Oh!" She smiled and put her hand in his. The moment their flesh touched a spark ignited.

"What was that?" he asked.

"I believe it is called energy," she said with a smile.

Caleb chuckled. "Looks like it's going to be real interesting having you around, Rane— I mean Connery."

She grinned in return. For the first time since Shen's death she had hope. And as her teacher had always told her, where there was hope there was possibility. She prayed he was right.

Chapter Three

ꟹ

While Connery took a shower and changed into the clothes Caleb had found for her, some things his sister-in-law Ana had left at the ranch, he went through the refrigerator to see what he had to offer her in the way of food. Saying a silent thanks to his housekeeper Hannah, he pulled out a plate of fried chicken, containers of potato salad, green beans and corn.

Hannah had been working for him ever since his father took office and Caleb took over running the ranch. She was the wife of his ranch foreman Clyde, and one of the best cooks in three counties. Not only did she always make sure he had plenty to eat, but she kept the place as immaculate as Clara, his step-mother had done all his life.

He filled two plates and put them into the microwave to heat. He leaned back against the counter. He wondered what his family would say if he told them a woman fell out of the sky and damn near drowned him? They'd probably call him loco. Hell, he was having a little trouble believing it'd happened.

He and Connery had decided to head back to the ranch during the night. They could both probably use a good night's sleep, and he wanted to do some checking before daybreak, just to see if he could find out anything about the military helicopter she told him about.

Not that he didn't believe her. Exactly. He just wanted to check. He got his laptop from the office and brought it to the kitchen, accessing the local news site. There was nothing about a crash of any kind or a missing woman.

Acting on impulse he called his father.

"Hey, Dad," he said as soon as the call was answered. "Listen, have you heard anything about any plane crashes around here?"

"What makes you ask, son?"

"No real reason. Just thought I heard an engine when I was packing it in for the day at the lake. Sounded like it was having engine trouble. But I never saw anything…"

"You heard this where?"

"At the west end of TR Lake."

"Caleb, you know that if there was information about a crashed military helicopter I couldn't tell you about it. Hell, boy, if the two pilots had miraculously escaped when the bird hit a substation and blew up, blacking out power for fifty square miles, I couldn't tell you. Couldn't say a damn word if both of the pilots claimed that a woman died in the crash. Sorry, boy, but I just don't have any news to share with you."

Caleb grinned. Charlie took his position as governor seriously, but his loyalty to and trust of his sons was still rock solid.

"I hear ya. Well, thanks anyway, Dad. Love to Clara. Talk to you later."

He hung up the phone and leaned back in his chair. Things were really getting strange. The beeper on the microwave sounded and he rose to take the plates to the table. He was pouring two glasses of iced tea when Connery appeared in the door.

"Whatever that is, it smells delicious."

The sight of her had him overfilling the glass. Tea slopped over the rim and onto the kitchen counter. "Shit!" He put down the tea pitcher and made a grab for the towel, but she beat him to it and started mopping up the mess.

She smelled of soap and woman. Clean and inviting. Her long hair was still wet, hanging nearly to her waist. Even without the enhancement of makeup she was stunning.

And the clothing he'd given her would have made most women green with envy to have achieved such a look. The jeans, an old pair of Ana's, were a bit loose and hung low on her hips. The T-shirt was tight across the chest, emphasizing her full breasts, and fell a good three inches short of her navel, displaying her tight torso and an interesting belly ring in her navel.

It was enough to have things south of the belt taking way too much of the blood supply from his brain. All he could do was stare. And breathe. Damn, she smelled good.

"Thanks," he finally managed as she moved to wring out the wet cloth in the sink and rinse it out.

He took the glasses of tea to the table. "Hope this is okay."

She took a seat and looked down at the plate in front of her. She picked up her fork and pointed to the chicken leg on her plate. "What's that?"

"Chicken."

"That is a breed of domesticated fowl, correct?"

"Uh, yeah."

She shuddered and pointed to the potato salad. "And this?"

"Potato salad."

She speared a chunk and popped it into her mouth. Her eyes closed as she chewed and a moan of "hmmmm" came from her throat. She opened her eyes, grinned at him and dug in.

Caleb watched in amazement. Aside from the chicken, that went untouched, Connery cleaned her plate in a matter of minutes, *hmmming* the whole time like it was the best food she'd ever tasted.

She put her fork down on her plate, lifted her glass of tea and drained it.

"That was so delicious," she said with a smile. "Did you prepare all of this?"

Caleb shook his head with a smile. "Nope. My housekeeper Hannah deserves the credit."

"You have a housekeeper? Well, she is quite an accomplished chef and that…potato salad is the most marvelous thing I've ever tasted. Thank you."

"Rain— Shit on a stick! I mean Connery. I've got to get used to that. Anyway, I talked with my father and apparently a military helicopter went down, crashing into an electrical substation and blacking out power for miles. The two pilots survived, and from what I know, claim that a woman died in the crash."

There was no reaction at all from her at the news. Her expression did not change in the least. Either she was really good at concealing things or she was in shock.

"Why would they claim you were killed?"

She stared at him without expression. "Come on," he encouraged. "I swear you can trust me. I just need to know how you ended up in that lake and why…" He shook his head and ran one hand back through his hair. "Why when you hit the water it moved out like something big and round had hit it."

Connery watched him for a few moments then leaned back in her chair. "Caleb, there are some things that are best left unexplained. You already know too much. And you're such a wonderful man. Smart, compassionate, sexy as…as sin, and you have a good life. Getting involved with me could be disastrous. While I appreciate everything you have done for me and all you have offered, I have to remind you that the best thing for you and everyone you care about is for me to just walk out the door and disappear and you to pretend that you never saw or heard of me."

The words "sexy as sin" hit him like a dose of Viagra. One moment his mind was completely focused on the mystery of her and the next he had a raging hard-on and could barely think of anything but jumping up, throwing her over his shoulder and taking her to his bed.

Christ on a crutch! He shifted in his seat, trying to get more comfortable and will his erection to subside. "Darlin', that's the absolute worst way to dissuade me. Not that I don't appreciate the compliments, but right now I'm sitting across the table from the biggest mystery I've ever encountered and I'm a true-blue sucker for mysteries."

"Curiosity killed the cat," she said.

"And satisfaction brought it back," he countered and was rewarded with a rise of color on her face.

She pushed back and stood. "Trust me, Caleb, there's nothing I'd like more than to discover the satisfaction I've no doubt you could deliver, but the longer I stay the more dangerous it is for you."

He stood and rounded the table to her. "Why don't you let me decide if you're too dangerous?"

She looked up at him and for a moment, a wistful expression appeared on her face. He put his hand on top of her shoulder. "Just level with me. If it's too much, I'll back down. But at least let me make the decision for myself."

It had been a while since she'd trusted anyone, but the urge to trust Caleb was getting stronger every moment. Was it because of the chemistry between them, or was it what she saw in his eyes? That look of honesty and integrity that shone like a clear light.

Help! She was afraid and didn't know what to do. She needed a sign.

"I have to be outside," she said in a choked voice, feeling suddenly claustrophobic. "Please, the walls are crowding in."

Caleb took her by the arm and led her out the back door onto a wide porch with wooden rocking chairs padded with thick cushions. The stars twinkled overhead in the clear sky and a breeze lifted her drying hair. She pulled away from him and went to the railing circling the porch.

Closing her eyes, she put both hands on the rail and raised her face, taking in a long, slow, deep breath. The sound of the wind and the night creatures filled her mind, soothing and comforting. For a long time she stood rooted in place, sending out a silent plea for guidance. Finally she opened her eyes. And a star shot across the sky.

"Penny for your thoughts," Caleb said softly from beside her where he leaned against one of the wooden columns that supported the roof of the porch.

Connery looked at him for a moment. Did he have any idea how truly gorgeous he was? Like some legend sprung to life, a god of old, capable of conquering the strongest opponent or soothing the most horrific fears from a frightened heart.

"Tell me about this military transport again," she said

"All I know is that it went down at a substation and blew up."

"But the pilots are unharmed?"

"Yeah, they're fine."

"Thank the stars."

"You were worried about people who were holding you captive?"

She nodded. "Those men were simply following orders. They believed it was for the greater good. I could not bear the responsibility of their deaths."

"And all of this is because you can…levitate stuff?"

"No."

"Then what?"

She sighed and dropped her head for a moment then looked up at him. "Because of that," she said, "and other things."

"What other things?"

When she didn't answer he took hold of her upper arms and leaned down, looking her square in the eyes. "Come on…Conn. What other things?"

"You do not want to know."

"Oh yes I do."

She chewed her bottom lip for a moment, her eyes searching his. "Very well. Things such as this."

And with that she vanished.

"Holy fuck," he breathed. "How're you doing this?

"I have no idea," she answered, becoming visible again and dreading the barrage of questions she knew would be forthcoming.

But instead of questions, he pulled her to him, engulfing her in his embrace. "Don't be scared, Conn. I won't let them find you. You're safe here. I give you my word."

She wanted to believe that. More than she could express. But at the moment, expressing anything would have been a monumental task. The feel of his hard body against hers and his arms holding her tightly had her body singing like electricity on a wire.

"You must release me," she managed to whisper.

"What's wrong?" He ended the embrace but kept his hands on top of her shoulders.

"You affect me, Caleb."

"Affect you?"

"Yes," she looked up at him. "Sexually."

"And that's bad? Baby, you've been affecting me since I woke up and saw you kneeling beside me."

"It's not the same."

"Oh? Well what's different about it? Sexual attraction is pretty simple."

She did not know how to say it and it not sound insulting. "Desiring may be simple. But acting upon it presents many complications."

"Like what?"

"Like whether you would be able to satisfy my needs."

He chuckled then laughed out loud. "Honey, if that's all you're worried about, then you've got no worries at all because I promise you that when we're done, you'll definitely be satisfied."

She admired his confidence and was tempted to test his claims. But now was not the time. She still had much acclimating to do in order to fit in and sex would only distract her from what she needed to learn.

Not willing to insult his manhood, she smiled at him. "I will keep that in mind. However, right now there are more pressing matters to attend to. If I am going to act in the role of your assistant, I need to learn about the care of animals. And I need to learn to speak in the same rhythm and cadence of the natives of this area. Otherwise, I will be unable to blend in and if I do not blend in, then I could attract undue attention."

"Babe, you'd attract attention if you didn't mutter a word."

She couldn't help but smile, and felt a warm flush stain the crotch of her jeans at his words. "I doubt that. But I do need to learn and you are the only teacher I have. So, will you teach me of animal medicine?"

"Sure, what do you want to know?"

"Everything."

"That's a tall order, honey. I guess I could dig out my old textbooks and you could start on them. But there's no way you'll know it all by morning."

"Books would be excellent," she agreed enthusiastically.

"Okay, I think I have them packed in a box in the attic. I'll go look."

"Thank you, Caleb." She stood on tiptoe to brush her lips against his. He gathered her to him and slanted his mouth across hers. Despite her intentions to not fall victim to desire, she could not stop her lips from parting beneath his. Could not stop her tongue from twining with his. It was a kiss that promised of great passion, and also great tenderness. She wanted it to last forever, but he pulled back.

"A promise," he said.

"A promise?" She did not understand.

"Of what's to come."

She actually felt her knees go weak. He gave her a sexy grin and went inside the house. She turned and looked up at the stars. If only she could find a way to remain here and explore the possibility of passion and emotion he offered. Closing her eyes she sent the wish skyward.

Chapter Four

ꟹ

Connery had been awake all night, reading the books Caleb had provided her and accessing the documents on the Internet site he'd connected to so that she could read professional articles on the topic of animal medicine.

She'd finished the material long before dawn but was not sleepy. She didn't require a lot of sleep. She'd spent the intervening hours going to different sites on the Internet, reading excerpts from popular fiction, watching bits and pieces of shows on the television and trying to decide the best course of action. For the first time in her life she found herself drawn to a man. And not merely for sexual gratification. Caleb promised more and she longed to explore that attraction, and the emotion he evoked in her. She wanted to remain with him, here on his ranch.

But that created conflict within her. Unless the government was convinced beyond all doubt that she'd died in the crash, they would be searching for her. And that would put Caleb and everyone on the Circle R in harm's way. While the government of his country professed to be a proponent of human rights, when it came to certain things, they were quite apt to ignore the rights of the individual in order to achieve their means. She had no argument with them. In the defense of one's homeland, sometimes harsh measures were required. But she was no threat and did not want to be treated as such.

She had to find out if they were convinced she'd died in the crash. It was the only way she'd be able to stay.

A knock at the door had her turning from her place at the window. "Yes?"

Caleb opened the door. "You're up."

"Yes."

He entered the room and walked over to the bed where the books he'd loaned her were scattered on the spread. The laptop screen displayed an article from a university site.

"How'd you fare with the reading?" he asked.

"Very well, thank you." She walked over to the bed and started stacking up the books. "I appreciate you allowing me to read your books. They were quite informative."

"You…" He reached up and ran his hand through his hair, an affectation she was coming to recognize as something he did when he was uncertain or confused. "You're finished?"

"Yes." She finished stacking the books into three neat piles.

"All of them?"

"Yes," she said then realized her blunder and looked at him anxiously.

He regarded her in silence for a moment. "You read all of these books? In one night?"

Connery looked away. Once again she found herself in the position of having to explain things she had no answers for.

"Connery?"

"Yes, Caleb," she said and met his eyes. "I read all of them. And all of the documents on the site you opened for me and all of the documents those linked to. And I watched your television and listened to your local newscasts so that I might learn to speak as you do. And yes, all in one night."

"How's that possible?"

"I don't know."

His hand went to his hair again which made her feel a little agitated. "Caleb, I'd explain it to you if I understood it. I don't know how I'm able to do these things that seem so odd to others. This is how I've been as long as I can remember so it's normal to me. I know it seems strange to you—to others—but to me it's just natural."

"Like becoming invisible and levitating."

"Yes."

He sat down on the edge of the bed and patted the spread beside him. "Come here, Conn. Let's talk."

She took a seat on the end of the bed and angled to face him. "What's up?" she asked, using a phrase she'd learned from the television.

Caleb smiled at the question. "Not bad. You're already sounding more like a local. I spoke with my father this morning and apparently the military's shut down the crash site. No civilians allowed and no information is being shared. The pilot and co-pilot have been moved to an undisclosed location but they're still claiming that the woman they were transporting was killed in the crash."

She nodded but made no comment and after a moment he continued. "There was a small mention sent out via the Associated Press that a military helicopter crashed but the crew survived. No mention of a woman being on the craft."

"Then we have no way of knowing if they truly believe me dead."

"No, I'm sorry."

"Then I should go."

"Why?"

"Because if they do think I'm alive, they'll search for me. And that places you and everyone here in danger."

"Connery, our government isn't going to just come in here and kill people. And even if they are looking for you, there's no reason for them to look here. We're miles off the flight path."

"Someone could discover you were at the lake and want to question you." She saw surprise register on his face and realized he'd not considered that. "I do not want you to lie for me, Caleb. If they come, you must be able to say truthfully that I am not here."

He leaned forward to reach for her hand. As before, his touch elicited a flash of scintillating energy that slithered through her veins like Kudalini, rising hot and overwhelming.

"Christ on a crutch," she whispered, unconsciously mimicking his tone and cadence.

Caleb smiled and lifted her hand to his lips. "I'm gonna take that as something good, if you don't mind."

Conn returned his smile. "This might be a lot more difficult than I imagined."

"What?"

"Being around you. Honestly, Caleb, you affect me."

"Likewise," he murmured, running his lips over her knuckles.

She couldn't take it. Even this simple act was too potent. It overwhelmed her, robbed her of her ability to think rationally. Clearly they would not be able to effectively carry on their planned masquerade with so much sexual energy arcing between them. At least she couldn't.

And that meant there was only one option. Shoving aside doubts, she angled to face him and draped her arm around his shoulder to run her hand into his thick mane of hair.

His eyes widened slightly in surprise as she leaned in close and whispered, "Will you allow me to make love to you, Caleb?"

"Absolutely," he replied without hesitation.

"Then so be it." Her lips closed on his softly.

Caleb pulled her onto his lap, molding her body against his as he plundered her mouth. Her hands roamed over his shoulders and back, her lips soft and pliant beneath his and her luscious ass rocking back and forth, inflaming an erection that already had him straining painfully in his jeans.

When she pulled away from the kiss, her lips trailing over his face and down his neck, he could have sworn he felt sparks of electricity tingle on his skin. Her hands moved to his shirt, working nimbly at the buttons. Each inch of soft and warm skin she exposed, her lips touched. It was like liquid fire radiating out from each touch until he felt suffused with a heat that had his belly tightening and his dick throbbing.

Slipping off his lap, she stood beside the bed, leaning forward to continue trailing her lips over his skin as she pushed the shirt off his shoulders to bare them. He helped, pulling the shirt off and letting it fall on the floor.

"Magnificent," she whispered as she straightened and looked at him. "Have you any idea what a perfectly beautiful man you are?"

He opened his mouth to return the compliment but she came to him, wrapping her arms around his neck and filling his mouth with her questing tongue. Her taste was sweet and exotic and unlike anything he'd ever experienced. Her firm lush breasts pressed against his chest, the hard nipples giving testimony to her excitement.

He could not resist cupping her breasts, his thumbs tracking slowly over the hard buds of her nipples that strained against the thin fabric of her T-shirt. He was rewarded with a sound not unlike a purr that came from her throat.

Not breaking the kiss, he reluctantly moved his hands from her breasts to pull off his boots and socks. When he stood and reached to loosen his belt, her hands quickly pushed his aside, leaving him free to return to the pleasure of fondling her breasts as she quickly divested him of his jeans.

Once he stepped free of the denim pooled around his ankles, she ended the kiss and stepped back. Her eyes moved slowly down the length of him and back up, stopping on his eyes and holding.

"As I heard last night on television…hot damn!"

Caleb grinned and reached out to take hold of the bottom of her T-shirt and strip it up over her head. Before he could toss the garment aside she was sliding out of her jeans.

"The feeling's mutual," he murmured, taking in her nude beauty and taking note of the hairless state of her sex. That in itself was a major turn-on. He couldn't resist reaching out and tracing his fingers over the bare temptation.

"Damn, that's some wax job, darlin'," he commented at the silken feel against his fingers.

"Wax job?" she asked as her hands started a slow trek from his chest to his groin.

Caleb was momentarily distracted by the question. "Your pussy, babe. All the hair's gone. And it's way too smooth for a shave job, so you had to have it waxed."

"Oh," she laughed and let her hands drop lower to fist his erection. "No, *darlin',* that's all natural, just like the rest of me."

Caleb felt his eyebrows rise and his dick throb. He'd never heard of a woman naturally having no body hair. Sure as shit, Conn was a horse of a different color.

"Well, damn," he breathed just before she pressed up against him, rubbing her hard nipples against him and wedging his dick, still gripped in both her hands, between them.

"I don't want to talk, Caleb," she whispered against his skin and then nipped at the firm swell of his chest. "I want to feel you, and taste you, and take you inside me."

"You're singing my song, honey," he replied but resisted when she started to push him back on the bed. "Baby, there's a couple of things we need to clear up before we start a hard ride."

"What things?" She stepped back and regarded him with a look he read as frustration.

"Things like STDs."

"What is an STD?"

Caleb groaned and sat down on the bed. "You don't know about STDs? Damn, Conn, are you from another planet? Sexually transmitted diseases."

"Oh. Yes, I learned about such diseases. Dreadful. In the worldwide HIV or AIDS epidemic, the continent of Africa has the unfortunate distinction of having the highest prevalence of reported cases of infection, at well over five million people. There is not a continent on the planet that does not have a substantial number of such cases. It appears the prevalence rates are far higher in developing countries where treatment is less accessible. For example, among the female population, syphilis rates can be from ten to one hundred times higher in developing countries. Gonorrhea and chlamydia rates also prove to be markedly higher and—"

"Honey, I'm not talking about statistics," Caleb interrupted. "I'm talking about you and me and whether either of us is infected."

"Oh, well then you have no need to fear. I carry no disease of any kind."

Caleb smiled and shook his head. "And you know this because?"

Conn was taken aback by the question. She'd always known if there was a disease, infection, virus or bacteria trying to attack her. She assumed everyone was the same in that respect. Clearly she was mistaken.

She took a seat on the bed beside Caleb. "Are you disease free?"

"Yes."

"And you know this how?"

"I have regular tests and I practice safe sex."

"You are referring to such things as condoms?"

"So you know about that?"

"Yes, I saw an advertisement for Trojan. Apparently a preferred and dependable brand. And you use these things in your sexual activities?"

"Yeah."

She grimaced at him. "Doesn't that detract from the tactile experience?"

Caleb chuckled and nodded. "Yeah, it is kind of a dampener."

"But since neither of us carry a disease—"

"Honey, I'm not calling you a liar, but how can you know you're not infected if you haven't been tested?"

"My body tells me when it is in danger from any attack."

"No way."

"I would not lie about such a thing, Caleb. However, I do not wish to cause you discomfort and I would gladly undergo whatever testing is required, but I cannot risk such a procedure. I deeply regret that I cannot enjoy the delights of your magnificent body, but fully understand your reluctance and—"

"Hey now, hold on," he interrupted. "I didn't say we couldn't enjoy ourselves, just that we have to steer clear of certain things until we're sure."

"Such as cunnilingus."

"Yeah, afraid so."

She thought about it for a moment then smiled up at him. "Well, that only applies to you, Caleb. You did say you had undergone the tests and are disease free, correct?"

"Yeah."

She rose and stepped in front of him putting her hands on his shoulders to push him back on the bed. "Then there is nothing stopping me from pleasuring you, is there?" she asked right before she lowered down and ran her tongue over the head of his penis.

Caleb opened his mouth to respond, but that one lick sent a bolt of heat through him strong enough to have only an expulsion of air escaping his lips. She straightened with a sexy smile on her face. "This would be much more comfortable if you were fully on the bed."

He wasted no time scooting back so that he was stretched out on the bed. Conn's eyes moved over him in such a heated manner that it was almost tangible. She climbed up on the bed, straddling his body, her moist sex settled firmly on his belly, creating a burn that had his cock pulsing.

When she started to speak softly, her voice was fully her own, that exotic husky tone and musical accent. "I want you to lie very still, Caleb. Let your body relax and loosen. I will be as gentle or rough as you wish, but want only to please you. Can you submit to that?"

"I think I can manage," he quipped, thinking she really was quite unusual. Most women were interested only in the pleasure a man had to give them. At least from his experience. Ride the wild bull seemed to be the current theme. The longer and harder you were and the more time you could stay in the saddle, the better the women seemed to like it. To have a woman wanting nothing more than to give him pleasure was not only an unexpected treat, it was downright unprecedented.

"Did you know," she said softly, leaning forward and bracing herself on her left arm, tracing her fingertips lightly along the side of his face. "That there is a common misperception that men only have sexual feelings in their penis?"

She lowered, her breasts lightly pressing against his chest. Her lips grazed his face and traced slowly to his ear. "For example," she whispered. "There are numerous nerve endings in the ear. Making it a highly erogenous area."

Caleb couldn't have agreed more when her lips closed on his earlobe and her tongue played with the pliant flesh.

"Hmmm-ummmm," he hummed, gathering her long hair in his hands and smoothing it back over her shoulders.

"Not simply the ear itself," she whispered then ran her tongue along its rim. "But the area surrounding it."

Her lips moved to a point just below his ear and he could have sworn he felt his heart beat in that one place as her lips and tongue caressed it. Slowly and gently her lips moved down his neck and along the edge of his collarbone, stopping at the hollow of his throat then working upward, over the peak of his chin.

When she reached his mouth and sucked his bottom lip into her mouth, biting lightly, he couldn't stop his hands from tightening in her hair.

That sound like a purr came from her and a spicy sweet smell rose in the air. He could feel the wetness from her pussy on his belly and the hard nubs of her nipples pressing against him. Combined with the sudden burst of pleasure that came from her tongue invading his mouth, her hands fisting in his hair to hold him captive, Caleb felt like he was about to pop a testicle, he was so worked up.

Conn took her time, exploring his mouth, tasting and biting until at last she gave an excited purr and sat up, her eyes at that half-mast stage that is a true signal of desire.

"Interestingly," she crooned, tracing her fingertips over his chest to circle his nipples, "some men have very sensitive nipples."

Her fingers circled then fastened on his nipples, squeezing lightly, then more firmly, at the same time, rocking on his belly so that he felt the slick slide of her pussy on his skin.

"Others find it less stimulating," she continued, leaning down to clamp her mouth on one nipple.

Caleb had never been particularly sensitive in that area, but Conn put a new spin on things. By the time her mouth was sliding down the center of his torso, he was pretty sure that if she even touched his dick, he'd come like Old Faithful, spewing a geyser.

Conn's tongue painted a trail of fire from his torso to groin, then she stopped and repositioned, spreading his legs so that she knelt between them, her weight on her elbows and knees so that her ass was higher than her head.

The position alone was erotic enough to have his balls tightening and his dick throbbing. She gathered his testicles in her hand, lifting them and blowing lightly on the hot skin beneath them.

Caleb was surprised at the way his body jolted. How could something as simple as a breath feel that good? When her fingers squeezed the tissue between his testicles and anus, massaging up and down, pre-cum beaded on the head of his dick.

"Hmmmm," she murmured and ran her tongue over the head, then blew on it, the sensation making a shiver dance over his skin.

"I'm going to take you to the edge of climax, Caleb," she whispered. "But I don't want you to come. You have to resist it."

And with that she took him in her mouth. Her fingers played over his scrotum, perineum and between his buttocks to circle and tease his anus. And all the while her hot, wet mouth worked on him.

His balls were as hard as stone, drawn up tight, and his belly was starting to tense, his body arching up as orgasm pressed closer.

"No," she whispered and slowed, running her tongue over the head of his cock and around it, but not taking him in her mouth. "Not yet."

"Darlin', you're killing me," he replied in mock complaint.

"Not even close," she replied and started over.

By the third time, Caleb's entire body was a sizzling network of nerves that were about to drive him crazy. He'd been as submissive as he could be, but the need was too great to submit further.

He sat up, slung his leg over her and got off the bed.

Conn watched as he left the room. She didn't understand. She knew he was enjoying it. His body told her that. So why did he leave?

She started to get up and follow but before she could get off the bed, he was back, sliding a condom on.

"My turn," he said and rolled her over onto her back, spreading her legs with his knees as he knelt between them. "I'd love to return the favor, honey, but right now all I can think about is sinking into that sweet, hot pussy and riding you long and hard."

Conn felt a burst of wetness from her vagina at his words and the look on his face. Here was a man who meant exactly what he said. She could only hope that he lived up to his words.

She reached out to take his penis in her hand and guide it to her channel. The moment he was in position, she lifted her legs to wrap them around his waist, pulling him down onto her and his penis deep inside her.

He was thick and long. She felt the initial resistance of her body to the penetration and gasped.

"Too much?" he asked, easing up on the pressure he was exerting.

She shook her head, willing her body to accommodate, rolling her hips to aid the slow push he gave. "Take me," she moaned as need suddenly erased all but the hunger. "Feel my hunger." She reached up and pulled him down to meet her lips.

Caleb had heard those words before, but never had it caused him to lose his mind. No sooner had their lips met than everything but the feel and smell and look of her vanished. There was no sense of time or place. There was only the two of them, joined. Hearts pounding in unison, breaths fast and hard, the slap of flesh on flesh as he stroked inside her.

He felt something swell inside him, something he didn't recognize. It was erotic and powerful and hungry. He pushed up, braced on his hands so that he could look down at her.

Her eyes were dancing with light, a swirling mix of colors that was almost dizzying to see. But he couldn't pull his eyes away. The lights seemed to suck him in, until he was blind, lost in a whirlwind of color and sensation.

The feelings grew stronger, electric, overwhelming. The approach of orgasm like the rumble of a giant train getting ever closer. He couldn't tell if the feelings belonged to him or her. There didn't seem to be a distinction between the two. He could swear that he felt her inside him, inside his mind. Like they were one mind.

He heard her cry his name at the same moment all control was stripped from him. Like a leaf caught in a hurricane, he surrendered to the storm of sensation, letting it take him where it would.

When at last the tempest began to fade, sight returned. Conn was watching him, the lights fading in her eyes.

Caleb gave in to the weakness that followed and rolled over onto his back, pulling her close to his side. For a few minutes he simply drifted in the satisfied glow, closing his eyes and letting his pulse and respiration normalize.

When he opened his eyes she was watching.

"Darlin', I don't know what you call that, but it's for damn sure, I've never felt anything like it in my life."

"Does that mean you're eager to repeat the experience?"

"Oh yeah, it most definitely means that."

She nodded and sat. "Then we have to have a way to have my blood tested to prove that I am not infected with any disease, because next time I don't want anything between us. You were quite correct. It dampens the experience."

Caleb couldn't help it. He laughed. And when Conn's brows drew together in a frown, he laughed harder. She started to get off the bed, but he pulled her down beside him, wrapping his arms around her.

"I fail to see what is humorous," she muttered against his chest.

Caleb cleared his throat and released her so that she could look up at him. "Conn, I'm sorry. It's just that—well the truth is, if what I just felt was in any way dampened, then I'm not sure I could survive the full experience because...well because...damn, woman."

She stared at him with a confused frown. "Because damn woman? That is a good thing?"

Caleb's laughter returned. "You're damn skippy, baby. That's a very good thing."

Chapter Five

Pandora turned away from the man seated across from her. Azarth's visit had been unannounced and unwelcome. It vexed her that her informants had not discovered the girl's whereabouts before Azarth's arrival. For that was the only reason he was there.

"There can be *no* other explanation," Azarth insisted. "The tests conducted by the government facility prove beyond all doubt that she is of V'Kar."

"There are many of V'Kar on this world," she replied, returning her eyes to his.

"And all accounted for from the reports gathered from all factions."

"Mistakes happen."

"This is no mistake!" He jumped to his feet. "This is your doing! You and your damnable Sisterhood. Your infernal unending games. You've done this and I want to know why."

She rose slowly, never breaking eye contact, making sure he felt the power she projected. "It would serve you well to remember to whom you speak, Minister."

He stared angrily at her for a few moments then slumped back into his chair. "Have you any idea the difficulty this creates? There are far too many who know of her existence to merely erase records. We would have to alter the memory of scores of people to eliminate knowledge of her existence. Not to mention the fact that we'd have to wipe out the entire Alliance, a task you well know to be impossible. Their numbers are too vast."

"That is preposterous as you well know. Should we find the need to have information altered or deleted, we merely have to activate the cells within the respective branch of whatever world government possesses the data.

"And…" She held up her hand for silence as he opened his mouth to speak. "Perhaps it would be prudent to look at the situation from another perspective. If—and mind you, this is in no way an admission, merely a thought on a hypothetical—if this female does exist and is not a V'Karian that can be accounted for, then we must assume that she has either been sent here from V'Kar as an emissary or spy."

"That possibility has already been explored and discounted. The Sisterhood controls the gate. Passage is impossible without their permission. Without your permission, Mother Superior. Therefore it stands to reason that if there is another of us here on this world, it is because of a direct dictate from you."

"There are other possibilities, Azarth. However, if it will assuage your concerns, I will have the Sisterhood provide a detailed accounting of the whereabouts of our entire conclave."

Azarth barked a laugh. "As if I would trust such an accounting. Don't assume that high and mighty look with me. We both know that you and your conclave of witches are not above lies and subterfuge if it suits your purpose."

"Such a high opinion you have of us, Azarth. I'm sure I'm blushing from the barrage of compliments."

He scowled and fell silent for a few moments. "Then let us set aside our respective titles for a moment. Not Mother Superior to Minister of Science and Medicine, but one lover to another. Tell me the truth. Is this female one of your acolytes?"

She smiled, thinking how well he knew her. Approach her from a political stance and he knew he would get nothing from her. Appeal to her as her lover of more years than she could count, and he knew she would feel compelled to speak the truth. At least as much of it as she felt was safe for him to know.

"Azarth, upon my honor I do assure you that this female of whom you speak is not now nor has ever been a member of the order. Nor is she a resident of any of the worlds of V'Kar."

"Then who is she?" he asked.

"Hope."

"Hope? For what?"

"Our salvation."

He stared at her for a long time. She knew there were questions swirling through his mind. She could hear them. Just as she knew that he was certain that she would provide no more answers. They might be lovers who had been together longer than humans had walked this green world, but still they were separated by position. He belonged to the J'Zahn, the ruling council of V'Kar, who answered only to the Emperor. And she was the leader of a group more powerful than the J'Zahn and the emperor combined. For she controlled the Sisterhood, the most powerful and feared body in this galaxy or her own.

At length Azarth stood and offered his hand. "I pray that your actions are grounded in wisdom and are instituted for the welfare of our people, for this will surely see rise to tensions between the factions here on Earth."

"There are always tensions between the factions, my darling," she replied, placing her hand in his and rising. "Just as there are always battles to be waged and won against the Alliance. But make no mistake. Regardless of the actions of our people here, or the interference and inconvenience created by the Alliance, our mission has not altered from its original course. You and I are here for one reason. To save our people. All the people of V'Kar. Should there exist a being who can further that cause, I submit to you that it is our responsibility to safeguard that person at all costs. For not only our lives, but the life of an entire star system depends upon it."

"Then so be it," he whispered and lowered his head over her hand.

Pandora smiled and went into his embrace when he raised his head. It was clear that she would have to take a personal role in assuring that her plans did not fall asunder. But for the moment, she could indulge herself in the pleasures her lover was most skilled at providing.

* * * * *

Caleb took the rutted old trail path to the house and left his truck parked out behind the house. He'd been out all day helping with the roundup and was hot, sweaty and tired. He was eager to get clean and see Conn. He'd left her in charge of the clinic today. She'd already proven herself capable of handling just about anything. And she had a radio she could use to call him in case of an emergency.

Conn was certainly acclimating to being on the ranch. It'd been only a few weeks and already everyone had come to accept her as one of their own. Hannah was even teaching her to cook.

And he was having the most amazing sex of his life. Tonight if he was lucky he'd have her for the first time without a condom. They'd ordered every home HIV test on the market and done all of them this morning. When he'd called her later in the day she was excited to tell him that they all came back negative.

The sound of voices from inside the house drew his attention as he mounted the steps. He knocked the dust off his boots and hurried inside.

Conn was at the kitchen counter, pouring iced tea into glasses. At the table sat his half-brother Chase and Chase's wife Ana. Conn turned at the sound of the door closing. "Caleb!"

He could see the look of anxiety in her eyes and understood it all too well. It was one thing to be around the people who worked on the ranch. They were going to accept whatever story Caleb told them about Conn. His family was another matter.

"Hey." He resisted the urge to gather her in his arms and tell her everything was going to be okay. No use in letting on to Chase or Ana how close he and Conn really were.

"Hey, bro." He greeted Chase with a handshake then walked over to lean down and give Ana a kiss. "Hey, beautiful. What brings you here?"

"Escape," Ana said with a smile. "There's a houseful of teenagers at our place and we couldn't take the music any longer. Besides, Chase wanted to pick up that horse."

Caleb laughed. "You still figuring on training that mare for barrel racing?"

"Yep," Chase replied and cut his eyes at Conn. "So, Miss Hoffman here tells us that she's your new vet assistant."

"Yep." Caleb avoided Chase's eyes and headed for the sink to wash his hands. Call it whatever you wanted but Chase had a way of seeing through a lie. Caleb had never known if it was due to his mixed heritage or something of Ana had rubbed off on him. Chase's mother was Charlie's first wife, a full-blooded Apache. And Ana was a witch.

"I invited your family to stay for dinner," Conn said softly, surprising him more by speaking in an almost perfect imitation of his accent, than by her statement. "I hope that's okay. Hannah said there's a casserole in the oven, and a rack of ribs and I made a broccoli salad and cooked some fresh…snap peas, I think she called them."

"Sounds good." Caleb gave her a smile, hoping it would ease her anxiety. "Here, let me help you with those glasses."

They distributed the glasses of tea and took a seat at the table. Caleb sat down between Ana and Conn, and Ana wrinkled up her nose at him. "Honey, you need a shower in the worst kind of way. Why don't you run on upstairs and clean up? Chase and I'll entertain Conn."

Leaving Conn alone with Chase and Ana was the last thing Caleb wanted to do but he saw no way to refuse without it seeming suspicious. "Good idea," he said and lifted his glass to drain it. "Be back in a few."

He hated the pleading look he saw in Conn's eyes when he looked at her. Hoping he hadn't made a huge mistake, he took the stairs three at a time.

Conn watched Caleb leave the room with a sinking feeling in her stomach. She turned and looked at his brother, Chase. There was something very primal and male about him. He was probably the most intensely sexual male she'd ever seen.

His dark eyes seemed like endless wells of mystery and his equally dark hair was long and worn loose. Caleb had said that he and Chase were half-brothers. Whatever race Chase belonged to must be one where there were people of great power because there was an air of power about him.

"So, what's the lowdown on you and my little brother, darlin'?" he asked.

Conn looked from him to Ana and back to him. "As I mentioned previously, I am employed as a—"

"What happened to your accent?" Chase interrupted.

Conn felt like a bird caught in the gaze of a viper. She'd made a terrible blunder. How to undo it, she hadn't a clue.

"I...I..." She looked at Ana to find Ana smiling at her. And in that smile was something Conn had not expected. Acceptance. How was it that she would sense something like that from Ana? And why did it have such strength and assurance?"

"It's okay," Ana said and reached out to put her hand on top of Conn's. "We've all had secrets from time to time, or had to hide who and what we are. But you're safe with us, Conn. In fact, why don't we ignore Chase's question for the moment and let me tell you a little about this family."

"Ana," Chase growled in a tone that sounded distinctly like a warning to Conn.

Ana didn't appear to take it as such. She just smiled and waved the warning aside. "Simmer down, cowboy. We're treading on safe ground here. Trust me."

"If you say so," he relented and leaned back in his chair to watch.

Ana turned her attention back to Conn. "To start with, I'm a witch. Not the stir-your-cauldron, do-evil-deeds and scare-little-children variety. I'm a white-lighter. Chase and Caleb have two other brothers, Cole and Clay. They're twins. Cole's married to a skin-walker. At least that's what the Navaho call them and she's part Native American like Chase—only different tribes. She's what you might call a were-cat because she can take on the shape of a mountain lion. Clay's wife Rusty is also a witch. Another white-lighter. She doesn't use her power too much except for communicating with animals and she's really adept at that."

Conn felt like pinching herself. Was this real? She'd never met anyone who claimed to have abnormal abilities before. And to talk about it like she was discussing the weather? It was unbelievable. And exciting. And it was like a lever that magically appeared and lifted some invisible weight from her.

"You..." She looked at Chase for verification. "This is true?"

"'Fraid so," he replied.

"Oh! Oh!" She jumped up and ran around the table to hug Ana. "Oh thank you, thank you!"

Ana laughed and returned the embrace. "You're very welcome. But I don't know what for."

"For being honest," Conn replied and reclaimed her seat. "I've been so afraid ever since I arrived."

"Of what?" Chase asked.

"So many things," she said with a sigh. "When I fell into the lake—"

"Whoa, darlin', back up there," Chase interrupted. "Let's start this at the beginning. Like how you and Caleb met."

"That is an excellent idea," Conn agreed enthusiastically and began to recite the events that led her to being on the ranch.

She was just starting to tell about the morning after she read all Caleb's medical books when Caleb entered the room. "Conn!"

"What?" She turned at the sound of alarm in his voice.

"What're you doing?"

"Telling your family how we met and I came to be here."

"Conn, honey, I don't think—"

"It's okay," Chase said. "She knows all the Russell dark family secrets."

"You told her?" Caleb asked, moving to take a seat beside Conn.

Chase shook his head and jerked his thumb in Ana's direction. Ana just smiled and raised her hand like a kid in a classroom. Caleb looked around at everyone. "So you know everything."

"Well, except for what happened that morning after she read all your books from college," Ana said with a mischievous grin.

"Uh, I don't think you need to hear that part," Caleb replied.

Conn looked at him in surprise. "I don't understand. We are being truthful. Is there shame in two people engaging in sex and—"

"I'm starved," Caleb cut in and bounded to his feet. "What say we get some grub on?"

Ana and Chase both laughed, making Conn feel even more confused. Ana looked over and smiled at her. "Don't be offended. Caleb's been such a rake for so long he's scared you'll spill the beans and the truth will be out that a date with Caleb isn't really a night riding the wild bull."

"Ana!" Caleb bellowed, making Chase laugh even harder.

"Spill the beans?" Conn asked. "Riding the— Are you referring to the size of Caleb's penis and his ability to sustain an erection for an extended period of time? If so then I can assure you his reputation is solidly intact because he is very well endowed and—"

"Conn!" Caleb yelled, causing Chase to nearly double over laughing and Ana to lay her head on the table and howl.

"What?" Conn shouted to be heard over all the noise.

"They don't need to know that," he insisted loudly.

"But Ana said…I thought you wanted everyone to know that you can sustain an erection for hours and that the size of—"

Her eyes flew open wide as his hand clamped over her mouth. "Honey, there are just some things you don't want to discuss with your family, okay? And the size of my…well, you know—that's just not a topic meant to be discussed with family. Okay?"

She nodded and he removed his hand. She looked at Chase and Ana who were still snickering and suddenly she understood. And understanding allowed her to see the humor in it. And also freed her to do a little teasing of her own.

"I promise not to tell any of your family that you're hung like a horse and sex with you is some world-class fuckin' and ain't that some fly shit. You have my word."

Ana and Chase lost it. She collapsed against him laughing and Chase howled and pounded the table with his fist. Caleb sputtered, turned red and looked at her in shock. "World-class fuckin'…ain't that some fly shit?"

"It was in a song on one of the films you have on DVD."

Caleb shook his head and turned away from all of them, busying himself with pulling things from the oven. Conn looked at Ana and winked and Ana gave her a big smile. "You know, Conn, personally I'm going to enjoy having you around. Welcome to the Circle R, sister."

Conn looked at the hand Ana extended across the table. She reached out to clasp it, but hesitated and looked at Chase. He smiled and nodded and when she clasped Ana's hand he placed his on top of theirs. "Welcome, Conn."

"Thank you," Conn replied gratefully. In that moment she felt closer to being a part of a family than she'd ever known and she couldn't help wishing that it would last.

Chapter Six

ഇ

Conn waved one last time to Ana and Chase as they drove away then turned and grabbed Caleb's hand. "Come with me," she said excitedly. When he didn't budge at first tug, she added, "Please? It's important."

He let her lead him to the den, where the only light came from the dying flames in the fireplace. She stopped at the sofa and pushed him down then stepped back a couple of feet.

"Ana said that your brother's wife, Rusty, is a…skin-walker. That she can shift from human to animal form. Correct?"

"Yeah." He wondered where the question was leading.

"So can I."

"Huh?"

"Tell me an animal."

Caleb wasn't really sure he was ready to delve into something like this, but curious if she could really do it, he decided to play along. "Okay, let's see. A grizzly."

"Grizzly?"

"Bear."

"Oh, yes. *Ursus arctos horribilis*, also known as the silvertip bear, a subspecies of the brown bear that—"

"Yeah, that one," he interrupted, having learned that unless he did, he'd get an encyclopedic lesson on the animal.

She grinned at him. "Like this?"

Caleb blinked once, then again. Standing before him on hind legs, front legs pawing the air was a bear. A very big grizzly bear. Much as it shamed him, he actually shrank back into the cushions of the couch when the bear landed on all fours and lumbered over, sticking its face in his.

"Uh—I believe you," he said, pulling his head back as far as possible from the big snout and mouthful of teeth.

"Shit!" His eyes slammed shut on their own as the bear's face came closer. The feel of something on his face had him jumping, then his eyes flying open. Conn was leaning over him, her warm full lips working over the side of his face.

"Christ on a crutch, Conn!" He pulled her down on his lap. "How'd you do that?"

"I don't know," she said and repositioned so that she was straddling his lap. "I wish I did. Maybe I should let Ana try to perform the regression technique she mentioned."

"Maybe," he agreed. "But right now, is there anything else you can do besides invisibility, levitation and shape-shifting?"

She gave him a look sexy enough to have him almost bursting the seams of his jeans with the raging erection it inspired. "I can make you orgasm without intercourse."

"Well hell, honey, you wiggle on me a couple more times and I'm gonna be damn close."

"I mean by not touching you at all."

"Now that I find hard to believe."

"Want me to show you?"

Caleb wasn't ready for that kind of sexual experience. He preferred to think of himself as a hands-on guy. "Actually, I'd rather we do it the old-fashioned way."

Conn's smile was immediate. "Some world-class fuckin,' ain't that some fly shit?"

Caleb chuckled at her imitation of the song then sobered. "Conn, what we do—it's not just fucking. Not for me anyway. I need you to know that."

Her smile vanished and she jumped up and hurried from the room. Caleb was shocked and for a moment just sat there.

What'd he do wrong? He got up and went in search of her, finding her standing out in the backyard, looking up at the sky through the limbs of the ancient Emory Oak.

"Conn?" He walked up behind her but didn't touch her.

She turned to face him. "I'm sorry, Caleb."

"Look, if I said something wrong—"

"No. No. Caleb, my most fervent wish is to be cared for, to know love and to be part of a real family. When you say our sex is more than a simple act of gratification it turns my mind to those things I wish for and it frightens me because this may not be the meaning your words convey."

Caleb couldn't stand the tremble in her voice, the raw emotional need that gleamed in her eyes. It opened a wound in his heart. He took hold of her shoulders. "Honey, you don't have to be afraid. Conn, I know it doesn't make a damn bit of sense. I don't even know who you really are, but that hasn't stopped me from falling in love with you."

The astonishment in her eyes shocked him. How could she not have known that he was a goner for her?

"You…love me?"

"I sure do."

"Oh, Caleb," she whispered with tears suddenly springing from her eyes. "I love you."

"Then why the tears?"

"Because I have not been honest with you."

Caleb felt something equivalent to a lead weight suddenly land in his gut. "What do you mean?"

"When we met. I told you that my name is Raenea Thotthoft?"

"Yeah."

"That is not true. It is only what I was able to spell using the letters assigned to me by Shen."

"That's about as clear as mud."

She sighed and looked down. "Shen never called me an actual name. He always referred to me as 'Not of the earth'."

Caleb was glad she wasn't looking at him because at the moment he was a little at a loss for words. If the man who'd raised her had called her such a thing, what exactly did it mean? She was an alien?

He had a hard time buying into that. Even being part of a family that included several witches and a shape-shifter.

She looked up at him and he hoped she didn't see the doubt in his eyes. But Conn saw too much.

"You think I am being dishonest."

"No, baby, I don't. I don't doubt for a second that Shen called you that. But that you might be an alien? I admit I have some trouble with that."

"As do I," she replied. "Caleb, I do not know where I'm from, but it's clear that the abilities I possess are not typical human capabilities. And the idea that perhaps I am not native to this world might explain why your government is so set upon finding and imprisoning me."

A sudden sick feeling took hold of Caleb. "They performed tests on you, didn't they? Blood tests and things like that?"

"Yes."

"Shit on a stick."

"You're upset with me."

"No." He took her hand. "Conn, honey, it doesn't matter to me where you came from. Pittsburgh or Pluto. I love you. But we really need to find out what the government has on you."

"How?"

"I wish I knew."

She moved in to wrap her arms around his waist, resting the side of her face on his chest. He hugged her close and for a long time neither of them spoke or moved. When she pulled back and looked up at him, her violet eyes were swimming with light.

"Have a condom handy, cowboy?" she asked in a flawless accent.

Caleb grinned at her. "Well, seeing as how we don't need them anymore, why don't we take this inside and—"

She didn't wait for him to finish. He laughed as she headed for the house. He closed in on her and swept her off her feet and into his arms. "I want you so much," she whispered before her lips locked on his.

The kiss stopped him dead in his tracks. She squirmed and wiggled in his arms, getting herself wound around him so that her arms circled his neck and her legs were tightened around his waist. And all the while her tongue warred with his for dominance, her exotic taste more of an aphrodisiac than he'd ever tasted.

"Fuck!" he grumbled into her mouth as he stumbled, trying to navigate his way to the back steps.

Conn laughed and released him from the kiss, focusing her attention on his neck and ear.

Caleb hurried up the steps and into the house. To hell with going upstairs to the bedroom. He carried her into the den, stopping in front of the fireplace. She unwound her legs from his waist and slid down his body, her hands moving behind him to grab his ass.

He wound one hand in her long hair and pulled her to him for another searing kiss. She purred in her throat when he unfastened her jeans and peeled them down her thighs, one hand moving between her legs to stroke her slick sex.

The sound of hunger that came from her and the way she moved against his questing fingers had him as randy as a young stud during a first mating. She looked up at him as his lips abandoned hers.

"Tonight you're all mine," he said. He'd waited long enough to have all of her and tonight he fully intended to have his fill.

"I wouldn't have it any other way," she agreed in a voice rough with desire.

"Then shuck those clothes, darlin'."

"After you, sugah," she drawled and toed one boot off, kicking it aside.

It didn't take either of them long. In seconds their clothing was strewn across the floor and he was reaching for her, winding one hand in her hair to pull her head back. She arched against him, presenting him with the perfect moment to feast on her breasts.

Conn let out a slight hiss when he bit lightly on her nipple, but instead of moving to stop him, she fisted her hands in his hair, encouraging him. With one arm supporting her back and the other gripping her breast, he teased the hard nub, licking and flicking it with his tongue then sucking it into his mouth.

"Ummmmm," she purred and worked one hand down his body to fist his erection.

Caleb raised his head long enough to lower her down onto the thick rug in front of the fireplace, spreading her legs as he knelt between them. She started to pull him down on her but he took her hands in his and stopped her.

"Not so fast, quick draw. I been waiting a while to taste you and I don't plan on rushing."

"Heavens no," she agreed, moving her hands to trace her fingers up her inner thighs to her wet sex.

Caleb bent over, spreading her sex, his big fingers gentle as he traced between the lips then spread her labia more. When he lowered his head and lapped at her, she felt something inside her belly swell, a heat that took only a moment to engulf her entire body. She wiggled against his mouth and gasped as his tongue worked over her clit.

Surprised at how quickly her body reacted and how close she was to orgasm, she was doubly surprised that he recognized it and sat back on his heels.

"Baby, you gotta hold off a little."

"Easy for you to say," she quipped in return, knowing from the smile on his face that he knew she was teasing. Just looking at Caleb was an erotic experience. His broad muscular chest and rippled abdomen, his tanned skin and those brawny arms and big strong hands were a feast for the eyes. As was his face. All male and at the moment wearing an expression of desire hot enough to start a fire.

As her eyes moved over his body, she felt her nipples tingle in excitement. She raised her hands to her breasts, letting her thumbs track slowly over her nipples. She knew it was a turn-on for him to watch her fondle herself.

Her hands moved lower, framing her sex as she bent her knees. Just as she started to spread her pussy to expose her clit, his hands moved to stop her. "You're trespassing," he warned and grabbed her behind the knees to push her legs back toward her chest and spread them wide.

She wasn't about to protest when his mouth staked a claim on her pussy. His tongue laved her slow and easy and then faster. Conn was certain she'd never felt so on fire. He sucked her labia, plundered inside her, his tongue sending sparks of energy through her that had her literally whimpering for release.

It was marvelous and frustrating and unbelievable. She wanted to come yet she didn't want it to end.

And it didn't appear that he was about to let it end. Every time she came close to a climax, he'd stop. Finally she reached her limits. "Please, please," she gasped. "I need to —"

The next sound out of her mouth was a low drawn-out moan. His tongue worked over her clit, building the fire until her body started to tremble with the onset of an orgasm.

As she plummeted over the edge, he pulled her to him, sliding into her wet depths. Conn moaned, lost in a void of sensation, feeling her pussy clench on him as the orgasm rolled through her. Before it could fade, she grabbed his arms and hoisted herself up so that she straddled him as he knelt on the floor. The feel of him fully hilted inside her was enough to have another wave wash over her.

"Baby, you come so pretty," he murmured. "Come for me again."

"My pleasure," she replied, then gave him a sassy smile. "But first…"

She lay back on the floor, pulling him down on top of her and then rolled them both over so that she straddled him.

By the stars, has anything ever felt so good or looked so magnificent? she thought as she reveled in the moment. Leaning down, she flicked her tongue over his nipple then lightly bit it, moving her hips in a slow ride.

The slight intake of breath that came from him had her moving a bit stronger, straightening to prop her hands on his chest, squeezing him with the muscles of her vagina then easing up, only to start again, slightly rocking her hips as her inner muscles contracted on him.

"Conn…honey," Caleb groaned, "You're gonna make me come."

"That's the idea," she purred, rocking a little faster.

She couldn't explain it. Didn't understand it. She'd never felt the desire to please anyone this way, to lose herself in the sensations of another. Yet with Caleb, that's the way she felt. She could feel his need, his pleasure, and she wanted to give him more.

It was almost frightening. Like an addiction, it was so strong, this need. She did not care that she didn't understand it. Surrendering to it was the path toward greater pleasure. For both of them.

Caleb rolled over onto his side, taking her with him. "Darlin', you're gonna do me in and I'm not ready for it to be over. What say we take advantage of that hot tub on the porch?"

Conn grinned at him. "I love your hot tub."

"Yeah, I know you do," he said as he untangled from her and got to his feet, pulling her with him.

Naked and giggling, they ran outside. The night air was cool on her damp skin. She lifted her hair, feeling the whisper of air on her neck as Caleb started the jets in the tub.

Conn was naked and in the water by the time he lifted his leg to get in the tub. He'd no sooner stepped into the water than she was on her knees in front of him, taking his erect shaft into her mouth.

"Slow. Down." He gently pushed her back and sank down into the water. Damn if the woman couldn't call up a climax in him faster than a snake striking.

"I like the way you taste," she said and submerged. A moment later he felt her mouth on him. And it felt good. He leaned back and closed his eyes, abandoning himself to the sensations.

A climax began to build. And at the exact moment he realized it, another thought intruded. She'd been under water an awfully long time. Caleb took hold of her shoulders and lifted her up.

Conn's hands replaced her mouth on his cock. "Damn, woman, you part fish?"

"What do you mean?"

"You were underwater a good long while."

"Another hidden talent?" she asked with a sexy smile, stroking him a little faster.

"Well you're sure full of 'em," he said around a groan as the climax suddenly spiked hot and fast, so strong that he didn't think he had the will to control it.

But she did. "Not yet," she whispered. "I want you to resist the need as long as you can. Until the hunger tears so hard at you that you have no strength to resist. Let me show you pleasure beyond anything you've known, Caleb."

"I'm all yours," he replied. How sexy and unusual it was to have a woman talk to him in such a manner, control the action without really exerting control other than a few huskily spoken words that promised of passion and satisfaction.

"Sit up on the next step," she urged and added when he raised his eyebrows in question, "I don't want you to fear I might drown, and ruin the experience."

Caleb slid up a step and leaned back, the motion lifting his groin up enough that his erection stabbed up out of the water. The cool night air whispered on his wet skin, bringing a slight shiver. But when Conn's mouth closed on the head of his dick, a spike of heat shot through him hot enough to dispel any sensations of cool.

He couldn't resist fisting her long hair and driving his dick deeper into her warm wet mouth. Her nimble fingers played with his balls, working around and behind them to circle and tease his anus.

Her mouth and hands played him as expertly as any musician upon their instrument of mastery. His hands tightened in her hair. Much more and he wouldn't be able to hold on. She already had him teetering on the edge.

"Darlin', please." His voice came out in a constricted growl as he fought against the rising tide that threatened to send him tumbling into freefall.

She raised her head, slithered up his body and claimed his mouth in a kiss that was almost as powerful as the sensations she'd given when she had her mouth on his dick.

He could taste himself on her, that slight tang of pre-cum. Oddly, combined with her exotic taste, it was intoxicating.

When she released him from the kiss, she sank back down with a sexy grin and started again. Caleb lost track of the number of times she took him to the brink then pulled him back. His body was taut, need vibrating through him like the current from an electrical tower.

"Conn, honey," he moaned. "Darlin', I can't…"

Her answer to his unfinished plea was to suck harder. And faster. And all the while that unusual purr accompanied the sound of water slapping against the sides of the tub and the bubbles from the jets breaking the surface of the water.

Caleb moved his arms out to his sides, gripping the edge of the tub as his body tightened and arched. Held captive in the wet warmth of her mouth with her fingers fondling and teasing his balls and ass, he was too far gone to hold on.

He plummeted. Sudden and powerful and overwhelming. Reality faded. There was only sensation and in that feeling was Conn. Right there with him. She was part of the orgasm. He could feel her with him. It was amazing. It carried him higher and further than he thought possible and to a place where nothing else existed. And then further.

Lights exploded in his mind, colors dancing and swirling. He couldn't identify or understand it. He didn't want to. She was with him. And they were locked in a cosmic dance of pleasure and oneness that he never wanted to leave.

Conn felt him surrender and followed, keeping her mind close to his as he soared through the realm of sensation. Though a novice to this level of sensation, he showed no fear, but embraced the experience, giving himself to it and to her.

Something hot and driving seized her. Something she'd never experienced. Something calling to a primal part of her she'd never known existed. She couldn't fight it. Didn't want to. It was elemental to who and what she was.

Slowly she rose on her knees, her hands moving from his still pulsing cock to trace up his body. She pressed against him, running her tongue over the hollow of his throat and up the side of his neck.

His pulse pounded fast and hard beneath the surface. She could feel it as her own, hearing the singing of the blood in his veins. That blood called to her in a voice that was both foreign and familiar.

Wrapping one hand around his cock, she climbed atop him, guiding him to her wet channel.

He groaned and surged to erection at the touch and she slid fully onto him, rocking back and forth to create a friction that was as sublime to her as it was to him.

Her mouth opened against the side of his neck, her tongue tracing over the racing pulse point.

"Conn," he whispered, his arms moving to grip her hips and pull her more firmly onto him.

The sound of her name on his lips robbed her of all reason. Coherent thought fled. In its place was only need. She tried to push away, suddenly afraid. But the call was too strong. Her sense of self fled and she was taken by a force she did not know how to battle.

Caleb sensed a change in her a split second before he was taken spiraling into an even higher sphere of sensation. He sensed fear. Then need. Need so strong that it nearly robbed him of breath.

He tried to speak, to call her name, to hold her tighter and drive deeper inside her. He wanted to give her as much as she'd given him. But before he could do more than register the thought, something took him.

And there was no more thought.

Conn came back to reality before Caleb opened his eyes. She pushed back from him, breathing hard. And that's when she saw it. Blood. On his neck.

Fear took hold of her with sickening force. Her throat seized, cutting off her air. Her hands trembled as she cupped them and lifted water to his neck, washing away the smeared blood.

What she saw had her gut twisting. There were puncture wounds on his neck. Well, there were for a moment. But they were already closing. Within moments the wounds had sealed.

Unconsciously her tongue ran over her teeth. The feel of sharp, rather elongated incisors had her eyes widening in shock.

She reached out to run her fingers over his neck. That's when he opened his eyes. The smile he gave her turned into a look of concern. He straightened, grabbing her by the arms. "Conn? Honey, what happened?"

"What do you mean?" Her heart felt like it was trying to lurch out of her chest at the question.

"There's..." He reached up and ran two fingers over her chin then raised them in front of his face to look at them. "Honey, this is blood."

Conn wanted to vanish. To be sucked into a tornado and be carried away. How could the most potent sexual experience in either of their lives be so destroyed? That completeness and love she'd felt inside that sphere of complete pleasure and oneness was not what either of them had imagined. How could she tell him that she might have discovered the answer to not who she was, but what?

How could she tell the man she loved that she feared she was a vampire?

"Caleb...I..." She couldn't find words. "I...bit you."

His eyes widened then narrowed. "You bit me?"

She nodded. "On the neck."

His hand moved to his neck. One side, then the other. "There's nothing there, Conn. Maybe you bit your lip, honey."

She shook her head. "I saw it, Caleb. I saw the marks. They were right there on the left side of your neck. And they just…closed up and vanished. I think…" Her eyes filled with tears and a look of anguish came on her face. "I think I'm a vampire."

If anyone had told Caleb that he'd be following the most incredible sexual experience of his life with the woman he loved saying she was a vampire, he'd have laughed and asked what they'd been smoking.

Nothing could have prepared him for this.

"Conn, that's…crazy. There's no such thing as vampires."

"Then how do you explain this?" She bared her teeth at him.

"What?"

"These!" She tapped on her incisors and gasped in surprise, running her finger over them. They were normal.

"Caleb, I swear to you that a few moments ago I had elongated incisors. Just like the images of fictitious vampires. And I bit you. I do not remember doing so, but I did see the evidence of it. There were two small puncture wounds. And blood on your neck. "

"Honey, I don't know what to say to you. Maybe you just imagined it or—"

"Caleb, I am scared."

Being this kind of afraid was new for Conn. She'd always known there were things outside herself that deserved respect and even fear. But to fear who you are was something she'd never considered. Shen had called her *Not of the earth*. She'd often wondered about it, and even considered that perhaps she wasn't native to Earth. That she could accept. But the idea that she might be some evil creature such as was written about in mythology, a creature who lived off the lifeblood of others? That was more horrifying than anything she could imagine.

Caleb sank down into the water and held her trembling against him. "Conn, listen. Let's say you did bite me. And the bite miraculously healed. That doesn't mean you're a vampire. Think about it. In all the myths and legends, vampires exist solely on blood. They sure don't get green around the gills at the idea of eating meat. And they don't wolf down a quart of potato salad for a snack."

"But the marks—"

"Like I said, maybe it happened. I'm not saying it didn't. It's a sure bet that something happened because you took me somewhere I've never been before and that's no joke. But still, a vampire? Honey, you go out in the sun all the time. Vampires aren't supposed to be able to do that. Sunlight destroys them. I just don't think it fits, Conn. Besides, do you remember biting me?"

She thought about it. "No. I just remember being filled with...need. And a little afraid. Then that disappeared and we were together and floating in a sea of sensation and love and nothing else mattered."

"I felt that too," he said. "And I did feel something else for a split second, but I can't explain it. Something just...took me. And the next thing I knew you were with me and we were in that place and I didn't want to leave."

"But I know it happened, Caleb."

"Okay, so let's see if we can make it happen again."

"What?"

"Well, obviously it was brought on by sexual arousal, so let's see if we can make it happen again. Only this time if you feel it, try to control it."

Conn wasn't certain that was the answer, but she didn't have a better plan so she nodded and started to lower her face to his groin. He stopped her.

"Only this time, it's my turn.

"I'm all yours," she agreed and wondered if he knew just how true that was. For she was certain. What had happened might be frightening, but it had connected her to him in a way deeper than anything she could have imagined. Whether she wanted it or not, she knew to the core of her soul that she was forever bound to him.

Chapter Seven

ℵ

Pandora's smile faded when she saw who awaited her in the luxurious parlor. The woman stood as Pandora entered. Beautiful and as youthful and powerful as she had been the last time Pandora saw her nearly twenty years ago.

"Stay away from her," the woman said before Pandora had crossed the threshold.

"What a delightful surprise." Pandora chose to ignore the threat. "And how foolish. But then you always were rash, Resa. Prone to leap before looking, as the humans say."

"Cut the crap and let's get down to it," Resa replied and took her seat. "We know she's been spotted and the only reason I'm here is to warn you that if you renege on our bargain—"

"I need neither your warnings nor your reminders of our agreement," Pandora interrupted, taking a seat adjacent to Resa. "And might I add that the agreement was not with you, but with your mate. Odd that he sends you instead of coming to me himself."

"He's not that stupid. The situation hasn't changed. The Emperor still favors his second born, leaving the Heir Apparent in perpetual exile. The only way for him to return and claim what is rightfully his is for us to succeed in seeing this through. And that will not happen if he is spotted. Unless, of course, you've failed to filter the information released to the V'Kar on this world and someone knows that he has not returned to sit at the left hand of the Emperor."

"Failure, as you well know, is not an option," Pandora replied. "But let us not rehash issues we've covered innumerable times. You come seeking assurance. I would like to oblige, but the truth is, her existence has been noted by many."

"Meaning?"

"Meaning that we must devise a plan to make the respective Earth governments aware of her existence believe that she is no longer among the living."

"Agreed. What do you propose?"

"At present I am uncertain of the best course of action. I have a man in position within the national security sector of this country. According to his latest report, all that is known is that the aircraft transporting her crashed, leaving two survivors. Even under drugs, the survivors remember only that she perished in the crash. The description they gave of the woman was of a tall, heavy-set woman with sandy-blonde hair and brown eyes. None of which describes her. Which means her powers of persuasion and mind control are strong."

"Then you're certain she lives?"

Pandora noted the way Resa's hands gripped the arms of the chair, giving testimony to her anxiety. She could exploit that anxiety if she so chose, but it would not further her cause. Resa was the one being in the universe who held the trust of the Heir Apparent. And Pandora needed his cooperation.

"She lives."

"Where is she?"

"My dear, that is information that can only bring you pain. You cannot see her and should you be given her location the temptation would be too strong."

Resa slumped in her chair, a gesture uncharacteristic. "You're right. I know. But I have to know that she's safe. You must give me your word that she will be protected."

Pandora reached out and placed her hand on top of Resa's. "Protecting her has been a priority for more than twenty years. It will continue to be so. We need her. She could be the key, Resa. A key in the puzzle that once pieced together will be the salvation of V'Kar."

Resa nodded sadly. "Yes, I know. But there are times I wish she wasn't."

"We all have a destiny to fulfill, Dhampir," Pandora deliberately used the old term, knowing that it would have more of an effect than all the sympathy in the world.

Resa's eyes hardened and her spine straightened. She stood and looked down at Pandora. "Yes, we all have a destiny to fulfill. See that you fulfill yours, Mother Superior. Because if harm comes to her, nothing will protect you from my wrath."

Pandora inclined her head in acknowledgement. Resa did not possess power as great as her own, but nonetheless she was a formidable woman. One Pandora would rather have fighting with her than against her.

She watched Resa stalk from the room then summoned her aide. "I want to see our operative from within the national intelligence sector."

The aide nodded and hurried to do Pandora's bidding. Pandora leaned back in her chair and closed her eyes. One thing Resa's visit had proven was that time was a luxury she did not have. She needed to conceal Raenea's existence and she needed to do it fast. It was time to use the resources of the humans to achieve that goal.

* * * * *

Caleb gritted his teeth and counted to ten. He wasn't in a good mood to begin with and it seemed that fate had it in for him and was dumping one problem after another on his plate today.

He and Conn had tested his theory, and while she had not sprouted fangs, chewed on his neck or disappeared in a puff of smoke at sunrise, she was still upset over what had happened and now obsessed with trying to find out who she really was.

And that was a can of worms neither of them wanted to open because as soon as they started searching for answers it would expose her. And then the military would be after her.

His heart hurt for her. Not knowing who you were and where you came from would be hard enough. But to be possessed of super-human abilities and paranormal fears about your identity had to be nearly impossible to deal with.

"Caleb!" Bobby, one of the ranch hands yelled, getting his attention. "The guy's here for that mare."

That wasn't news that brought a smile to Caleb's face. An old acquaintance of Caleb's father had shown up a while back looking for a horse for his granddaughter. Ordinarily, Caleb would have told him to go elsewhere. Hinson Daws was a mean-spirited old man who had a reputation for being hard on animals.

That didn't set well with Caleb, but his father had asked Caleb to cut Hinson some slack. Hinson Daws had a lot of clout in the state and Charlie needed that clout to get certain legislation passed that would benefit the state.

Caleb didn't like being used as a political tool, but did as his father asked and agreed to sell Hinson a sweet little mare.

Little did he know when he made that deal that Conn would take a shine to that mare and the mare to her. The mare followed her like a puppy and responded to verbal requests from Conn like a trained circus animal.

Conn was going to be quite unhappy to see the mare go. But what choice did he have?

Hinson waddled around the corner, bellowing as he approached. "You got that horse ready, boy?"

Caleb gestured to the ranch hand, Bobby. "Get the mare loaded up for Mr. Daws, Bobby."

"Yes, sir."

"So, word has it you got you a filly shacked up in the main house with you," Hinson said and spat.

"That so?"

"That's what I hear."

Caleb walked past him, forcing the man to turn and follow.

"So, who's this gal anyway?" Hinson puffed, struggling to keep up. "Your daddy know 'bout this, boy?"

The urge to turn and drive a fist in the old man's face was strong but Caleb just gritted his teeth and kept moving. He saw Bobby leading the mare toward Hinson's trailer. Conn was with them, and he could tell from the way Bobby cut a pleading look his way and the way Conn's mouth was moving, that she wasn't happy about what was happening.

Just then Hannah hurried up to him. "Caleb, there's some people at the house. Government folks. They want to talk to you."

Caleb felt acid bubble in his gut. Acid caused by fear. It could mean only one thing. They were here about Conn.

"Tell them I'll be there in a few minutes," he said and watched her hurry away.

He reached the truck a few steps ahead of Bobby and Conn. Hinson's man, Joe Stilwell, got out of the truck as Bobby stopped in front of it. "I'll take it from here."

Bobby looked at Caleb and at his nod, handed the lead to Stilwell.

"Wait!" Conn hurried over to Stilwell as he started to tug the horse toward the trailer.

"Who the hell are you?" he snarled.

"I just want to say goodbye," Conn said softly.

Stilwell snorted and gave the rope a viscous tug. The mare balked and started backing up, prancing nervously. That made Stilwell angrier and he tugged harder, cursing and yelling at the mare.

"Stop!" Conn shouted. "You're scaring her."

"Shut the fuck up!" He tried harder, succeeding only in making the mare rear up, pawing and whinnying in fear.

"Caleb, make him stop!" Conn screamed.

"Conn, honey." Caleb made a grab for her arm but she evaded and dodged around the mare to Stilwell.

"Stop that!"

"Lady, get the fuck away from me or I'm gonna put you on your ass!" he shouted, then yelled at the horse who reared and pawed, her whinnies sounding more like anger than fear.

Things were getting out of hand. Caleb started toward them to try to settle things down and suddenly things got a whole lot worse. Hinson Daws, who no one had been paying attention to, walked up behind the mare with a prod and proceeded to shock her.

"Get the nag in the damn trailer!" he shouted at Stilwell.

Caleb felt his blood pressure rise. Shocking or beating a horse was not something allowed on the Circle R. And the idea of selling a horse to a man who would do such a thing made him see red.

But apparently not as fast as it did Conn because before Caleb could make a move, she'd screamed in anger, run over to Hinson Daws and knocked the old man flat on his ass with a solid roundhouse.

If that wasn't enough, she'd snatched the prod from his hand and she jammed it against his ass when he rolled over and tried to push himself up.

"You are not taking this horse!" she shouted.

Caleb made a grab for her but she dodged him. He grabbed hold of Daws to drag the lard-ass to his feet. And when he did, Conn turned on Daws' man.

"You're not taking that horse anywhere. Let go of that rope right now!"

"Fuck you!" Stilwell snapped and took a swing at her.

Caleb turned just in time to see Stilwell throw a punch. He let go of Daws who hit the ground again with a loud grunt, and a split second later Bobby exclaimed, "Holy shit!"

That about summed it up. Daws was on the ground wheezing and Conn had his ranch hand Stilwell by the throat, lifted up off the ground, his legs kicking weakly, his face pasty and his eyes quickly rolling back in his head.

If that wasn't enough, half the ranch had responded to the commotion and was watching. All in dead silence.

"Conn!" Caleb grabbed her free arm but she didn't budge an inch. It was like she was made of lead, immovable and mad as hell. Lights danced in her eyes.

"You will *not* harm this horse," she hissed at Stilwell who was kicking weaker with each passing second.

"For Christ sakes, Conn, you're killing him!" Caleb shouted and yanked her arm hard.

Her head whipped around and for a moment the force of her anger was turned on him. He actually staggered back a step, feeling a sudden loss of air in his lungs.

"Conn," he gasped. "Stop."

She blinked and gasped. "Caleb!" She released Stilwell who landed in a heap on the ground and threw herself at Caleb, wrapping her arms around him as if to hold him up.

"It's okay." He pried her off. "I'm okay. But we've got a mess on our hands, honey, and you'd better skidaddle 'cause sure as shit old Daws is going to be raising hell in about five seconds or so."

"No, this is my fault. I won't let him take it out on you."

"Conn, go," he ordered and when she stiffened, added, "we can't afford to have him call the law."

She didn't say a word but turned and marched to the front of the truck where she stopped, crossing her arms over her chest, her eyes flashing fire. Caleb saw everyone watch her. Saw the shock on everyone's faces. And knew that nothing was going to be easy from this point on.

Bobby and another ranch hand got Daws to his feet. Caleb checked on Stilwell. He was coming to. Mad as hell but not hurt.

"Boy, you just bit yourself off a world of hurt," Daws wheezed. "You think for one red-hot second that you're gonna get away with letting some two-bit slut attack me with a cattle prod then you got yourself another think coming."

"Mr. Daws, now settle down. This was all just a misunder—"

"Don't you take that tone with me, boy. That little tramp attacked me and I'm gonna see her locked up. Best thing you can do is say 'yes, sir' and tie that bitch up 'til the sheriff gets here. Stilwell! Get the goddamn sheriff on the phone!"

Stilwell coughed, wheezed, climbed to his feet and stumbled to the truck.

"Mr. Daws, there's no need to call the sheriff." Caleb tried to be calm even though his heart was racing. "I'm sure Conn just overreacted. She's grown fond of the mare and—"

"Boy, one more word outta your mouth 'cept 'yes, sir' and I'll come down on the Circle R so hard, when I'm done with you, Charlie Russell won't have a fucking ranch to come home to! Stilwell! You got the damn law on the phone?"

"I don't think that will be necessary," a smooth male voice announced from behind Caleb.

Caleb whirled to face the tall, dark-haired man in the black suit and dark sunglasses. Beside him stood a stunning woman with platinum hair worn in a tight bun, equally dark suit and dark glasses.

"And you'd be?" Caleb asked.

The man reached inside his jacket and produced his identification. "Marcus London, NSA. We must speak. Now."

Caleb gestured around. "Well, as you can see I kind of have a little situation on my hands at the moment."

The man stepped close to Caleb, lowering his voice so that no one else could hear his words. "Not of the earth, Mr. Russell. Does that ring a bell?"

Caleb's heart sank. Much as he wanted to, he couldn't think of anything that was going to save Conn now. "Conn, honey?" He turned and held out his hand to her. "We need to go inside and have a talk with these nice folks."

She didn't seem to hear him. Her eyes were wide and her face pale. She was staring at the newcomers with an expression he couldn't begin to identify.

"Conn!" he barked and she started.

"Honey, go on up to the house and wait for me. Please?"

Without a word she turned and walked away.

Which did not please Hinson Daws at all. "Whoa there, boy. That bitch ain't going nowhere. She attacked me and I'm gonna see her—"

"You are going to do nothing," London said, advancing on Daws. "Aside from getting in your vehicle and leaving. This is a matter of national security and should it be discovered that you have discussed or revealed anything that happened here today, the consequences could be quite severe. Do we understand, sir?"

Daws swallowed nervously and nodded.

"Then I suggest you leave immediately, sir."

Daws gestured to his man and both of them got in the truck. Caleb watched them pull off then looked around at his people. "Y'all go on back to work. Bobby, take the mare back to the stables. Everything'll be fine."

"What's this all about, Caleb?" Bobby asked.

"Go on back to work, Bobby," Caleb said. "It'll be okay."

Bobby nodded but didn't look convinced. Caleb turned to face the pair in the dark suits. "So what now?"

"Now you invite us in and we have a discussion," London replied.

Caleb saw no way to refuse. "Fine, come on in."

In the history of bad days, this one was chalking up to be a real prize winner.

* * * * *

Caleb didn't bother with manners. He entered the house, leaving the agents to follow him inside. Conn was waiting in the front room, standing in front of the window, watching. Hannah was lurking in the hall.

"Hannah, why don't you call it a day." Caleb tried to put as much calm and assurance as possible into his voice.

"I don't mind staying."

"That's okay. Everything is fine."

"If you say so."

Caleb watched her turn and head back toward the kitchen. He went over to Conn, draping his arm around her waist and pulling her close to his side. He waited until he heard the back door close before speaking. "Honey, these people are with the NSA and they—"

She completely ignored him. "Who are you?" she asked the couple in a low menacing tone.

"Honey, I told you," Caleb said. "They're with—"

"No, they're not," she cut him off. "These people are..." She looked up at him. "Caleb, they're like me."

It wouldn't have surprised him any more if a bomb had gone off under his feet when the woman stepped forward and said, "You're right."

"What?" Caleb hugged Conn closer. "You're telling me you're not with the NSA? Then who the hell are you and what do you want with Conn?"

The woman gestured gracefully toward the seating arrangement. "Might we sit?"

"Have at it," Caleb growled, keeping his position.

The couple took a seat on the sofa and the woman removed her glasses. Her eyes were the same strange violet color as Conn's. She smiled at Conn. "You have long sought answers, Raenea, and I am here to answer them. Please sit."

"Why do you call me Raenea?"

"That is your name, my dear. Raenea Belenus, daughter of Constantine Belenus of the D'Harahn, Heir Apparent to the Throne of Shadallah, the crown prince of V'Kar."

"Say what?" Caleb asked.

The woman cut him a smile. "Perhaps it would be best if we spoke with Raenea in private."

"No," Conn said. "Anything you have to say to me you can say in front of Caleb. He's my…mate."

The man who'd introduced himself as Marcus London, removed his glasses. Like Conn he also had violet eyes.

"What makes you apply that term to this human?"

Conn stared at him for a moment. "It's applicable."

The couple exchanged a glance and the woman spoke up. "Very well. We will speak. However, Mr. Russell, do not doubt that should you think to reveal any part of what is said here today, you will not live to speak of it again."

"Don't you threaten him," Conn hissed, eyes flashing with light. "You hear me? I want answers and if you've answers for me then speak them. But never threaten Caleb again. Do you understand?"

"She is much like him," the woman remarked to the man.

Conn went weak against Caleb, but only for a moment. Then she moved away from him to cross the room and stand in front of the man. "Like him? You know my father? Who are you?"

The man stood. "I am Azarth, Minister of Science, and I have served your father for longer than humans have walked upright on this world."

Caleb felt his own knees go a little weak and decided it was a good time to have a seat. He took a chair by the window.

Conn stared at the man for a long time, reaching out with her mind to probe his thoughts. And met a wall too thick to breach.

"You will find it far more difficult to infiltrate the thoughts of your own kind than that of humans, Raenea," Azarth said with a smile and sank back down on the couch.

"You could tell?" That was a shock. No one had ever felt her invade their mind before.

"There is much for you to learn," the woman replied, earning Conn's attention.

"Such as your name," Conn said.

"You may call me Pandora."

"And what role do you serve, Pandora?"

Pandora smiled. "Let's just say that in the system of V'Kar, a female may rise to positions of great power."

Conn heard the deception in the tone. "In other words, you are not going to be honest."

"My words are true."

"Your words are evasive," Conn said, falling back on her normal speech patterns and accent. "If I cannot trust you to be truthful about your identity and position then what is there to inspire me to trust any other words you might speak as truth?"

Azarth chuckled, earning an annoyed glance from Pandora. "She has a valid point," Azarth commented.

"Indeed," Pandora said. "Very well. I am SyFeth, of the Sybelle De'Fane V'Kar. In the language of these people, Mother Superior of the Sisterhood of V'Kar."

Conn looked to Azarth for confirmation and he nodded. "The Sisterhood is the most powerful and feared organization in this galaxy or our own. As Mother Superior and the oldest of the V'Kar, Sy—pardon, Pandora wields enormous power and holds information—and secrets—not even the ruling body of V'Kar, the J'Zhan or the Emperor is made privy to. She is, in effect, the most powerful woman in the known population of the Universe."

"Lofty," Conn murmured, "but illogical. If indeed you wield such tremendous power then why not dispatch an underling to do your bidding? Why come to me yourself, in the guise of a human? And why be here on this world if the galaxy you rule is so powerful and vast?"

"Excellent questions and questions worthy of a daughter of the throne," Azarth commended.

Pandora regarded her in silence for a long while then smiled. "In time perhaps you will become privy to certain knowledge, Raenea Belenus. But for now my concern is simple. To erase all knowledge of your existence from human minds and records and ensure that you are not harmed or terminated."

"Why?" Conn asked. "Why would someone of such power be concerned with a single life? With my life? Of what benefit am I to you or your worlds?"

Pandora sighed lightly. "I can see that dealing with you will be equally as vexing as dealing with your father. Very well. The simple truth is, the worlds of V'Kar have lost the ability to reproduce. Since before humans crawled from the primordial soup of this world, our worlds have suffered infertility."

"Then how is it that your worlds survive? Unless, of course, you're immortal."

"Close," Azarth replied, and at the sharp look from Pandora, chuckled. "Oh, come now. It is no secret. In human terms we are virtual immortals. And in answer to your next question, Raenea, our system suffered a cosmic cataclysm that poisoned our peoples, rendering them infertile. Yet here on this small green world we may have found a key to ending that sterility."

"And I factor into this how?"

"You are the child of the Heir Apparent, a D'Harahn, the most pure bloodline of all V'Kar, and a mutant. A woman fathered by a D'Harahn and a human witch. Amazingly your mother's genetic makeup is more than ninety percent D'Harahn and you, Raenea, are the first child ever to have been born of a mixed union who has not only survived, but possess nearly complete D'Harahn genetics."

"I'm a test result," Conn whispered, then her voice grew stronger. "Then where are my parents and why don't I remember them?"

Azarth sighed. "When you were the human equivalent of ten years old, your existence was discovered. It sparked much internal turmoil between the various factions of V'Kar on this world, bringing us to the brink of war. It was decided that in the best interest of all, you should be hidden.

"An accident was staged and from all reports your parents were gravely injured and a report was issued that your father was recalled to the home world to sit at the left hand of his father, the Emperor. The reports stated that despite her half-breed status, your mother accompanied him. You were reported dead."

Pandora picked up the tale. "I arranged for a suitable guardian and mentor and erased all knowledge of your parents from your mind. It was the only way to protect you."

"Hold on," Caleb spoke up.

Conn turned to look at him as he stood and walked over beside her. "I've been listening to all this and yes, it all sounds like science fiction to me, but knowing what Conn can do, I can't entirely discount the possibility that maybe you people are from another galaxy. So for the sake of argument, let's say that everything you've said is true."

"Very well," Pandora agreed.

"Okay, so it still boils down to a load of shit," Caleb announced. "If Conn is who you say and what you say then why would any of your people want to harm her? She could hold the key to your sterility problems. I'd think every single one of you would want to protect and safeguard her. So, I'm betting there's more to this tale than you've said. Just who is it that she needs to be protected from?"

"An intelligent man," Azarth said and smiled at Conn. "And correct. While our peoples might be willing to go to war to discover the secrets hidden within your genetics, none would raise a hand to harm you. But there are those who would."

"Who?" Caleb asked.

"The Alliance," Pandora hissed the words. "An organization founded when man worshipped at the feet of the Pharaohs, dedicated to the eradication of our race."

"The Alliance," Conn whispered, feeling a cold shiver slide down her spine. "Why do those words inspire fear inside me? Have I ever encountered them?"

"It was you they were trying to kill in Mexico when Shen was murdered," Pandora answered.

"Why do they want to kill me?"

Azarth and Pandora shared a look. Pandora turned her head, looking to one side while Azarth answered. "Because they believe our people to be something of myth and legend. They covet our abilities, and because they cannot discover a way to harness these abilities for themselves, they fear us. And what man fears, he tries to destroy."

"Something of myth and legend?" she asked, then looked quickly at Caleb. "Vampires!"

"Yes," Azarth confirmed her guess.

"Well are we?" Conn asked.

"Hardly," Azarth scoffed then added, "however, there are certain proteins in human plasma that are very fortifying for our kind."

Conn shivered. "What are you saying?"

"Simply that if injured or wounded, human blood has a healing effect that is almost instantaneous."

Conn thought about it. "Well that could apply to anyone on this planet. If a human is injured and suffers blood loss they require transfusions."

"We take it in another fashion."

"No. Oh no," Conn groaned. "We are vampires!" She looked at Caleb. "I told you. I saw the marks on your neck. Oh merciful heavens, I bit you!"

A laugh from Azarth had her turning on him. "You think that's funny? Well I don't. No one should have that done to them against their will. And I wasn't injured or wounded or sick. I was…"

"Yes?" Azarth asked.

Conn couldn't bring herself to tell him what inspired the act. It was too personal.

"It is also an act of mating," Pandora spoke up. "An act that binds us to another."

"Mating?" Caleb asked. "How does something like that act as binding?"

"When a V'Kar takes the blood of another, he or she takes a part of that person's essence, if you will. And, in turn, imparts something of their own essence to the other. In other words, Mr. Russell, should you have a genetic test performed it would be discovered that you carry alien DNA."

"What?"

"You and Raenea have mated, in the most primitive and binding way possible for one of V'Kar."

Suddenly memories that had been long suppressed resurfaced. Conn staggered, nearly overwhelmed. Memories flooded in, or at least fragments. Her parents, her childhood and the knowledge of her kind and their enemies, the Alliance.

"Oh, Caleb," Conn whispered. "I'm so sorry. I didn't know."

He pulled her close to his side. "No worries, honey. I can't think of anyone I'd rather be bound to." He looked at Pandora and Azarth. "But this business about the Alliance concerns me. Is there any chance they could find her?"

"They already have," Azarth said in a deadly serious tone and bounded to his feet. "Take her and flee. You must protect her at all costs. Go. Now."

"Hold on!" Caleb protested then jumped when the front door crashed open.

"Go!" Azarth shouted and flew into action.

Caleb had never seen anything move as fast as Azarth and Pandora. Men poured into the house, bearing swords and crossbows and daggers. And met with whirling disturbances in the air that sent them flying.

Conn yanked on his arm, nearly causing him to fall, she pulled so hard. Together they raced through the house and out the back door, headed for the stables. What met Caleb's eyes nearly doubled him over. His people were scattered on the ground like lifeless dolls.

He had to stop. Bobby was lying near the barn door. Caleb felt for a pulse. "He's alive."

"They didn't want to kill them, just render them unconscious so they would be unaware of what transpired," Conn said.

"What?" he yelped.

"Azarth told me. With his mind. Now the question is, do we stay and fight or run?"

"Run," Caleb said and jumped to his feet, racing into the barn. Conn flew into high gear, moving as fast as she could, which turned out to be rather swift because in a matter of seconds, she had two horses saddled.

"Hell, you can probably outrun them without a horse," Caleb commented as he mounted.

"Caleb, are we doing the right thing?" she asked, suddenly unsure. "What if those people kill Pandora and Azarth? What if they do something to the people here to try to find out where we've gone?"

She stepped back from the horse. "No, we can't leave. We have to stay and fight."

Caleb came down off his horse and grabbed her. "Listen to me. You heard him. You agreed. We have to go. I have to protect you. I can't let them get you, Conn. I can't."

"It's a little late for that, cowboy," came a deep voice from the door.

Caleb turned to see a tall, muscular man with a crossbow aimed at Conn. He stepped in front of Conn. "Get off my land."

The man laughed. "That only works in the movies, cowboy. Now step aside. Or not. Doesn't matter much to me."

"You'll have to get through me and I won't make it easy," Caleb warned.

"No!" Conn shouted from behind him.

Caleb felt her move but never saw her. Apparently neither did the man with the bow because one minute he was aiming at them and the next he was flat on his ass and Conn held the bow in one hand and the arrow in the other, with the point of the arrow pressed against the center of the man's chest.

"Leave this place now and do not return if you value your life," she growled.

"Go ahead, kill me," the man laughed. "There's thousands more. And we'll never stop coming until you're dead, vampire bitch."

Conn knew that to be true. As unbelievable as it was and as heartbreaking, there was no way she could stay with Caleb. The Alliance would not rest until they saw her dead.

Or believed her dead, she realized. Tossing the arrow aside, she knelt down beside the man, gripping his head in both hands. It was the most horrible act she'd ever committed and it sickened her, but she forced her way into his mind, projecting the images she wanted to plant firmly and permanently.

He screamed and thrashed, but her strength was greater than his, fueled by the need to protect Caleb and their chance at love.

When at last the man's eyes rolled back and he went limp, she rose and turned to face Caleb.

"My god, Conn, what've you done?"

"Made him believe that I'm dead. Caleb, we have to go to the house. We have to neutralize all of the attackers."

"What?"

"It's the only way. Please."

"Conn, this is way out of control."

"I know, but unless they believe me dead they'll never leave you in peace. Please, we have to ensure that no one here is in further danger from them."

Caleb hesitated for a moment then nodded. She grabbed the unconscious man by the back of his jacket and started dragging him as she started for the house. Conn felt a growing sickness inside her. The Alliance may not have succeeding in killing her, but they might have effectively killed her chance at a life with Caleb.

Chapter Eight

ꟗ

The scene inside the house was something from a nightmare. That was the only way Caleb could describe it. Azarth and Pandora stood in the midst of the carnage. Bodies were lying strewn and broken. There was no blood which shocked him. But there was the unmistakable smell of death. Everywhere. His stomach recoiled and he had to step back outside to catch his breath.

Conn left the unconscious man just inside the doorway, making Caleb have to step over his body to go outside. She remained inside with Pandora and Azarth. When he reentered the house a few minutes later they all stopped talking and looked at him.

"They agree," Conn said. "With their help we can make him," she said and pointed at the unconscious man, "believe that after he was overcome, others came to his aid and killed me. He alone escaped."

"So you think he's just going to wake up and leave this?" Caleb gestured around them at the bodies. "You don't think he'll call for help?"

"He will not awaken here," Pandora said. "We will move him to another location."

"And what about this?" Caleb gestured around again. "If they were dispatched here then what makes you think they'll believe they found nothing and then got lucky and found her somewhere else?"

"They will believe what we want them to believe," Pandora said and smiled at the disbelief on Caleb's face. "Trust me, human. We've been doing this since before your kind—"

"Crawled out of the primordial soup," Caleb interrupted. "Yeah, I know. Still, there's a lot of dead bodies here."

"We have people en route now," Azarth replied. "Within hours it will be as it was before the Alliance attack."

"As it was?" Caleb shouted. "As it was? Are you fucking insane? A dozen people died here and you think anything can ever be as it was?"

Conn heard more than his words. She heard his heart. And hers came close to shattering into a million small pieces. He was right. Nothing would ever be as it was. Caleb would never forget the deaths that occurred here. He would never forget seeing her forcing her way into that man's mind to break him and impose her will on him. He would never see her in the same light again. From this moment on when he looked at her he would see only an alien who brought death and destruction with her.

"You're right," she agreed. "But we have to make it appear so for the others who live and work here. They cannot suspect anything more than what they saw. Government agents arrived and took me into custody."

"They're not government agents. They're fucking—"

Conn fought back the tears that threatened. "Go on, say it. They're aliens. Some kind of freaks or vampires."

"That's not what I was going to say."

"Yes, Caleb. It is."

She sensed the presence of others and looked in the direction of the door. A moment later people began to file into the house. Silently they started gathering up the bodies. Caleb watched them with a look of distaste on his face that hurt her to see.

She turned her back on him. "Can you make sure that everyone on this ranch remembers me being taken into custody and nothing else??"

"Yes," Azarth replied.

"Then please do so," she said quietly. "I would like a few moments alone with Caleb."

Azarth and Pandora left and she turned to face Caleb. "Could we take a walk, please?"

"Gladly," he said without hesitation, but did not take the hand she offered. She walked through the house and out the back door, stopping beneath the shade of the ancient oak.

"I am so sorry, Caleb," she said when he stopped beside her. "I've brought death into your home and I can never undo that."

"It wasn't your fault," he said in a tone she read as grudging, and knew from the connection she had with him, aptly described what he was feeling. She had no doubt that he cared for her. Deeply. But at the moment he also resented her. It was because of her that all of this had happened and it was human nature to seek something to be angry about when horrible things happened beyond a person's ability to control.

Intellectually, she understood. Emotionally, she was devastated. She'd hoped the bond was stronger between them. Apparently she was wrong.

"It is because I am here that this happened. I must leave, Caleb."

Her words struck a chord inside him he didn't want played. Right now he needed to be mad, to let anger consume him so he didn't have to feel that sickness that was curled in his belly, wanting to expand and take him over completely.

But the thought of her leaving was like acid washing through him, bitter and sharp. "No." He shook his head, wanting to take her into his arms but unable to escape the image of her in the barn and the feral light that danced in her eyes as she tortured that man into submitting to the dictates of her mind.

"I love you, Conn. I do. It's just that right now…"

"I know," she whispered. "And I love you, Caleb. Too much to stay. You look at me and see some monster, a creature that brings death and torment and pain. You see me bending another to my will even when it causes excruciating pain. And that image will, in time, wash away all feelings of love you have for me, leaving only revulsion and anger, which will evolve into hate. And I cannot bear for you to hate me. I will leave with the others, as soon as the repairs to your home have been completed."

"Conn, no." He took a step toward her but stopped short.

She looked up into his eyes and saw his pain. She felt it as if it was her own. And she knew she could not let him live with it. Steeling herself against her own pain, she stepped up to him.

"I love you, Caleb. I always will. But I will not destroy you."

He flinched when she reached up and stroked the side of his face, then closed his eyes and tried to relax. She felt his struggle and she wanted to scream against the unfairness of it, shove it from her mind and pretend that none of the ugliness had happened. But there was to be no forgetting for her.

Caleb, on the other hand, did not have to remember. He must have sensed her intent because his eyes flew open and his hand clamped on hers, trying to pull it back from his face.

But Conn was stronger. She knew that now. And she'd rather force this on him than have him live with bitterness.

"Forget," she whispered, pushing a tendril of energy into his mind.

"Don't," he gasped. "Conn…don't."

"I'm sorry," she sobbed and pressed deeper. "I love you, Caleb."

His mouth opened in a silent howl as she pushed past his defenses. Within moments it was done. When his body went slack, she caught him, and propped him gently against the trunk of the old oak.

In sleep his face was relaxed and peaceful. She knelt down and kissed him, lingering so that in the long years to come she could remember the feel of him, the smell and taste of him.

"It is time," Azarth said from behind her.

Conn rose, swiped at the tears on her face and turned. "When he wakes he will believe that I have been taken into the custody of the NSA."

"That is acceptable," Azarth said. "Should he try to pursue you, he will meet only at dead ends, for even if that particular agency did have you, they would never admit to it. You are, for all practical purposes, dead to him."

That stabbed her in a way that made her breath hitch and suddenly it was all too horribly real. She'd mated with Caleb. Shared her spirit with him and she was bound to him for the duration of her life. And she would never be with him. Never have love in her life. From this day on, she would be alone.

"You are not alone, Raenea," Azarth said, putting his hand on her shoulder. "We will place you with those of our own who will protect you and be your companions. They will teach you all you've forgotten of our people and you can live a full and productive life."

"But a life without love."

Azarth made no comment. She didn't expect him to. They both knew she was right.

* * * * *

Something hard was poking him in the back, messing up the spicy dream. He and Conn were at the lake, making love in the water. Damn, what the hell was that? He rolled over and started to bunch his pillow up under this face. All he got was a face full of grass. Which had his eyes flying open.

"Oh shit!" He pushed himself up and ran for the house. How had he gotten out there? The last thing he remembered was being in the front room with Conn and those NSA agents.

He came to a sudden stop as the thought registered in his mind. They took her! How the hell had he gone to sleep? They'd taken Conn and there wasn't a damn thing he could do to stop them. So how in Sam's Hill had he fallen asleep? Much less gotten outside?

He didn't have any answers and at the moment that wasn't nearly as important as finding Conn. There had to be some way to find out where they'd taken her. He ran inside and snatched up the phone.

His father answered on the second ring. "Somebody better be dying."

Caleb hadn't stopped to consider the time. It was just a few minutes past four in the morning.

"Sorry, Dad. I need help."

"You hurt?"

"They took Conn."

"Yeah, I heard from Hinson an hour after he left the ranch. That little gal caused quite a mess, Caleb. And if the NSA has her, there's no way we're getting her back. I don't want to be hard on you, boy, 'cause I know you're hurtin', but the sooner you write her off the better."

"I just want to know where she is."

"And you ain't gonna get that, Caleb. You know what it means when the NSA takes someone into custody? It means they own her until they're convinced she's not a security threat to this country. And they don't arrest people who are just ordinary law-abiding folks, son. If they have her they probably have a good reason. Now I'm gonna hang up and I suggest you go back to bed or get your ass in gear and tend to what you can tend to, like the Circle R. G'night."

The distinctive click of Charlie hanging up had Caleb slamming down the phone and kicking the refrigerator hard enough to leave a sizeable dent. There had to be something he could do to figure out where Conn had been taken.

An idea came to him. He grabbed his keys and headed out.

* * * * *

Chase's house was dark when Caleb pulled up in front. But a light went on before he reached the front porch. The door opened to reveal Ana, sleepy eyed and wrapped in one of Chase's old shirts. The legs of what appeared to be a pair of men's boxer shorts peeked from between the held together folds of the shirt.

"Sorry," Caleb said as she pushed the screen open for him.

"What's happened?"

He followed her into the kitchen and took a seat at the table as she started preparing a pot of coffee. "The NSA showed up and took Conn."

"What?" Coffee grains spilled onto the countertop as she whirled to look at him. "When? What happened?"

"What the devil's going on in here?" Chase bellowed from the hallway. A few moments later he walked into the kitchen, his jeans unbuttoned and his feet bare. "What the hell's going on?" he asked.

"The NSA took Conn," Ana said and turned her attention back to the coffee.

Chase blew out his breath, slung his hair back over his shoulders and took a seat across from Caleb. "Let's have it."

"It was a day out of hell. Hinson showed up to pick up a horse Dad insisted I sell him. It was a mare Conn had gotten attached to. It balked and Hinson shocked it. Conn went at him and kicked his ass."

Chase barked a laugh and Ana snickered. Caleb would have laughed, but all the humor had been sucked out of him. "Hinson was hollering about calling the law and out of the blue these two agents showed up. London and…something.

The woman never gave her name. Anyway, they blew Hinson off with some bull about national security and him keeping his mouth shut or else, then they went inside with Conn and me.

"And announced they were taking her into custody. That she was a fugitive from justice and a threat to the security of this country."

Caleb propped his elbows on the table, covering his face with his hands for a moment. "There wasn't anything I could do. I just stood there, Chase. Stood there and watched them take her away."

Chase reached across the table and put his hand over Caleb's. "You both knew there was a chance it could happen. Question is, how did they know where to find her?"

Caleb hadn't considered that. "Damn if I know. But I gotta find her."

"Sorry, bro, got no influence with the government."

"I was thinking maybe Ana could help."

"Ana?"

Caleb looked at Ana who had turned and was leaning against the counter, watching him. "Maybe you can hypnotize me or something and I'll remember something one of them said that will give me a clue where they've taken her."

Ana crossed the room and took a seat beside him, placing her hand on his arm to give it an affectionate squeeze. "Honey, that's a long-shot at best, but I'll try."

"Then do it."

Ana glanced at Chase. After a moment he nodded.

"Chase, would you get me that big candle from on top of the fridge?" Ana asked as she got up and went to the pantry. She returned with an incense burner and a box of long fireplace matches.

After pouring a sprinkle of powdered incense into the metal burner, she lit it. It sparked then billowed, filling the room with a sweet yet spicy smell.

"What you want me to do with the candle?" Chase asked.

"Light it and set it on the hutch behind Caleb, then turn off the lights."

In a minute they were all sitting at the table with the light from the single candle casting dancing shadows around them.

"Caleb, I'm going to strike this match. I want you to watch it burn."

He nodded and she struck the match. It flamed to life and she held it in front of him. "Watch the flame. See it consume the wood. The shorter the match gets, the more relaxed you feel. You're feeling a little sleepy and that's okay. Just keep your eye on the flame. When the flame dies you can close your eyes and sleep. You're perfectly safe and relaxed. Just watch the flame."

Caleb was feeling a little sleepy, which was odd. He'd never been more wide awake in his life. He guessed panic did that to a person, and sure as shit smelled, he was feeling more than a little panic.

He didn't see the flame die. He didn't even remember closing his eyes. But he knew they were closed. He just didn't feel the need to open them.

Ana's voice was soft and soothing. She led him through the day. Funny, but he could remember it all so clearly now. Especially the look in Conn's eyes when Hinson shocked that mare. And the way she screamed his name, looking to him to make it right and save the horse.

It made his chest hurt, like something had ballooned inside it and needed to escape. He didn't realize what that something was until he felt wetness on his face. Was he crying?

He must have been because Ana said it was okay. He just needed to remember the NSA agents and what they said before they left with Conn.

Suddenly things weren't so clear anymore. He couldn't remember exactly what they said. He couldn't even remember

Conn saying anything. And why didn't he remember seeing the car drive off? Surely he didn't just stand there and let them take her without watching her leave?

Confusion set in and with it the relaxation of a few moments ago fled. He opened his eyes. "It doesn't make any sense."

"Chase honey, turn on the lights," Ana said softly.

"Why can't I remember?" Caleb asked.

Ana regarded him in silence for a moment, gnawing absently on her bottom lip. "Maybe that's not what really happened."

"What?" Caleb's voice was joined by Chase's at almost the same moment.

Ana leaned back in her chair, arranging her arm so that she supported her right elbow in her left hand. Her right hand cupped her chin and her index finger tapped at her lips.

Caleb waited. And waited. Finally he couldn't take it. "Well?"

The lip tapping stopped. "I wasn't going to say anything because...well, because I wasn't sure. But tonight, after we went to bed, I had a strong flash. It was Conn. She was in...the mountains. But not here. It was different. She wasn't locked up. There were people with her. People who had eyes the same color she does. But she was sad and crying."

"They had eyes the same color! Those NSA people. But what does that mean?"

"Probably that they're not with the NSA," Ana said. "In my vision I got the sense that the people she's with are like her."

"But why would her own people take her away?"

"To protect her," Chase said, earning Caleb's attention. "Think about it, little brother. Conn's on the run. The military isn't convinced she's dead and it's only a matter of time before they get a lead that brings them straight to the Circle R. Now, let's suppose it was us. If I knew you were in danger, I'd snatch you out from under the military's nose."

"Especially if you weren't human," Ana added.

"There's no proof that she's..." Caleb couldn't bring himself to say it. Didn't want to believe it. Conn couldn't be an alien.

"Caleb honey, you have to be realistic," Ana said soothingly. "The things Conn can do? That's beyond anything I or any other witch I know can master. And she does it without effort. I think she just may be from another world. And if she is and her people have found her, chances are you won't find her. No matter how long you look."

It was the last thing Caleb wanted to hear. "No, you're wrong," he barked and shoved his chair back as he stood. "I am going to find her."

"Caleb!" Ana started after him as headed for the door, but Chase put his hand on her arm and stopped her.

"Let him go, Fancy. This is something he has to work out on his own."

Caleb stopped at the door and looked back. "You're right. And I will. I'll find her."

Chase nodded. "Walk well, little brother."

Caleb nodded and hurried from the house. He had no clue how he was going to find Conn, but one thing was for sure. He wasn't going to stop looking until he did.

* * * * *

"Enough, please!" Conn exclaimed and jumped up from where she sat in the luxurious study of the villa to rush out onto the balcony.

She'd listened for days on end to the tales of the V'Kar worlds. She'd read the histories, seen the marvelous holographic images showing historical events, listened to endless recollections from everyone at the villa and through it all, her mind could not help wandering to a ranch in Arizona where the man she loved suffered.

Had anyone told her that mating would forge a connection so strong that even separated by thousands of miles she'd feel his pain, she would have become a recluse and hidden away from the world. For surely it was better never to have known love than to give yourself so completely that you went through life feeling the pain and anguish your mate suffered.

Pandora and Azarth had tried counseling her. Azarth had assured her that in time Caleb's anguish would ease. He would forget her and go on to love another. And, he reminded her, she needed to learn to answer to her true name and forget the name Caleb had given on her.

She didn't believe him. Nothing was working the way they'd promised. Not only was Caleb furious and worried, he was determined to find her. And he no longer believed that she'd been taken into custody of government agents. She felt his resolve and frustration. Just like she felt bits and snippets of his memory returning.

Azarth was adamant that it was impossible. No human could counter the control imposed by a V'Kar. Caleb would never remember what really happened. Conn disagreed. She could feel it happening.

And she didn't want to be Raenea of V'Kar, daughter of the Heir Apparent. She wanted to be Conn Hoffman, veterinarian assistant and Caleb Russell's lover.

Azarth stepped out onto the balcony behind her. "We should step up your training. There are techniques for controlling rampant and unwanted emotions I can teach you that—"

"I don't want to control my emotions!" She turned on him with rage flaming hot and bright. "Don't you get it? I don't want to forget him. I don't want to be some…some princess or tool or key or potential savior. I want to be Connery Hoffman. I want to be with Caleb!"

"That isn't possible, my dear."

"Oh but it is." Not until she'd uttered the words did she realize it was far more than a protest or argument. It was a statement of intent.

"I'm leaving. You can either help me get back to Arizona or I'll find my own way. But one way or other, I'm going back." She could not voice her fears. That despite her need to be with Caleb, there was still the possibility that he might see her as a freak, something to be feared and loathed. Regardless, she had to go to him. If he sent her away then she'd have to find a way to accept it and exist without him.

"That would be ill-advised. Your safety would be compromised should you return and we cannot guarantee—"

"I'm not asking for your guarantee or your advice. I'm sorry, but this isn't a negotiation. I'm going. The only question is will you provide me transportation?"

"Raenea, we've been over this before. The same danger awaits you if you return that existed before you left. The Alliance will have eyes on the Russell abode, and at the first sign of your return—"

"I know the danger. It doesn't matter. He's my mate. I can't forget him no matter what techniques you teach me. You said it yourself. When the people of V'Kar mate it is an irrevocable bond that can't be broken. Well, I've bonded. No, it wasn't with someone from V'Kar. It was with a human. But there's human blood in me if what you say about my mother is true. And even if there wasn't the result would be the same. He's my mate. It's done and it can't be undone."

When Azarth turned and placed his hands on the railing, dropping his head with a heavy sigh, she moved beside him and put her hand on his arm. "I appreciate your position. I do. And I appreciate all you've taught me and all you offer. But in matters of the heart, I don't have a choice, Azarth. Mine has been given and if he'll have me after what I did, I'll stay with him. If they come for me…well, we'll cross that bridge when and if it's necessary."

Azarth studied her for a long time, searching her eyes. She met his without hesitation, letting him inside her mind when he probed. She wanted him to see her determination, as well as the depth of her emotion. One of the lessons he'd stressed was the passion and devotion of the V'Karian heart. Well, here was a prime example for him. Her heart belonged to Caleb and she'd rather live one day with him than ten thousand years without him.

At length Azarth sighed and broke both mental and eye contact. He looked out over the scenery. "You are much like your father. He would have given up the throne rather than give up your mother."

"Thank you for telling me that. It's the nicest thing anyone has told me about him."

He turned and smiled at her. "If you insist upon returning, at least let me assign a detachment to you. Bodyguards."

"No."

"My dear, whether you want protection or not, I cannot simply leave you unguarded. The Alliance is still a great threat."

"No. I don't want any of…any V'Kar on the ranch."

Azarth smiled. "Very well. But help will be close in the event it is needed."

Conn returned the smile. "Fine. Give me a phone number and I'll use if it I need to. But nothing more. Deal?" She stuck out her hand.

Azarth chuckled. "You've become quite adept at that accent, and the mannerisms."

"So do we have a deal?"

Azarth took her hand. "Yes, we have a deal. If you agree to a bit of patience. There are preparations to be made and research to be done before you return."

"What kind of preparations and research?"

"I merely want to explore options before you make your final decision."

"I'm not going to change my mind. I have to be with him, Azarth."

"I am not arguing with you, my dear. I merely want to present you both with options. I ask that you allow me a bit of time to complete what I need to do."

"And then I can go back?"

"Absolutely."

Conn let go of his hand and hugged him tight. "Then please hurry with what you have to do."

"I will endeavor to move as expediently as possible."

She nodded and released him. As he moved away to enter the villa she turned and leaned on the rail as he returned inside. Now that she'd made up her mind, she felt better. But what she'd face when she returned gave her cause for nervousness. If Caleb's memory fully returned before she did, then she might be going back to a man filled with too much anger to see she'd acted out of love.

Which meant she ran the risk of Caleb turning his back on her. The thought of that made her sick with worry. But better that he make the choice. At least then she wouldn't have to live with making the choice for him. She'd just have to try to find a way to survive without him.

Chapter Nine

ꟙ

Caleb threw the beer bottle at the old oak, taking no satisfaction in the way it exploded on the bark and rained to the ground with the rest of the collection that littered the ground.

Not much mattered to him these days. Nothing except the brief flashes of memory that plagued his mind. And even those moments provided no comfort. He didn't know what was real. Had Conn been taken or had she left on her own accord? He kept going back to one moment that had flashed through his head a week ago. Conn's hands on his face. Feeling something crawling into his mind and her voice. "Forget…I'm sorry…I love you."

Was that real? Had she used her abilities somehow to make him forget what really happened? Had she left him because she wanted to? Because she felt she was protecting him? Did she love him or was that nothing more than something he'd cooked up in his head?

He groaned and leaned forward in the lawn chair, his elbows on his knees and hands covering his face. What the hell was he going to do? He couldn't go on like this, not able to concentrate or sleep or be civil to anyone around him. Another month of this and he'd be a worthless alcoholic. Or insane.

He had to find the answers. But where?

"Start with me," came a voice from behind him. A voice he thought was nothing more than a wishful imagining until he felt her hands on his, pulling them away from his face.

"Conn!" He was out of the chair, pulling her to her feet from where she knelt in front of him to engulf her in his arms.

"Caleb." Her voice was a choked whisper against the side of his neck.

For a long time they stood locked in each other's arms, not speaking, just clutching one another. At length, she gently pulled back.

"I'm so sorry, Caleb," she said, tears tracking down her face.

"What happened?" he asked. "Things are…jumbled in my head."

Conn's throat constricted painfully, choking back the sob that rose. What had she done? Caleb had aged five years. His eyes were hollow and ringed with dark circles, his face unshaven and his hair a matted mess. His clothes looked like they'd been worn for quite some time and he'd definitely lost weight.

She'd done this to him. It made her sick. "Caleb, there's a lot I need to tell you. But you need to be rested and possessed of a clear mind. Let me take you inside. You can bathe and I'll prepare you something to eat. And after you've eaten and slept, we'll talk."

"Talk now," he barked. "Tell me what happened!"

"Not now," she insisted quietly, feeling a stab of guilt as she utilized the skills Azarth had shown her how to employ and sent a tendril of energy into his mind, a suggestion that he was hungry and tired."

His eyes narrowed and his jaw tightened and she wondered if maybe she'd failed. Then he blinked, blew out his breath and nodded. "You promise you're not going to leave again?"

"I promise."

He nodded again, took her hand and went inside with her. As he mounted the stairs to head for the shower, she went into the kitchen and picked up the phone.

Ana answered on the second ring. "Hi," Conn said.

"Conn! Oh my god. Conn. What happened to you? Where are you? Caleb is half crazy and—"

"I'm with him, Ana," Conn cut in. "At the Circle R. I'll explain everything. I promise. After I've explained to Caleb. I just wanted you to know I'm here."

"Thanks, honey. You call if you need me."

"I will. Thank you, Ana."

She hung up the phone and looked in the refrigerator to see what she could heat up for Caleb. By the time she had two plates filled and heating in the microwave, the table set and tall glasses of iced tea poured, she heard the soft pad of bare feet enter the room. She turned to look at him.

And her breath caught in her throat. Standing there with wet hair, wearing only a pair of faded jeans, he was every bit as potent as the first moment she'd set eyes on him.

"You can't imagine how much I want you at this moment," she admitted.

"The feeling's mutual," he said with a hint of his old self that faded too quickly to be replaced with a look of anguish.

"Were you taken from me, or did you leave me, Conn?"

She knew then that dinner would be a forgotten affair. She could see the need in his eyes and the determined set of his jaw. He'd go without nourishment, but answers were critical to his well-being.

"Yes."

"Yes...," he stammered in shock. "Yes? Yes what? Yes, you left because you were forced or because you wanted to."

"Because I saw no other way to protect you and the other people on this ranch."

"What does that mean? The NSA threatened me and my employees?"

"No."

"Then what?" he yelled and snatched up a glass of tea from the counter, hurled it across the room and stalked over to her.

"Those people were not agents of the government."

"Then who the hell were they?" He grabbed her by the arms and lifted her slightly as he pulled her a little closer.

"You're hurting me," she said softly.

"You damn near killed me," he growled in reply.

That effectively smothered anything she could think to say. He was right. She'd wronged him and deserved whatever anger he felt. But there was more than anger in his voice and in the tension in his body. There was hunger.

"And you're the most magnificent man I've ever known," she whispered. "The one man I want and need."

The tight-fisted grip he had on her arms loosened to become a slow caress on her skin that flamed the fire inside her brighter. "You're so beautiful, Caleb," she said as she reached up to trace her fingers across his chest. "So perfect."

"There's nothing perfect about me, Conn."

"Oh, but there is," she argued, moving her hand from his chest and down his abdomen, feeling his muscles tense. She reached the top of his jeans and slowly unbuttoned them, keeping her eyes locked with his.

His eyes were filled with heat and longing as she unzipped his jeans and pushed them down over his hips. "I've missed you so," she said, letting her fingertips glide up the inside of his thighs to his manhood then move away. She felt him shiver at the light caress and repeated it but this time when she reached his erection, she took him in her hand, squeezing and stroking in a slow rhythm.

His eyes closed and his head titled slightly back. She knelt in front of him, taking him in her mouth and was rewarded with a lusty groan. The movement of her tongue and mouth had him tensing. She felt his need and knew that he would not last long. But she did not stop until his hands fisted in her hair and tugged her to her feet.

His lips claimed hers in a kiss that was near brutal in its hunger, need so hot and urgent that gentleness was momentarily forgotten. She understood and did not protest when his hands grabbed her shirt and ripped it open. Nor did she protest when his hands closed on her breasts, pressing them together and lifting them high. His mouth closed on one nipple, sucking and biting as if in a frenzy.

She gasped at the small jolt of pain, but did not fight against it. She was his and would give him what he needed.

As if suddenly realizing how rough he was, he stopped, turning his attention to undressing her. When she stood nude before him, he stepped back, his eyes leaving a tangible tingle on her skin as they traveled down her body.

"You're so beautiful," he whispered hoarsely then let his eyes meet hers. "Are you mine, Conn, or is this some trick? Are you really here or is this just another trick my mind is playing on me?

"I'm here, Caleb." She took his hand and placed it against her heart. "This is real. As is my love for you. And I am yours. For as long as you want me."

The thrill that raced through her when his hands cupped her breasts was as strong as the first time he touched her. "Caleb. My love," she breathed as he leaned down, his lips touching her neck.

His lips moved slowly up her neck to her ear. At the same moment he sucked her earlobe between his lips, his fingers moved to her nipples, stroking and squeezing. She exhaled with a trace of a moan and arched against him.

Caleb's lips abandoned her ear to focus on her breasts. Holding them firmly, he moved his mouth from one to the other, his tongue teasing the hard nipples. Conn felt her breath quicken when one of his hands moved down her body and into the slippery folds of her sex.

She was wet when his fingers penetrated her and she gasped at the wash of longing his touch evoked. "I want you. Please," she whispered, not in the least embarrassed to beg.

His answer was to scoop her up in his arms and carry her to the den. He lay her gently on the thick rug in front of the fireplace then moved away to strike a match and start the prepared wood in the fireplace. A small flame danced and he returned to her, kneeling between her legs. Putting his hands under her thighs, he lifted her, spreading her legs.

Conn raised her arms up above her head, the weight of her body on her shoulders as he lifted her higher. When he lowered his mouth to her and his tongue lapped at her sensitive, erect clit, tremors of sensation rippled through her.

"Ahhh, Caleb," she breathed as the sensations intensified. His hands moved her legs apart even more, his tongue taking her closer and closer to release. She fought to control it, but was powerless against the pulsing wave that engulfed her, making her cry his name and tremble in its wake.

Caleb released her and knelt on his hands and knees above her. Conn grabbed his hair and pulled his face down to hers, licking at his lips and sucking his tongue into her mouth, tasting the heady mixture of his unique flavor mixed with the taste of herself.

At the onset his kiss was one of controlled passion. But when she writhed against him the kiss turned hungry and rough. She responded eagerly to his hunger.

"Please," she whispered when he pulled back from her lips to look into her eyes.

His eyes gleamed in the reflection of the fire. Still kneeling between her legs, he took hold of her arm and flipped her over. His hand fisted tightly in her hair to pull her head back. She complied with the unspoken command and got onto her knees.

This was one time no thought was given to protection. He rubbed the head of his cock against her wet sex, spreading her lips then pushed inside.

Conn cried out in pleasure and Caleb's hands moved to encircle her and lift her, impaling her on his thick cock. Conn moaned in lust and moved against him, rolling her hips as he pumped inside her.

His hands traveled up to cup her breasts as his mouth moved down the side of her neck. She raised one arm and felt behind her to grab his hair. Turning slightly she pulled his face to hers, licking at his lips. And in that moment, for the first time since she'd been back, felt their connection.

Caleb groaned, feeling her in his mind. Feeling her love and her fear and the pain she'd suffered from being parted from him. He crushed her against him in a kiss that conveyed all of the emotion inside him. The fear, confusion, need, anger, hunger and love. It didn't matter that she saw what was inside him. She was his love. His mate. He knew it like he knew the sun would rise in the morning. She was his and because of that, he was complete.

His fingers tangled in her hair, pulling her head back to expose her neck. He bit at her ear, the tender flesh at its base and moved lower to the junction of her shoulder.

Conn pressed back harder against him, her lush ass moving in slow erotic circles as she rose and fell on his throbbing dick. His mouth opened against her neck, feeling the rapid beat of her pulse beneath his lips and tongue. The overwhelmingly sexy movements of her firm ass against him and her tight pussy squeezing him as she took the length of him slowly, increased his hunger to a fevered pitch.

His lips sought hers and he was not gentle, or in control. He wanted to devour her, to taste every part of her, to have her trembling with need. Her response to his hunger was a fire that burned as bright as his own. The kiss became a battle, each seeking to fill their own desperate need.

Conn broke free, her lips swollen and red. She moved forward onto her hands and knees and he followed, staying hilted inside her. With feline grace and flexibility she twisted so that she faced him, her legs circling his waist to pull him deeper into her tight channel.

Caleb worked his hands under her ass to lift her, driving deeper inside her. She almost robbed him of all control with the way she undulated against him, soft gasps and moans accompanying the sight of her hands snaking down her body to play with her clit. Her violet eyes were darkened to the color of a thunderhead, hooded with desire and her skin glistened with a sheen of perspiration and a flush of need.

She was the most intoxicating sight he'd ever witnessed. Caleb took her hands to pull her to him. She wound around him like a python, all muscle and grace as his lips ravaged her mouth.

She acquiesced, but briefly. Then she became the dominant, fisting both hands in his hair to imprison him in a searing kiss that made his balls pulse and his control weaken.

He stroked deeper inside her, gripping her ass tightly to drive her down the length of him. She arched back, offering her breasts. His tongue moved between them and then beneath her right breast, nipping at the soft underbelly before moving up to take the nipple in his mouth. She screamed as a climax ripped through her and she ground around him, gasping his name.

He was going to lose it. He could feel it. "Slow down, honey," he groaned and slid free from her wet sex. He knelt between her legs, sliding his hands up her legs to her hips then higher until he cupped her breasts.

She moaned in pleasure and arched against him as he pressed her breasts together and ran his tongue into the crease and then up to tease one peaked nipple. Conn writhed against him.

"More," she panted. "Please, Caleb."

More was exactly what he had in mind. He let go of her breasts and slid his hands slowly down to her sex and then back up, barely brushing the sides of her pussy. She quivered and stretched in pleasure as his hands traveled over her body, across her belly, circling her breasts in ever decreasing spirals until his fingers rubbed across her nipples.

Then he reversed the direction, working steadily down her body and back up. And as he worked slowly up her body again he lowered himself onto her. Inch by inch until he was stretched over her, his flesh barely in contact with her slick hot body, his weight supported on one arm.

She wiggled sexily, brushing her nipples against his chest and pressing her pussy up against his erection, sandwiching it between their bodies.

"You feel so damn good," he murmured against the side of her neck then proceeded to lick and bite his way to her ear lobe. "I can't get enough of you." When his lips moved to hers, she rewarded him with a kiss so passionate he nearly came. But he wasn't about to let it end. He assumed control, plundering her mouth, tasting her, feeding off her.

They were both breathing hard, bodies pressing and grinding against one another in increasing fervor. His hard cock rubbed against her belly, throbbing with as much intensity as the pulse-pounding thrum of her pussy.

They had no awareness other than that of their joined lips, mouths and writhing bodies. When their lips parted, Caleb rose over her to look down into her eyes. And saw what he wanted in their violet depths. Felt it in his mind and his heart. She truly was his. His woman, his mate. She would take and match all he could give.

The knowledge ignited a fire inside him so hot that his body burned with need. When he slid his hands to her hips and pulled her to him, impaling her on the length of his cock, she raised her arms above her head, arched up and surrendered to his need.

The fire died away and night gave way to day before their passion was finally spent. With the sound of Conn's whispered "my love" echoing in his mind, he succumbed to sleep.

Chapter Ten

ꟙ

Conn was feeling more than a little anxious as she and Caleb descended the stairs of the ranch. She'd returned two weeks ago and since her return neither she nor Caleb had left the house. No one aside from Ana and Chase knew she was there. It had to be that way.

Caleb had even sent Hannah and her family on a three-week paid vacation to make sure that the house was empty.

Conn had explained everything to Caleb. Where she came from, the political situation on the worlds of V'Kar, why the V'Kar were on Earth and about their greatest enemy on Earth, the Alliance.

As a credit to him, he'd accepted her at her word. She suspected it would have been more difficult if she had not mentally joined with him, giving him access to her thoughts.

Their greatest difficulty to overcome was the fact that she'd left to protect him. She understood. As a man it went against the essential male grain to have a women feel she was in the position of protector as it was a man's natural inclination to see himself in that role.

It'd taken some time, but in the end he agreed that had the situations been reversed he probably would have done the same thing. Relief couldn't come close to describing the weight that lifted from her when he said he understood.

But they still had some hard choices to make if they were going to ensure the safety of the people on the Circle R and all of Caleb's family. And the best solution meant revealing information that was sure to be not only a shock to all of the Russell family, but to bring to the forefront old family anger that had lain dormant for many years.

Caleb had called his father and all of his brothers and asked for a family meeting. Everyone had arrived two days ago and since then Conn had told them everything, not sparing a detail. She wasn't sure it was wise, but Caleb had insisted on full disclosure and she was not able to go against him on that.

Having two witches and a shape-shifter in the family had certainly dulled what could have been a shock. Still, even with paranormals as family members, announcing that not only do aliens exist but that they'd been walking the earth for countless centuries was not the easiest story to make seem believable.

In the end they had believed her. Well, after a few demonstrations of her abilities and a lot of inside information that Azarth had warned her might prove dangerous for them to know.

Last night the discussion had ended with Caleb announcing that he and Conn had a plan to keep the Alliance from targeting the ranch and their family but they'd discuss in the following morning.

Now it was time to face the music and Conn felt this aspect was going to be far more of a blow to the family than having been introduced to a woman from outer space, as Caleb's brother Cole put it.

Caleb stopped at the door of the kitchen and gave her hand a squeeze. "Don't worry. It'll be okay."

She could hear the voices inside the kitchen. There was a lot of speculation about what kind of plan Caleb could have in mind. She looked up at him. "Are you sure you want to do this, Caleb?"

"Absolutely. I love you, Conn."

"And I love you."

"Then let's get this show on the road, honey," he said with what she read as false bravado.

She nodded and they entered the room.

All talk ended and all eyes focused on her and Caleb.

"Okay, let's have it," Charlie said.

"Morning, Dad," Caleb said with a grin. "That coffee smells good. "

"Sit, sit," Clara said and rose from her seat. "I'll get it."

Conn and Caleb took seats at the table. Caleb placed the leather portfolio he had tucked under his arm on the table. After Clara had poured them coffee and taken her seat, Charlie spoke up again. "Well?"

Caleb looked from him to Conn then back again. "I think it might be best for Conn to explain."

"Please do," Charlie said to her.

"Very well," she said and folded her hands together on top of the table. She saw the eyes that followed the motion of Caleb's hand landing on top of hers.

"In order to explain, it is necessary that I delve into the history of the Russell family." She saw the way Charlie's eyebrows rose and the way the twins looked at each other. Only Chase seemed unaffected. But then she'd learned that Chase was like deep water. There could be much activity in the depths even when the surface was as pristine as glass.

"Specifically," she said, "Mr. Russell's brother Jack and his wife Alana."

"Hold on there, missy," Charlie said. "We don't discuss that…that bitch in this house."

"Sir, with all due respect, there is much you do not know about Alana and your brother," Conn argued gently. "Your family believes that Jack abandoned his place in the family to run off with some gypsy tramp, turning his back on the family legacy. In truth, your brother left in order to protect all of you."

"That's a load of shit," Charlie spat.

"On the contrary," Conn met his anger without flinching. "Alana was neither a gypsy nor a tramp. She was V'Kar. More specifically, a member of the Sisterhood. Your brother left because by staying he put you in the crosshairs of the Alliance's sights. He was willing to risk his own life for the woman he loved, but not the lives of his brother or his father.

"The only way to protect you and your family was for Jack to leave with Alana. The V'Kar number is strong in Florida and they offered to provide Jack with land and the funds to start his own ranch."

"That's such a load of cow shit!" Charlie exclaimed. "Jack's nothing but a whore-mongering renegade who lost his honor the day he turned his back on this family and took off with that slut."

"Hold on, Dad," Caleb spoke in a voice so quiet, yet so full of strength and power that everyone, including Charlie looked at him in surprise.

"She's not lying," Caleb said. "I know because I talked with Jack myself. He confirmed everything she said."

Charlie's mouth fell open then closed and he shook his head, clearly at a loss for words. There was loud silence for a long time.

When Chase spoke, Cole's wife Rusty was watching Charlie so intently that she actually started in her seat. "You always told us that nothing's thicker than blood. It's all you can trust in this life. Well, he's blood. Regardless of who he's married to."

"You mean your uncle is married to one of Conn's people?" Rusty asked, and when Caleb nodded she smiled. "Cool."

Chase smirked at her comment. "Let's say all this is true. What does that have to do with what's happening now?"

"Glad you asked," Caleb said. "I'm moving to Florida. The lady Conn told you about—Pandora? She met with Jack and Alana and they've arranged everything."

"You're leaving?" Ana asked in a voice choked with emotion.

Caleb nodded. "No other way, beautiful. If we stay, the V'Kar will try to protect us, but the Alliance is strong and there's no guarantee that they won't strike out at one of you to get to Conn."

"You moving to Florida won't keep them from striking at us if they mean to use us as leverage against you," Chase pointed out.

Caleb looked at Conn and his hand tightened on top of hers before he answered. "Two weeks from now information will be released that the woman who escaped the helicopter crash was an illegal alien with ties to a terrorist cell. She was five foot ten and had sandy-blonde hair and brown eyes.

"It'll go on to say that she showed up here impersonating a woman I hired as a vet assistant and when I found out that the real Connery Hoffman had been killed, I called the authorities who came and took Conn into custody.

"She was killed when the car the government agents were driving was forced off the road by a cell of terrorists. Many of them were killed in the battle as well and those who did escape are being sought by the government now."

"What?" Caleb's brother Cole, up until that point quiet, bellowed.

"I will not perish," Conn answered, "but the Alliance will believe that I have. When Caleb arrives in Florida, he will be introduced to a relative of Alana's who has come to stay with her, Constance Zane. An identity has already been arranged that will hold up to even the closest scrutiny."

Charlie shook his head. "Honey, I ain't calling you a liar, but that's a mighty tall order. And if what you say is true, then there are people who've seen you and can identify you."

"I think not," came a voice from the door. All the men jumped. Chase was already out of his chair with fists clenched. "No, it's all right," Conn exclaimed and stood. Azarth stood framed in the doorway.

More than one person at the table started. Azarth entered the room. "Forgive the intrusion, but I felt it prudent to visit and lend my assurance to all of you that the plan Raenea—forgive me, Conn—has set in motion, will indeed succeed."

"Just who the hell are you?" Charlie asked.

"Forgive me." Azarth inclined his head. "I am Azarth, Minister of Science and Medicine."

"So you're an alien?" Cole's wife Rusty asked.

"From your perspective, yes," he answered with a smile.

Rusty and Clay's wife, Scout, shared a look and grinned. Charlie did not smile. In fact, his frown deepened. "I'm not going to ask you to prove that statement, sir, but I will ask you to prove to me that this plan has a chance in hell of succeeding and keeping this family safe from your enemies."

"Of course. May I?" Azarth gestured to chair that sat beside the refrigerator.

"Sorry, let me get that," Caleb answered and pulled the chair to the table.

"Thank you." Azarth took a seat. "The identity that has been secured for Conn is one that will never be put to question. I feel sure she has mentioned Pandora to you?"

"The Mother Superior of this Sisterhood in your star system?" Ana asked. "Yes."

"Excellent. Pandora has lived on this world, as have I, since the time before the civilization of Sumer rose to greatness. In that era she was worshipped as a goddess, as she has been in many subsequent cultures. Today she is known as Pandora Gotleib, the majority stockholder of one of the most powerful communication conglomerates in the world.

"And as something of a recluse who guards her family with great care. As a contingency that something should go wrong when a member of her board of directors, Eric Zane, lost his wife and child during childbirth, information was released that the wife had died but the child had survived. At the time Conn was placed in Shen's care, additional information was released that this child was being schooled in the most exclusive and private academies in the world. Photos have been amassed over the resulting years of Conn, should the need arise to move her from Shen's care to Pandora's protection."

"Last week Eric Zane died and today a press release was issued that his only surviving heir, Constance, had sold all of her stock back to the majority stockholders. Mr. Zane's only surviving family aside from his daughter is his sister, Alana Zane Russell. Mrs. Russell flew to Zurich immediately following the death of her brother to help Constance settle the estate.

"Today information was leaked that Constance Zane would accompany her aunt to Florida where she would be staying for an indefinite period of time."

"Damn!" Cole muttered. "You people sure plan in advance, don't you?"

"But why?" Clay asked.

"I'd like to know that myself," Chase added.

Azarth looked around at everyone. "When you have lived as long as we have, you learn to always think ahead. Contingency plans are a necessity for one can never predict when a random element will wreak havoc with even the best-laid plan."

"You mean like Conn jumping out of that helicopter?" Ana asked.

"Exactly," Azarth said with a smile. "Had she stayed aboard the aircraft, she would have been taken into custody upon arrival by people loyal to us and we would have extricated her from further scrutiny."

"Guess that just wasn't in the cards," Chase said. "Fate has a way of intervening."

"Indeed it does, sir."

He looked around at everyone. "If there are no further questions, it is time for us to take our leave."

Caleb rose and extended his hand to Azarth. "Thank you."

Azarth nodded respectfully and accepted the handshake. Conn got up and when Caleb turned to her, went into his arms. "I'll try not to screw this plan up," she said.

Azarth chuckled. "My dear, this time I believe we have a plan that not even the daughter of the Heir Apparent can destroy. Although, as am I fond of saying these days, it would be wise not to underestimate your ability."

Conn chuckled. "Well, I'm sure that's a veiled insult, but today I can't be upset about anything. Thank you. For everything."

"I believe that if one of my kind chose to mate with a human, a member of this family would be a wise choice."

"Amen, brother," Conn chirped in a perfect accent that had everyone chuckling, even Azarth.

Charlie shook his head and leaned back in his chair. "I tell you what, I sure am glad I don't have any more kids. These four have given me enough surprises to kill a weaker man."

All the men laughed at the comment. Conn watched the interaction between the members of the family and was suddenly looking forward to the day that she could take her place as a member of the family and share such love and companionship.

"So when do you leave?" Chase asked Conn.

"Now," came a soft female voice leading into the living room.

Everyone started. Azarth extended his hand as Pandora entered. She placed her hand lightly atop his as he made the introductions. "This is Pandora, Mother Superior of the Sisterhood."

"No harm will come to your son," Pandora directed her statement to Charlie. "He and Princess Raenea—forgive me, Conn—are merely fulfilling their destiny. As unbelievable as it may seem to you, this *is* Caleb's destiny. And it is the way to ensure lasting protection to your family and a member of the royal family."

"You sure he'll be safe?" Charlie asked. "I'm still not sold on the idea of him spending time with that renegade Jack. Even if he is married up with one of your…followers or whatever.

"They will not be alone," Azarth answered. "Remember, our numbers are many and our plan well considered. Upon his arrival in Florida, there will be many to safeguard him from harm. As there will be here. With your permission, of course. I have volunteers willing to work on your ranch to ensure your continued safety."

"I only want my family to be safe," Charlie said as he stood and walked around the table to face Azarth. "Man to man, I have your word?" He stuck out his hand.

Azarth took it without hesitation. "Upon my honor, I give you my word."

"I hope for your sake your honor's worthy, sir. Because if something happens to any one of my family, including Conn, nothing on this world or yours is going to stop me from exacting vengeance. You get my drift?"

"Indeed, I do," Azarth nodded respectfully then looked in Conn and Caleb's direction.

"Are you ready?"

Conn hugged Caleb tight. "I'll be waiting for you."

"I'll be there, baby, don't you worry."

"I love you, Caleb."

"I love you, Conn. It doesn't matter where we live as long as we're together. And just so you know. I'm gonna marry you. If you'll have me, that is."

She grinned up at him. "Just try and get rid of me, Caleb Russell. Remember I can shape-shift and I'd hate to see you wind up with the world's biggest slug stuck to your fine behind."

Caleb laughed and hugged her again, then released her as Ana got up and ran over to Conn. "You hurry back, little sister," Ana whispered through tears. "And we'll have the biggest wedding this county's ever seen."

"Thank you," Conn replied, blinking back tears of her own, and looking around at everyone. "Thank you all."

She gave Caleb a long lingering kiss then nodded to Pandora. "I'm ready."

"Very well," Pandora said and nodded to the family. She and Azarth left the room. Caleb took Conn's hand and followed.

When they reached the dark sedan parked outside, Caleb paused and held Conn close. "Promise you'll be there waiting for me?"

"Upon my life," she vowed. "You don't think I'm going to let you weasel out of marrying me, do you? "

"Honey, that's the last thing I'd do. You call me on the phone Azarth gave me when you get there. And a hundred times a day until I arrive."

"I will."

Caleb looked at Azarth. "You make sure she's safe."

"Always. Now we must go."

Caleb grabbed Conn for one more kiss then reluctantly let her go. He watched until the car disappeared from sight then returned inside the house where the family was waiting.

"Son, I'm not happy about this," Charlie said the moment Caleb entered the room. "Not happy at all."

"It's going to be okay, Dad. They'll keep her safe and once I get there and spend enough time to make it reasonable, we'll come back and—"

"That's the part that rankles me, boy. You being there with that scoundrel, Jack."

"Just what is the deal with you and Jack, anyway?" Clara asked.

"Yeah," Chase added.

Charlie blew out his breath. "I told you. He's a renegade and a scoundrel."

"What does that mean?" Caleb asked, taking a seat.

"It means that when Pa was ailing and we needed him the most, he up and left. Took off with that gal and turned his back on the family without a look back."

"He was in love," Ana said softly. "And wanted to protect the woman he loved. Surely you understand that better than most, Charlie. Look what happened when you thought Clara's life was in danger."

Charlie shot her a heated look but it faded fast. He sighed heavily. "Still, he could've come back. Or stayed in touch. It's been…damn fifty years."

"Did you ever try to get in touch with him?" Caleb asked.

"Nope."

"Why not?"

Charlie opened his mouth as if to answer, then closed it and shook his head. "Too much water under that bridge, boy. You can't go back."

"But you can go forward," Caleb said gently. "Dad, it's time to mend those bridges and bring the family back together. Conn taught me that in a roundabout way. She's spent her whole life wondering why she was alone with no family. And longing to be part of one. And now she knows who she is, but still she can't be with her parents. Hell, she can't even see them for fear of putting lives at risk. But she can be part of a family and know what it means to have that love and support. And I want her to have as much of that as I can give. Including Uncle Jack.

"And I think you want it too. To mend things, I mean."

"So now you know what I want?"

"No, but I do," Clara spoke up. "And Caleb and Conn have provided the perfect opportunity for you and Jack to heal those old wounds. So you will mend the fence, Charlie Russell."

"Is that a fact?"

"Oh, it is indeed," Clara said with a smile. "Or you can take it to the bank that the Russell women will make sure you're miserable as an old goat tied at the shed 'til you do."

"Amen," Ana spoke up, followed by a chorus from Rusty and Scout.

Charlie shook his head, trying in vain to stop a grin from spreading on his face, but failing. "I swear, if it ain't my boys that are gonna kill me, it's you damn women."

Clara laughed and hugged him. "You better believe it, you old coot. Now, get yourself on the phone and call your brother. Me and the gals got some planning to do."

"What kind of planning?" Charlie asked as she got up from the table.

"Honey, we got a wedding to plan," she said as she got a notepad and pen from one of the kitchen drawers. "Girls, let's go into the den and put our heads together.

Charlie looked around at the men as the women got up to follow Clara. "Ain't that jumping the gun a bit? Caleb hasn't even left yet."

Ana spoke up from the door. "Planning a wedding takes time."

Charlie just looked at Chase who groaned and shook his head. "Don't even try to fight it. This is a battle you can't win."

Caleb laughed and leaned back in his chair, grinning at his father and his brothers. He couldn't wait for the next step in the plan.

Chapter Eleven

ꩭ

Caleb peeled off his wet shirt, pried off his boots and socks and fell face first into the pool. Damn if the Floridians didn't have it worked out. Spend a blistering hot day working on the ranch and come home and ease the heat in a nice cool pool. He'd have to remember to suggest that to Charlie when he and Conn got back home.

Jack and Alana had provided him and Conn with the use of their guesthouse so they could have their privacy and Caleb had enjoyed every moment of it. But there were times when he missed home.

He'd ended up spending longer in Florida than he'd planned. It was a whole new world. Ranching was pretty much the same no matter where you were, but the climate and landscape provided different challenges, and the breed Jack raised was different from the stock raised on the Circle R.

And getting to know his uncle had proven to be fascinating. Jack and Charlie were like night and day. Charlie was big boned, stocky and bellowed when he talked. By contrast, Jack was tall and wiry and rarely raised his voice.

Conn walked out onto the patio and spotted him. "Well, what have we here?" she asked with a grin and dived fully clothed into the pool.

Caleb grinned when she slithered up his body, her hands sliding over his skin to end up clasped behind his neck. She wound her legs around his waist and captured his lips in a kiss hot enough to rival the Florida sun.

"Ummm, salty," she murmured when the kiss ended. "Have a good day?"

"Yeah, it was good. How 'bout you?"

"Good. But Alana's a little down about us leaving."

"And you? You want to go back home, don't you?"

"I want to be wherever you are," she replied and nibbled his ear. "But I do feel bad for her, Caleb. With her boys gone…well, you know."

Caleb carried her over to the edge of the pool and climbed up to sit beside her, dangling his legs in the water.

"It's still kind of hard to believe. The part about her and Jack letting Pandora send their sons back into the past. I mean doesn't that set up some kind of paradox or something?"

"Apparently not. At least not from what I've learned from Azarth. As odd as it is, if they hadn't gone back into the past, then your—let's see, what is it? Your great, great, great, great, great grandfather wouldn't have left Florida to head west and start the Circle R."

Caleb shook his head. "Boggles the mind, doesn't it?"

"There are more things in heaven and earth, Horatio, than are dreamt of in your philosophy."

"Horatio?"

Conn chuckled. "From your English playwright, William Shakespeare, in Hamlet. Act one, scene 5."

"Been in Uncle Jack's books again, have you?"

She nodded enthusiastically. "He has a marvelous library."

"Yeah. Who would've thought that a rancher would have such a love for classic literature. But still, that whole time travel thing. I don't know if we want to tell the rest of the family that part."

"I think that should be up to Jack and Alana," she replied.

"Right you are. And right now I don't want to think about time travel or ill-tempered bulls or anything except getting clean and getting you in bed."

"What about dinner?"

"Dinner can wait," he said as he stood and took her hand to pull her to her feet.

"Hmmmm," she murmured as she rose slowly, working her way up his body, kissing and licking until her tongue traced its way up the side of his neck and she captured his ear lobe between her teeth. She moved her hand to cup his crotch.

"Hmmm doesn't even come close," Caleb said as he took hold of her hair to pull her up to meet his lips. He'd never get enough of the taste of her. She writhed against him, allowing him to take her mouth, her hard nipples raking across his chest, creating trails of fire on his skin.

His lips left hers and moved down the side of her neck and over the top of one shoulder. The scoop-necked gauze top she wore was easy enough to slide down off her shoulders, baring her breasts. His mouth gravitated to the tantalizing bud of her nipple. Conn purred and arched back when his lips closed around the sensitive tip. He supported her with his arms, bending her back like a bow.

The blast of energy that sizzled from her mind to his nearly weakened his knees with its power. Uninhibited, raw and primal, it was like a live wire in his mind that sizzled throughout his body. And it was an offer he wasn't about to refuse. He continued to torture her breasts, his hands moving down her body to peel off her shorts.

When one hand moved between her legs, his fingers spreading her sex and dipping into the silken wetness, she spread her legs, pressing against his hand, riding his fingers as he penetrated deeper.

The throaty moan that came from her announced that he'd not only found her secret spot, but that it was so alive that only one stroke had her working toward orgasm.

Caleb held onto her and stroked his fingers inside her, each movement driving her closer to the edge. A rush of wetness preceded a vibration that ran through her body before her pussy started to spasm around his fingers. Her hands gripped his upper arms, fingers digging into his skin as the climax rolled through her.

It was like an aphrodisiac. Everything about her was. He wondered if he'd ever get enough of her.

"Please," she gasped as the climax started to subside. "More."

Caleb didn't hesitate to comply. He pulled her over to a large round lounge, lay back and pulled her on top of him. "Take it, baby," he said, watching her eyes for reaction. "Let me see how much you want me."

Lights danced in her violet eyes and a sly, sexy smile came to her face. She straddled his body, taking his dick in her hand and slowly, inch by inch, impaled herself on his length.

Once fully seated, she started a rocking glide, back and forth, higher then lower, the movement slow and seductive. Caleb moved his hand to the junction of her thighs, his fingers working into the folds of her sex, imprisoning her hard clit between thumb and finger.

A gasp exploded from her at the touch. She arched back, bracing herself with her hands on his thighs. The sight of her, bowed back with breasts high and his dick filling her pussy, was enough to make a man lose his mind. Her pussy was hot and slick, gripping him as she rode him.

Harder and faster she moved. Her clit grew tighter and harder, signaling a coming release. Caleb fought to hold back his own climax as she vibrated on and around him. He rolled her clit, squeezing harder and she moaned loudly, a sound all female, no matter what the species.

At the moment of that moan he felt her orgasm. It literally radiated from her pussy, down the length of his dick and throughout his body. Unable to control it, he quaked beneath its power, his seed shooting inside her in great throbbing waves.

How long it lasted he had no idea. It could have been a moment or an eternity. He didn't know or care. He was lost in sensation, a climax that claimed both body and soul. He felt Conn with him, her passion and her love.

And as always, it shook him to his soul. He felt the claim he had on her and her acceptance of it. Moreover, he realized the claim she had on him. They were joined in a way he'd never dreamed possible.

When she sagged, melting down on top of him, her breath still fast and her heart pounding against his chest, he wrapped his arms around her, feeling complete.

For a long time they lay on the lounge, letting the last of the dying rays of the sun bathe them. Finally she sat up. "I'm starving."

His stomach rumbled and they both laughed. "Well, I guess I'm not the only one," she said and got off him. "What say we take this inside and get something to eat?"

"Did you cook?" he asked as he got to his feet.

"Why, I'll have you know that I fixed fresh squash, a roast and—"

"Let me guess. Potato salad."

"I love that stuff," she said with a laugh. "But I also made you rice and gravy."

"Well damn, come on then. We don't want good food like that going to waste."

She grinned and started for the door but he took her arm and stopped her. "Conn?"

"Yes?"

"I just want you to know that I love you and I promise we're going to have a good life."

"We already do," she said and stood up on tiptoe to graze his lips with hers. "And we will. One day at a time."

"Works for me," he replied and licked at her lips, parting them with his tongue.

"Hmmmm," she murmured, sinking against him for a moment then pulling back. "Damn, cowboy, you sure know how to make it tough on a woman."

"You ready for round two already?" he asked teasingly.

"Don't tempt me. At least not until I get some food in me. Then we'll see how much round two you have left." She turned and headed for the door. Caleb laughed and smacked her lightly on the bare behind.

"Then get ready, honey, cause once I get refueled, it's on."

She laughed and tossed him a towel. "Promises, promises. Are you nervous about going back? To the Circle R, I mean?"

"Actually, I think I'm ready. I miss my family. And I want them to know our son."

He reached over and put his hand on her belly. "Still hard to believe. Your stomach's flat as a fritter. You sure you're pregnant?"

"Positive," she said with a smile.

"Then all the more reason to go back where we belong," he said.

"As Constance Zane," she reminded him.

"Soon to be Constance Zane Russell," he said and grabbed her to pull her into a tight hug. "This is going to work isn't it? This identity switch?"

"Absolutely," she assured him. "We're safe, Caleb. Safe to live our lives, raise our children and be happy."

"Then bring it on," he said and swept her up into his arms. "In fact, let's celebrate."

"But what about dinner?" she asked as he carried her through the kitchen and toward the bedroom.

"Later, darlin'. Right now we got some world-class loving to do. That's got to beat out potato salad."

"Hands down, cowboy. Hands down."

Also by *Ciana Stone*

ꝏ

Acid Rayne *(with Nathalie Gray)*

An Unwanted Hunger

Hot in the Saddle 1: Chase 'n' Ana

Hot in the Saddle 2: Molding Clay

Riding Ranger

Saturday Night Fever

Sexplorations II: The Thing about Cowboys

Sexplorations IV: Finding Her Rhythm

Sexplorations VI: Working Up a Sweat

The Hussies: A Taste for Jazz

The Hussies: All in Time

The Hussies: Maxwell's Silver Hammer

The Hussies: Sin in Jeans

Wyatt's Chance

Also see Ciana's release at Cerridwen Press (www.cerridwenpress.com):

That Which Survives

About the Author

ഗ

Ciana Stone has been reading since the age of three, and wrote her first story at age five. Since then she has enjoyed writing as a solitary form of entertainment, and has just recently come out of the closet to share her stories with others. She holds several post graduate degrees and has often been referred to as a professional student. Her latest fields of interest are quantum mechanics and Taoism. When she is not writing (or studying) she enjoys painting (canvas, not walls), sculpting, running, hiking and yoga. She lives with her long-time lover in several locations in the United States.

Ciana welcomes comments from readers. You can find her website and email address on her author bio page at www.ellorascave.com.

Tell Us What You Think

We appreciate hearing reader opinions about our books. You can email us at Comments@EllorasCave.com.

Why an electronic book?

We live in the Information Age—an exciting time in the history of human civilization, in which technology rules supreme and continues to progress in leaps and bounds every minute of every day. For a multitude of reasons, more and more avid literary fans are opting to purchase e-books instead of paper books. The question from those not yet initiated into the world of electronic reading is simply: *Why?*

1. ***Price.*** An electronic title at Ellora's Cave Publishing and Cerridwen Press runs anywhere from 40% to 75% less than the cover price of the exact same title in paperback format. Why? Basic mathematics and cost. It is less expensive to publish an e-book (no paper and printing, no warehousing and shipping) than it is to publish a paperback, so the savings are passed along to the consumer.
2. ***Space.*** Running out of room in your house for your books? That is one worry you will never have with electronic books. For a low one-time cost, you can purchase a handheld device specifically designed for e-reading. Many e-readers have large, convenient screens for viewing. Better yet, hundreds of titles can be stored within your new library—on a single microchip. There are a variety of e-readers from different manufacturers. You can also read e-books on your PC or laptop computer. (Please note that Ellora's Cave does not endorse any specific brands.

You can check our websites at www.ellorascave.com or www.cerridwenpress.com for information we make available to new consumers.)

3. ***Mobility***. Because your new e-library consists of only a microchip within a small, easily transportable e-reader, your entire cache of books can be taken with you wherever you go.
4. ***Personal Viewing Preferences.*** Are the words you are currently reading too small? Too large? Too... *ANNOYING*? Paperback books cannot be modified according to personal preferences, but e-books can.
5. ***Instant Gratification.*** Is it the middle of the night and all the bookstores near you are closed? Are you tired of waiting days, sometimes weeks, for bookstores to ship the novels you bought? Ellora's Cave Publishing sells instantaneous downloads twenty-four hours a day, seven days a week, every day of the year. Our webstore is never closed. Our e-book delivery system is 100% automated, meaning your order is filled as soon as you pay for it.

Those are a few of the top reasons why electronic books are replacing paperbacks for many avid readers.

As always, Ellora's Cave and Cerridwen Press welcome your questions and comments. We invite you to email us at Comments@ellorascave.com or write to us directly at Ellora's Cave Publishing Inc., 1056 Home Avenue, Akron, OH 44310-3502.

ELLORA'S CAVE
ROMANTICA PUBLISHING

CPSIA information can be obtained at www.ICGtesting.com
Printed in the USA
LVOW131857210313

325445LV00001B/87/P